Truth and Solace

Love at Solace Lake, Volume 3

Jana Richards

Published by Jana Richards Books, 2018.

This is a work of fiction. Names, characters, places, and incidents either are the product of the author's imagination or are used fictitiously, and any resemblance to actual persons living or dead, business establishments, events or locales, is entirely coincidental.

Praise for Jana Richards

A LONG WAY FROM EDEN

"Jana Richards has penned a poignant romance that will have you believing in the power of love." N.N. Light's Book Heaven

SEEING THINGS

"Seeing Things is a book that will keep you at the edge of your seat." Alice Klein, Sime-Gen Reviews

THE GIRL MOST LIKELY

"Loved this book! Jana Richards writes with great wit and a sharp eye for detail, making her characters and story feel absolutely real." Jill Blake, Goodreads Reviewer

Get Your Free Gift!

GET **HOME TO SOLACE LAKE**, your free prequel to the Love at Solace Lake series when you sign up for Jana Richards' newsletter!

Prologue

MARGARET CATHERINE Lindquist stepped off the school bus in front of the old fishing lodge and trudged up the stairs to the front porch. She hoped Grandma hadn't noticed the arrival of the bus because she couldn't bear one of her interrogations. Not today.

She made it to her room undetected. After quietly closing the door and locking it, she leaned her forehead against the solid wood and allowed the tears she'd been holding back to fall. Staggering to her bed, she curled into a fetal position and clutched Mr. Jingles, the Teddy Bear she'd owned for every one of her fourteen years.

It wasn't fair. All summer, while Luke had worked at the fishing lodge for her grandfather, they'd been close. He said he didn't care that she was four years younger. He'd told her all his dreams for the future, kissed her like she meant something to him, made love to her in their secret place in the forest. Though it had been the first time for them both, they'd soon overcome their initial awkwardness and learned where to touch and how to please. It had been a magical summer.

But now it was September, and the magic was over.

Maggie was back in school, and she'd heard Luke was working at a restaurant in Minnewasta. A love of cooking was something they shared. Someday, he'd promised, he'd own a restaurant and she'd be his head chef.

The tears flowed harder. He'd lied to her about that, too.

When she'd received a crumpled note from Luke earlier in the day, delivered by one of his bosses' kids, relief and excitement had overwhelmed her. He asked her to meet him at the football field behind the bleachers during afternoon recess. As soon as the bell rang, Maggie ran across the school yard. She hadn't seen Luke in almost two weeks, not since Grampa Bill had caught them together in one of the outbuildings. He'd fired Luke on the spot and told him to get off his property. It had been agony not to see him. And she'd been afraid he blamed her for losing his job and getting him into trouble.

When she arrived at the bleachers, Luke was there. But he wasn't alone. He was locked in a passionate embrace with Cheryl Bradley. Cheryl was as mean as she was pretty. Maggie had confided to Luke about how Cheryl's nasty comments about her dead parents had hurt her. The shock and betrayal of seeing him kissing her made Maggie sick to her stomach.

"Luke! What are you doing?"

He'd casually hung his arm around Cheryl's shoulders, his eyes cold and hard as he stared at her. An involuntary shiver crawled up Maggie's spine. Luke had never looked at her with such disdain before. Such disgust.

"I'm leaving town," he said flatly. "Don't do something stupid like try to follow me."

"You're leaving? Where are you going?"

"Someplace far from here."

"But you'll be back, right? You said you'd wait for me, and we'd go away together. You said—"

"Forget it! You're a kid. I don't want you! Leave me the hell alone. Go home and play with your dolls."

With that, he'd grabbed Cheryl's hand and pulled her away. Cheryl glanced over her shoulder with a smirk full of smug triumph.

The rest of the afternoon passed in a blur. She tuned out Ms. Carter in math class last period, too shocked to make sense of anything she said. Now, all she could do was cry.

She must have done something to make Luke fall out of love with her.

She'd go crazy if she didn't know. She had to find out what went wrong. She had to talk to Luke and make him explain. Maybe she could make things right and he'd take her with him.

Maggie clamoured off the bed and pulled a beat-up suitcase from underneath. She could hitchhike back to town and go to Abby's house. Abby was Luke's mother, the only person who'd known about their relationship. Abby had been her mother's best friend, and Maggie trusted her.

She pulled her waist-length hair into a low ponytail and haphazardly stuffed her things into the suitcase. Praying her most prized possession survived the journey, she hastily folded the delicate crystal unicorn Luke had given her inside a couple of T-shirts and stuck it amongst some other clothes where she hoped it would be protected. She hesitated over Mr. Jingles and then, with one last hug, she set the Teddy bear back on her bed. Time to put away childish things.

If she hurried, she could catch Luke before he left town. It didn't matter that he'd broken her heart when she'd found him kissing Cheryl. It had to be a mistake. Maybe if she'd been able to tell him how much she loved him, he wouldn't have done this. She wished it wasn't so hard for her to say the words, but if she caught up with him, she could tell him now. She'd make him see they belonged together.

A little voice in her head screamed she was wrong, that he'd betrayed her and taken advantage of her innocence. No eighteen-year-old boy on the brink of manhood would want a girl of fourteen. And if he really loved her, he wouldn't be kissing Cheryl Bradley. She shoved the voice away and snapped the suitcase shut.

"Maggie, open up!" The doorknob rattled as her grandmother tried to open it.

"Go away!"

"Maggie, please. I know you're upset, but letting that boy go is for the best. Your mother would want what was best for you."

Rage poured through Maggie at Grandma Dorothy's words. If Grampa hadn't fired Luke and forbade him from seeing her again, he wouldn't be leaving her now. "How do you know what my mother would have wanted? She's been dead for twelve years!"

"Margaret Catherine! Watch your smart mouth!"

The doorknob rattled again and then gave way as Grandma pushed the door open. Like everything else in the fishing lodge, the lock was old and broken.

She eyed the suitcase. "What are you doing?"

"I'm leaving. I can't stay in this place a minute longer. I hate it, and I hate you!"

Grandma pointed her finger at her. "You're exactly like your mother! Headstrong and stubborn. And look where it got her! If she'd listened to me, he wouldn't have killed her!"

"He didn't kill her! It was an accident. Abby said—"

"Oh, Abby said!" Grandma Dorothy spat the words.

"She said it had to be an accident. Daddy loved Mommy too much to ever hurt her!"

"How does Abby know anything? Was she there? Did she see your father and mother out on the lake that day? If she had, she would have seen how he grabbed that oar and split open her head."

The death of her parents – murder/suicide, the police said – occurred a few months past her first birthday. Maggie had imagined the horrible image in her dreams a thousand times, but this was too much. She covered her ears with her hands and turned away. "I don't have to listen to you anymore. I won't!"

Grandma grabbed her arm and twisted her around. "You have to listen before you make a mistake as big as the one your mother made. I know you're going to try meeting up with that boy, but he's gone, and he won't be coming back. Good riddance!"

"Luke will wait for me. I know he will. He loves me and I love him. You can't keep us apart."

"I won't let you make the same mistake Miranda made. She tried to run away from her problems but in the end, they killed her. I won't let that happen to you."

Tears of anger and frustration and grief ran down Maggie's face. "No! Let me go!"

"You think he loves you? He was only using you." Grandma tightened her hold. "You're lucky he's gone. He would have ruined your life like that man ruined your mother's life."

Maggie struggled to free herself from Grandma's strong grip. She beat her fist against her shoulder. "Let me go! Luke loves me. I know he does. I hate you! I hate you!"

"You are so like your father, it breaks my heart!"

Grandma Dorothy's grip on her arm abruptly loosened, and she staggered backward. Her face turned a funny greyish color and she clutched her stomach as if she was going to be sick. "She wouldn't listen to me. She wouldn't give him up."

Maggie seized the opportunity to grab her suitcase from the bed. "I'm leaving and I'm never coming back!"

Grandma clutched the bedpost. "She should have listened to me. She never listened to me. Oh, Miranda, my darling girl. Why didn't you listen to me?"

She slumped to the floor.

Maggie stared at her, fear making her immobile. "Grandma? Grandma, what's wrong?"

Grandma Dorothy's breath came out in ragged puffs. She struggled to lift her head. "I'm begging you, Maggie, don't run away. Don't make the same mistakes she did."

Maggie dropped her suitcase and slid to her knees beside her grandmother. Anger and love mixed with fear as she reached out her hand to touch her arm. "What's wrong? Should I get Grampa?"

Grandma Dorothy grabbed a handful of Maggie's T-shirt, her eyes pleading. "He was no good for her, but she said she loved him. She couldn't give him up. And it killed her."

"Who couldn't she give up, Grandma? Who did she love?"

"Your father."

"I don't understand, Grandma. If she loved Daddy, why did she run away? Why would he kill her?"

Grandma Dorothy's body went limp. Maggie stared at her, unable to move. She knew Grandma had a heart condition. She took some kind of pills for it. She shouldn't have argued with her, upset her like that. This was her fault.

Oh, my God. I've killed her.

She uncurled Grandma Dorothy's fingers from her T-shirt and stumbled away from her body. Tears of guilt crashed down her cheeks as she ran out of the lodge and raced to Grampa's shed.

You're exactly like your mother. The words taunted her, even as they confused her.

Nothing Grandma said made any sense. What had she meant? What had her mother done?

Anger welled up in her chest. This was all Luke's fault. He'd abandoned her when she needed him most, and she never wanted to see him again.

Chapter One

TEN YEARS LATER

Dammit, she knew better. Some chef she was.

Water boiled bubbled over the top of the pot and flooded her new stove's pristine surface. The pot was too small for the amount of pasta Maggie wanted to cook, but the bigger pot was already in use and she figured she could get away with it, just this once.

Wrong again, Maggie.

She turned off the gas burner and yelped in pain as water splashed up and scalded her bare arm.

Damn, that hurt, but it served her right for being so careless and for thinking she could cut corners in the kitchen. *Stupid, stupid, stupid.*

Suddenly, a man was standing next to her at the stove, sliding a heavy lid over the pot and pushing it onto a back burner. She'd been too distracted to notice his arrival in her kitchen, but now as she looked up into his face, her heart jumped into her throat. Though she hadn't seen him in ten years, she remembered every angle of his face, every golden speckle in his grey-green eyes, every wave in his dark hair.

"Luke."

The old resentment burned in her chest, surprising her with its intensity. She thought she'd put it behind her. Put *him* behind her.

Without a word, he steered her to the sink, turned on the cold water and pushed her arm beneath the stream. The water immediately soothed her scalded skin.

"Keep your arm under the cold water till the pain goes away."

"What the hell are you doing here?"

The corner of his mouth turned up in the way her teenage self had always found sexy. Now, as a grown woman, it only made her angry.

"I'm here to apply for the job, but I wanted to talk to you first."

Maggie's mind went blank. She couldn't think with him looking at her, touching her. She could barely breathe. She hated that he still had that affect on her. "What job?"

"The job as your hotel and restaurant manager."

Her sister Harper and brother-in-law Ethan had been searching for someone experienced in the hotel business to handle the job. With the renovation of the fishing lodge Maggie and her sisters had inherited from their grandfather nearing completion, they needed help running the new and improved Solace Lake Lodge. Years ago, Luke's mother Abby told her he'd gone out to California to work in a hotel, but Maggie didn't know the specifics. She had avoided talking to Abby since she moved back to the lodge.

"I've been working at a boutique hotel in the Napa Valley for the last eight years. I manage the hotel and restaurant, and I oversee the wines we serve. I've taken special training in pairing California wines with food."

Maggie turned off the water and dried her arm on her apron. As soon as her skin dried the burn stung again, but she ignored it. "That's a very nice resume, but what I want to know is why you're back in Minnesota. Tired of all the sunshine, are you?"

"My mother is sick. Her doctors say she'd dying."

She stared at him in shock as guilt washed over her like a tsunami. Abby had asked to see her. Her sisters had visited and told her Abby asked for her repeatedly. But she'd been too childishly angry to go. After her grandmother's death, Abby had been her friend and confidant. She'd helped her through sadness and loneliness, and moments when Harper forgot she was her sister and not her mother. Abby had been her only connection to Luke and even though she resented the way he'd left her, she still craved news of him.

But then Abby married Reese and moved away. The abandonment had devastated Maggie. Someone was always leaving her.

And now she was losing Abby again.

"She's sick? How long...?" She couldn't finish the question.

"When the doctors discovered breast cancer, she had a double mastectomy, but it had already spread to her lungs. Her doctors say she's terminal, that she has less than six months, but I don't accept that diagnosis."

"What do you mean?"

"I've done some research, talked to cancer specialists. I'm trying to get her to continue treatment with a new doctor. I need to be here to help her. That's why I'm applying for this job on a temporary basis."

"Temporary?"

"I've taken a leave of absence, but I can't afford not to work. I'll go back to California when...when Mom has stabilized."

"But what about Reese? He's devoted to Abby. Surely, he's done everything possible for her."

"Reese is a good man, but he's accepted what the doctors here have told them about my mother's health. I think we need another opinion from someone who isn't going to give up on her."

Luke turned away on a deep breath. His pain reached out and touched her like a living thing. He'd always been close to his mother. Years ago, Abby had told her how Luke had been conceived during a brief affair she'd had in her twenties. She'd said she couldn't regret the affair because it had given her Luke, and he was the light of her life. It had been the two of them against the world—three counting her mother. They'd lived with Abby's widowed mother Phyllis in the small town of Minnewasta all through Luke's childhood and adolescence.

"Before I have my interview with your sister, I needed to talk to you. We have a history, and the way I left you...wasn't fair. If my being here is awkward for you, or makes you uncomfortable, I won't apply for the job."

She snapped to attention at his words. Abby needed Luke right now, and Luke needed to be with his mother. Her petty concerns meant nothing. "Don't be ridiculous. That was years ago and we were kids, or at least I was. Whatever happened back then doesn't matter anymore. Abby's care is all that matters now."

He nodded, but a look of anguish marred his handsome features. "Yeah. That's all that matters."

AN HOUR LATER, MAGGIE heard voices in the lodge's main entry as Harper and Ethan walked Luke to the front door. She stood behind the staircase where she could listen unobserved.

"How soon can you start?" Harper asked.

"I can start right away, but I want you to phone my references before you make any decisions," Luke said. "Don't give me the job because you feel sorry for me."

"Luke, please. Let us help."

"I'm serious, Harper. I want you to know for certain that I can do this job for you. I want to be an asset to the lodge while I'm here."

That was the Luke she remembered, the boy with so much pride and so determined to go his own way.

Without her, as it turned out. She closed her eyes, pushing down the anger and pain. She hated that his rejection mattered even now.

"We'll phone your employer in California if that's what you want," Ethan said. "I'll call you as soon as we've done that."

"Thank you. I appreciate your kindness."

They said their goodbyes, and Maggie heard the front door open and close. She ventured out of her hiding spot. "So, you're going to hire Luke?" she asked.

"Probably." Ethan put his arm around Harper's shoulders. Her sister leaned against her husband, looking as if she was about to cry. "I'll call his employer as a courtesy to him, but if the information on his resume is true, he's exactly what the lodge needs right now."

"Why didn't you tell me Luke was coming for an interview? I didn't even know he was back in Minnesota." Seeing him so unexpectedly had been a shock, one she'd wished she could have prepared for.

"We didn't know. He phoned shortly before showing up here. He said he'd seen our ad on an internet job site." Harper dabbed at her eyes with a tissue. "I can't believe Abby's doctors say she's terminal. She's never given any indication how sick she was."

"Luke said he's trying to convince her to see a new doctor and try another treatment." Maggie prayed this doctor could perform a miracle.

"Reese never said a word," Ethan said. "He must be going out of his mind. I know I would."

He pulled Harper into his arms and held her close, murmuring something in her ear. Maggie retreated back into the kitchen to give them privacy. Harper and Ethan shared a close, loving bond. Her sister had all but given up on the idea of finding love, but then Ethan swept into her life and changed everything for her.

No one deserved to be happy more than Harper. But sometimes, especially now that her other sister Scarlet was about to marry, Maggie wondered if that kind of happiness would always elude her.

Chapter Two

AFTER HIS INTERVIEW, Luke headed to his mother's house in Minnewasta. Despite his protests, Abby insisted on making tea. Her slow movements around her kitchen were painful to watch. He needed all his self-control to keep from jumping out of his chair and filling the kettle himself, but he knew she needed to do these small chores simply to prove to herself she still could.

Abby pulled two teacups out of the cupboard and set them on the table before she sat down. She looked exhausted, as if making the tea had taken all her reserves of energy. "Luke honey, can you bring the teapot to the table?"

"Sure, Mom."

He brought the teapot from the counter. "Can I pour you some?"

"Sure. I like it a little on the weaker side."

He poured tea for her and then for himself, even though he hadn't drunk tea in years and didn't much like the stuff. But she didn't have to know that.

"So, how did the interview go?" she asked.

"Good, I think. They're going to check my references and get back to me."

"They wanted to check your references? Why? Harper's known you all your life."

"That's not how I want to get this job. I insisted they check."

Abby smiled. "You always were too proud for your own good."

He smiled back. He'd had to be. Minnewasta was just small enough and just conservative enough that some people looked down on an unwed mother and her illegitimate son. Sometimes, stubborn pride was all he had.

"You shouldn't be turning your life upside down like this for me."

Luke reached over and clasped her hand. "I'm not turning my life upside down. I'm doing exactly what I want to do in the place I want to do it."

He'd been devastated by the news that his mother's cancer was terminal. Devastated and wracked with guilt. He hadn't been back to Minnesota to see her in many years. Sure, he talked to her on the phone or on Skype at least once a week, and she and Reese had made many trips out to California. But he'd only made a handful of trips home to Minnesota in the last ten years and none to Minnewasta. He'd been so adamant about putting the past behind him that he'd rarely made the effort to come to see her, or his grandmother. His actions shamed him now.

"Did you see Maggie?"

"Yeah, I saw her."

Luke had been blown away. The pretty teenager he'd once known was now a beautiful young woman. The waist length hair he'd loved to run his fingers through was gone, replaced by a short, pixie cut. He missed her gorgeous hair, but he had to admit the cut suited her petite frame. With the hair gone, her neck appeared long and slender, and her dark brown eyes were huge in her beautiful oval face.

"Would you ask her to come and see me? I've sent messages through Harper and Scarlet, but she's been a no-show. I think she's still angry with me."

That surprised him. "Why would she be angry with you?"

"Because I deserted her. We became very close after you left and her grandmother died, but it was better for Reese's business to be in Minneapolis and, frankly, he didn't want to live in Minnewasta. Maggie was only sixteen then, and she believed I'd abandoned her."

The same way I abandoned her. Luke sipped his hot tea, the taste bitter on his tongue. "I'll ask her, Mom."

"Thanks, honey." She paused to drink a bit of tea. "I saw her at Harper's wedding in June and we said hello, but not much else. She looked so grown up, and so pretty. Don't you think she looks pretty?"

"Yeah, she's pretty."

"So?"

"So what?"

"So, did any sparks fly between you?" Her eyes danced with mischief.

He laughed, happy to see a glimpse of the mother he'd loved, the one full of fun and good humor. "No, absolutely not. No sparks, flying or otherwise."

Abby leaned back in her chair and regarded him. "You may laugh, but I can tell you first love is a powerful thing. It stays with you all your life."

He rolled his eyes, making her laugh. "Are you speaking from personal experience? I hope you're not carrying a torch for my father, the sperm donor."

"No, not your father."

He waited for her to elaborate, but she kept her thoughts to herself. He was glad she wasn't secretly pining for Jerry Fields. Though he shared genetic material with the man, Jerry had never been a father to him, and he'd never been any kind of partner to his mom. Luke wanted nothing to do with him.

"Mom, I've been doing some research," he began cautiously. "Ever since you told me about the diagnosis you got from your doctors, I've been looking online for new treatments for lung cancer. There's been interesting developments recently."

Resignation etched his mother's fine features. "Reese has taken me everywhere, talked to everyone. And they all say there's nothing to be done."

"I've been talking to an oncologist in California who's had good results with a new treatment."

"I really don't have the energy to go to California, Luke."

"You don't have to. He's agreed to look at your medical files. All you need to do is give a blood sample and your permission for him to look at your records."

She touched his hand. "Honey, I know you're doing this out of love, but—"

"You can't give up, Mom." Luke gripped her hand, suddenly afraid. "You have to fight this. You can beat it, I know you can."

For a long moment, she stared unblinking into his eyes. Finally, she sighed. "All right, I'll let you send my records to this doctor."

Relief flooded through him. "Good. I'll arrange for a technician to come to the house to take a blood sample as soon as possible."

She held up her hand. "I'll only agree on one condition."

He should have known it wouldn't be quite so easy. "What condition?"

"I want you to meet with Jerry. Talk to him."

"Mom, come on—"

"No, you can't weasel out of this. If you want me to go through the process of talking to yet another doctor, you have to do something for me. I want you to see him. He's asked about you."

"Is that right?" He couldn't keep the sarcasm out of his voice. Luke leaned back in his chair and folded his arms across his chest. Jerry had no business bothering his mother. He had no business in their lives at all. "It's a little late to remember he fathered a son, isn't it?"

"He wants to make amends."

"I have no intention of paying him a visit." Over the last five years or so, Jerry had sent letters to him in California, none of which he'd opened. The man had had no time for him while he was growing up, and Luke had no time for him now.

"Luke, don't let old resentments fester inside you. Forgiveness would help you far more than it would help Jerry."

"I don't want to see him, Mom."

"Luke—"

Abby set down her cup with a clatter as a sudden coughing fit seized her. Luke jumped to his feet and brought her a glass of water, not knowing what else to do. The cancer was slowly destroying her lungs.

In a few moments, her coughing stopped. She drank some water and smiled weakly at him. "I think I need to lie down for a while, honey. I'm sorry to cut your visit short."

Luke kissed her forehead. "Don't worry about it. I'll be back tomorrow."

"That sounds good."

He helped her to her bed and eased her head onto the pillow, removing her slippers before pulling the blanket over her. "Can I get you anything before I leave?"

Her eyes drifted shut, her face a mask of exhaustion. "No, I'm fine. I'll sleep for a while before Reese comes home."

He kissed her forehead once more. "Bye, Mom. I'll see you tomorrow."

"Will you contact your father?"

He stared at her small, prone figure. Despite her illness, the determined, stubborn streak that had carried her through every adversity in her life shone through. Luke tipped back his head and stared at the ceiling. She was serious. Unless he met with Jerry, she wouldn't talk to the new doctor. And talking to the new doctor was vital.

Life or death.

"Okay, fine. I'll talk to Jerry."

"When?"

Luke rolled his eyes and resisted the urge to groan. "Soon. This week."

"Promise?"

"I promise. Geez, Mom."

The corners of her mouth turned up, though she didn't open her eyes. "Okay. Bye, honey."

"Bye."

Luke softly closed the door of her room, struggling to hold back tears. Why did this have to happen to her? She was the sweetest, most positive person he knew. She'd never hurt anyone or anything.

He couldn't come up with an answer. There were no answers to be found.

LUKE DROVE HIS RENTAL car the short distance to his grandmother's house, the house he'd grown up in. Nothing much had changed. Phyllis Carlsson's house was robin's egg blue with white trim and a red door, the way it had always been. A white picket fence still circled the front yard, although this was a newer version rather than the ancient one he'd had to paint every other summer. He'd been expected to do a lot of chores growing up, and they'd helped him become self-reliant. His Grandma's house represented happiness for him. And love.

He pulled his suitcase from the trunk of the car and headed to the front door. As usual, the door was unlocked and he stepped inside. "Hello? Are you home, Grandma?"

She emerged from the kitchen wearing a flowered apron and a big smile. "Luke! I'm so happy to see you."

She clasped his face between her hands and kissed him. Luke wrapped his arms around her and held on tight. He'd forgotten how tiny she was, how fragile. He buried his face in her soft white hair and inhaled a combination of vanilla and ginger. It had been a long time since he'd seen her. Too long.

"I missed you, Grandma."

"I missed you, too. But you're here now. That's all that matters."

A wave of guilt rushed over him. She'd only been able to make the trip out to California twice in the last ten years. He should have come home to see her instead of letting old hurts and fears stop him. She was getting up in age. There was no telling how long she'd be around.

He thought his mother would be around forever, but he'd been wrong.

Luke pushed the thought away. She was going to get better. He'd make sure she got treatment and everything would be fine.

He released her, and Phyllis gave him a grin. "I've been cooking since you called me. All your favorite dishes."

"You shouldn't have gone to so much trouble." He hoped his stay wouldn't be too much for her.

She waved away his remark. "Are you kidding? It's been fun to cook for someone else again. Cooking for one is boring."

His grandmother had been the best cook in the neighborhood when he was a kid. Her pies were legendary at community suppers and her cookies had been popular with all the kids on the block. Luke's personal favorite had always been her gingerbread cookies. They were sweet and spicy, and their moist chewiness melted in his mouth. He salivated thinking about them. "Well, in that case, I'm looking forward to all the goodies."

Phyllis beamed at him. "Supper's almost ready. Why don't you take your suitcase to your old room and get settled in? Supper will be on the table after you've had a chance to freshen up."

"Can I help with anything? I don't want you to wait on me."

She waved away his concern once more. "No, absolutely not. Go on and let me have my fun. It's not every day my grandson comes home."

He chuckled, his heart overflowing with love for her. God, how he'd missed his grandmother. "Okay, I'll let you have your way tonight, but that's it. I won't let you run yourself ragged."

She made a sound of disgust but softened it with a laugh. "Spoil sport."

Luke laughed and carried his suitcase to his room. Not much had changed here either. Grandma had painted the room a soft blue and his old twin-sized bed had been swapped out for a new queen-sized with a new comforter, but all his old track and field trophies were still displayed on a shelf. Those days seemed like a different life now.

He hung his shirts in the small closet and folded underwear and jeans into the ancient dresser he'd used as a kid. Most of his clothes were of the warm weather variety. Right now, the weather was unseasonably warm for November in Minnesota, but it could turn bitterly cold in a heartbeat. If he was going to make it through the winter, he'd have to buy some appropriate clothing. Like a parka. The thought of winter in Minnesota caused an involuntary shiver to race up his spine.

After washing his hands and face, he made his way back to the kitchen. Phyllis was setting a big pot on the table between two place settings of her best dishes. The pang of guilt jolted him once again. He didn't want to be treated like company. All he wanted to be was family.

He made himself smile. "That smells really good, Grandma. Is it your famous chili?"

She lifted the lid with a flourish. "It is. I hope this version is as good as you remember. It's been a while since I've made it. Well, come on. Let's dig in."

"Great, I'm starved. I missed lunch."

His plane landed in Minneapolis around noon, and he hadn't wanted to waste time finding something to eat. He called Harper Lindquist, then picked up his rental car and headed straight to Solace Lake for his interview. When he'd seen their ad online for a hotel and restaurant manager, he knew the universe was telling him to come home.

Grandma's chili was as delicious as he remembered. Combined with her homemade bread, it was a taste of his childhood.

Phyllis kept up a steady banter about the goings on in the community. After ten years, he barely remembered the people she talked about, but he enjoyed hearing about his grandmother's life and her friends. In return, he told her about his life and his friends in the Napa Valley.

They talked about everything except the reason he'd come home.

Luke helped clear the table and load the dishwasher, one of the few new additions to the kitchen. They washed a couple of pots and pans, and Phyllis untied her apron.

"Are you still a coffee drinker?" she asked.

"Yes, I am. I'd love some."

While the coffee brewed, she reached into the jar on the counter and arranged some cookies on a plate. She set the plate on the table and they both resumed their seats. "Your favorite, the gingerbread."

Even though he was stuffed from dinner, he couldn't pass up his favorite cookie. The remembered flavor sent his taste buds into ecstasy. "Mmm, delicious, Grandma."

"I tried tempting Abby with some of my cookies, but she has no appetite." Tears shone in her eyes. "It's not right she should die before me."

She suddenly looked very old and very sad. Luke reached for her hand and laced his fingers with hers.

"She's not going to die, Grandma. I've been talking to a world-renowned cancer specialist in California, and he's agreed to look at her medical records and determine whether she's a good candidate for a new therapy he's testing."

"Does your mother know this?"

"Yes, of course. I had to have her consent. She agreed to release her records to him and submit a blood sample."

Phyllis wiped at a stray tear. "I'm surprised. When the last round of chemo didn't have any affect on her cancer, the doctors said there wasn't anything further they could do.

Abby made her peace with the news. She's tired. She's been fighting for a long while now."

"I know, but this is something different, a new doctor and a new treatment. There's hope."

She squeezed his hand. "Your mother is very sick, Luke. I don't want you to get your hopes up too high."

"I won't."

He was lying. He was counting on this new doctor to perform a miracle. In the two years since she'd been diagnosed, Reese had taken his mother to some of the best hospitals and doctors in the state. Reese had done everything he could, but Luke wasn't ready to give up. He couldn't.

"I'm shocked Abby consented. What did you say to convince her?"

He shifted in his chair. "I may have promised to talk to Jerry Fields."

Phyllis threw her head back and laughed. "That's my girl. She drives a hard bargain."

"You're not kidding."

"It'll do you good to come to terms with Jerry. He wasn't much of a father to you growing up, but I believe he's changed and wants to make amends. You might be astounded by what you learn if you get to know him."

Luke didn't believe it for a minute. "I'm not interested in getting to know him."

"Look, you don't have to fall in love with the man. You don't even have to send him a card at Christmas. You only need to acknowledge he's your father. It's a fact of life and you can't deny it anymore."

Acknowledging Jerry Fields as his father was the last thing he wanted to do. But a promise was a promise.

Chapter Three

MAGGIE LOOKED UP FROM her grater when Harper entered the kitchen.

"What are you making?" her sister asked.

"Fennel cakes. I mix up the grated fennel with some bread crumbs and cheese, fry them in oil and then top with a bit of sour cream and smoked salmon. I'm trying to put together a repertoire of appetizers for some of the events we've got coming up. I thought I'd try them out on the family at dinner tonight."

Harper made a face. "Isn't fennel the stuff that tastes like licorice? I hate licorice."

"Give it a chance, will you? The bulb doesn't taste like licorice at all once it's cooked. It's light and bright, like a little bit of spring. Exactly what we need on a November day."

"Okay, I'll try it, but I won't promise I'll like it." Harper leaned her hip against the stainless-steel counter. "You know we've been trying to recruit a full-time hotel and restaurant manager, but nobody is willing to move to the wilds of Minnesota to take a chance on us."

"Yes, I know." They hadn't been able to find a head chef either.

"We talked to the owner of the hotel where Luke works. He's not happy about losing him, even temporarily, but he understands his reasons for coming home. He's says he's a hard worker, manages staff well and really understands the industry. He wants him to come back to California as soon as he can."

Maggie stirred Parmesan cheese and panko bread crumbs into the grated fennel. She couldn't look at her sister. "You mean as soon as Abby dies."

Harper sighed. "Yeah. I'm sorry, Maggie. I know how close you were to her as a kid. I really wish you'd visit her. She's been asking for you, and I know you'll be sorry if you don't go. I'll come with you if you want me to."

Her reasons for avoiding Abby now seemed childish and petty. "I want to see her, too. I might take you up on your offer, but I'm not sure what to say to her."

"All we can say is that we love her."

Tears welled up in Maggie's eyes, obscuring her vision. She blindly stirred the fennel mixture and blinked them back. She *did* love Abby. Like a mother.

"So, are you okay with us hiring Luke? Grampa Bill wouldn't tell me the whole story, but he hinted the two of you had gotten pretty close the summer I was away working in the city. He made it sound like he didn't approve."

"He didn't. Neither did Grandma." Maggie pushed back the tears and turned to face her sister. "Luke worked at the lodge that summer, mowing grass and tending the flower beds. I had a serious crush on him, my first ever. He was good-looking and nice and funny, and I fell head over heels. But he was eighteen and on the verge of leaving home, and I was fourteen. Grandma and Grampa didn't have to worry, though, because Luke didn't think of me as girlfriend material. More like little sister material."

Not the whole truth, but all she was willing to share. She really believed, even now, that she and Luke had had something special. But he used her, just as her grandparents had said.

Harper smoothed Maggie's hair. "I'm sorry you got your heart broken."

"I survived. And I grew up. Luke is an old friend, that's all. I'll have no problem working with him. In fact, I'm looking forward to it."

She hoped she was telling the truth. Even as she said the words, the anger that had been simmering in her chest since Luke's arrival made her clench her fists.

"I'm glad to hear it." Harper sounded relieved. "At least we're able to help Luke. I wish we could have him here indefinitely, but since that isn't in the cards, you and I and Ethan will need to absorb as much knowledge as we can from him while he's here. I'm hoping the restaurant and hotel will be running like a well-oiled machine by the time he leaves, and we'll be able to manage everything ourselves."

"We can do it."

"I think so, too. Ethan is smart and hard working, and he's got so many great ideas for the lodge. And I love the recipes you've developed for the restaurant so far, though I'm reserving judgement on the licorice-flavored appetizers."

Maggie laughed. "Have a little faith, will you?"

"I have all kinds of faith in you. That's why Ethan and I want you to be our executive chef. We want you to permanently head up the lodge's kitchen."

The laughter died in Maggie's throat. "I don't have enough experience to be executive chef."

"Perhaps you lack experience, but you certainly don't lack talent. I'm confident you've got what it takes to make our restaurant a success."

Panic swirled in her gut. "Harper, the restaurant is too important to leave in the hands of an inexperienced chef."

"You set up our kitchen, didn't you? Ordered the equipment and everything the restaurant needs, right?"

"Yeah, but—"

"How many new recipes have you developed for the restaurant?"

"About thirty," Maggie said reluctantly. "I was trying to get things ready for the head chef. They'll probably want to put together their own menus, though."

Harper ignored her. "And you've spoken to suppliers to ensure we can get a lot of fresh local ingredients."

"Well yeah, but—"

"But nothing. You've done everything an executive chef needs to do except to actually accept the position." Harper looked directly into her eyes. "I'm not gonna lie, Maggie. Ethan was very reluctant at first to make you head chef. But over the past few months, he's seen how hard you've worked, and he loves your food. He agrees with me that you're the best person for the job. Even if we could find someone with more experience who was willing to take a chance on us, no one else will have the same connection to the lodge as you. No other chef will want it to succeed as much as you."

Maggie massaged the spot between her brows where a headache was beginning to form. Harper was right. No other chef wanted the lodge to succeed more than she did. But almost every other chef in the world had more self confidence.

Harper laid her hand on Maggie's shoulder. "I don't mean to put pressure on you, but Ethan's been advertising for an executive chef since June without any success. We've interviewed a couple of people, but the only training one candidate had was working in a fast-food restaurant. And when we googled the other candidate, we found out he'd been in jail for fraud."

She hadn't thought it would be so difficult to find a chef willing to take over the kitchen. But the lodge was some distance from Minneapolis and totally unproven. No chefs were willing to put their reputations on the line.

"With Luke joining the team, Ethan and I think we need to make firm decisions about our staff. You've come through for us every step of the way, Maggie. For my wedding, for the wedding we hosted here last month on short notice, and with everything you've done to prepare the kitchen. We wouldn't ask you to head up the kitchen if we didn't think you could handle it. We know you can do this, and we'll support you all the way."

Maggie stared into her sister's eyes. She was truly grateful for the confidence she had in her. She owed everything to Harper, and to Ethan. Before they'd called her home, she'd been on the brink of financial disaster.

She squared her shoulders. *Step up, Maggie.* "If you need me to be executive chef, then that's what I'll be." She ignored the little voice in her head that screamed in terror at her words.

Harper beamed at her and squeezed her shoulder. "That's such good news, Maggie. I promise you, you won't regret it. You're going to be brilliant."

Brilliant? She'd settle for "didn't screw up too badly."

"I hope you don't regret it."

"Never. I want to tell Ethan the good news. I'll let you get back at it."

"See you at dinner, Harper. About an hour."

Maggie turned her attention back to her fennel cakes as she dropped spoonfuls of the mixture into the heated frying pan and flattened them with the back of her spatula. Since fennel blubs weren't readily available in Minnesota year-round, her plan was to develop a similar recipe using grated potato or zucchini for the pancake and smoked walleye for the topping.

Her stomach did an anxious somersault. Would Luke have faith in her cooking?

He'd probably worked with chefs far more experienced, and likely more talented. She'd wanted to be a chef since she was that fourteen-year-old girl who fell in love with an eighteen-year-old boy one summer. Luke had encouraged her dreams, had told her she could do whatever she set her mind to do.

Would he still feel that way?

Dread settled in her gut. She was no longer the girl who thought she could do anything. Life had disabused her of that notion. If she blew her chance as head chef at the lodge, she had no place else to go.

THE NEXT MORNING, LUKE parked his rental car in front of the lodge and let it idle a few minutes before getting out. Much about the old lodge looked the same, but so much was different, including a whole new wing of rooms stretching out on the right-hand side of the building. To the left of lodge, the conference and event center was being built. The two-story structure was hip-roofed and clad in a barn-board siding that made it look as if it had been there for a hundred years. The guest wing addition was built of logs and made to look and feel as if it had been part of the original structure. He wondered what old Bill Swenson would think of the changes. This place had been his pride and joy.

A wave of bitterness washed over him at the thought of the old man. He couldn't blame him for protecting his granddaughter. No, Luke had no one to blame but himself for hurting Maggie.

He pushed aside old resentments and turned off the ignition. Since he was staying in Minnewasta for the next few months, he'd need to get his own vehicle, preferably something used and cheap. He had a car and a condo back home in Napa to make payments on, and money was tight. He'd talked to Ethan Hainstock the previous evening and had accepted the contract offered. A very fair offer, considering his position was only temporary. He hoped he could make it all work financially so he could be here for his mother.

Thinking of the reason he'd returned to Minnesota put a lump in his throat. He couldn't fail her.

Harper was in the front entry to greet him as he stepped into the lodge. She reached out her hand to him. “It’s good to see you again. I can’t tell you how pleased we are to have an old friend working with us.”

Luke grasped her hand, feeling immediately more at ease. “I want to thank you for hiring me on such short notice. It wouldn’t be possible for me to stay in Minnewasta if I didn’t have work.”

“I’m grateful you’re here. But I’m sorry about the reason you had to come home.”

The lump was back in his throat. “Yeah. Me too.”

Harper squeezed his hand before letting it go. “We’ve arranged a meeting of the whole family this morning to introduce you to everyone and get you up to speed on where we’re at in construction and renovation.”

“Sounds good.”

He followed her into the dining room, which remained much the same as he remembered. The only difference was that the windows overlooking the lake now included three sets of French doors that led out to a large deck. Guests could enjoy a meal or a drink outdoors in good weather. Luke give them an A plus for that innovation.

He noted the new tables and chairs in the dining room that were modern while still retaining a rustic vibe. Also a good addition.

Four people sat at one of the dining tables, including his stepfather Reese. Maggie was on her feet, refilling everyone’s coffee cups. Ethan sat next to a man with dark hair and eyes much like his own. Beside him was Scarlet Lindquist. He hadn't seen her in years, but he remembered her from high school though she'd been two grades ahead of him.

Harper started the introductions. "Of course, you know Reese. He's been our general contractor on the renovations to the lodge and the new additions. You met my husband Ethan yesterday. Beside him is his brother, Cameron Hainstock. Cam designed and built eight new luxury cottages where the old ones used to be. Two are completely finished, and the interiors of the other six should be done by late spring."

Cam Hainstock rose and offered his hand. "Pleased to meet you."

"I'm glad to meet you, too. Maybe you can show me the cottages later today."

"I'd be happy to."

"You know my sisters," Harper said. "Maggie is our executive chef, and Scarlet heads up our marketing efforts."

He grinned at Maggie. "I always knew you'd make your dream of being a chef come true."

She didn't smile back. "Well, you know. Family connections."

Her comment stunned him. She made it sound as if she only got the job because of family nepotism. The Maggie he'd known was fiercely proud and confident in her abilities.

Harper didn't let the remark pass unchallenged. "Hardly. We're lucky to have you."

He extended his hand to Scarlet. "Nice to see you again. It's been a long time."

She shook his hand and smiled. "It has. It must be at least twelve years. It's good to see you again, too, Luke."

Harper sat down at the table and Luke took the seat next to her. Maggie poured coffee for them before sitting across the table.

"I thought we'd give Luke the Reader's Digest version of what's been going on here the last few months," Harper began. "As you've probably guessed, my sisters and I inherited the lodge from our grandparents. Unfortunately, the building was in disrepair and business had fallen off to the point where we either had to modernize or sell the property."

"I was all for selling," Scarlet said. "Without telling us, Harper started looking for investors. That's where Ethan came in."

Ethan picked up the story. "I came into some money a few years ago after winning a lottery. I was looking for investment opportunities when I ran across Harper's ad looking for investors for the lodge."

"Except Ethan didn't mention that he owned Hainstock Investments. He told Harper his name was Ethan James and he was an employee of the company," Scarlet said.

Ethan lifted his hands in surrender. "Hey, I was only trying to protect myself. I had some bad experiences in the past. I can never quite be sure how someone is going to treat me once they find out about the money." He smiled at his wife. "So anyway, I came out to Solace Lake and was immediately smitten. And I liked the lodge, too."

Harper returned his smile. "So long story short, Ethan came on board and the renovation process started."

"And Maggie and I forgave Ethan for lying," Scarlet winked at her brother-in-law. "Eventually."

He winked back at her. "I think I've redeemed myself. I introduced you to my brother, didn't I?"

Scarlet turned to Cam with an expression that lit her face. "All is forgiven, Ethan." Cam lifted her hand and kissed her palm.

"Getting back to the renovation," Harper said with a smile. "We hired Reese to do the renovations on the lodge and Cam to build the cottages. Reese, why don't you tell Luke what you've done? I know you want to get home to Abby shortly."

Reese cleared his throat and looked at Luke with sorrowful eyes. "Yes, I do. First, I want to tell you how much it means to your mother that you've come home. It means a lot to me, too."

Luke nodded, unable to speak. Everyone else at the table went quiet.

Reese cleared his throat once again and began to speak, all business this time. "The work on the lodge has been extensive. New roof, new plumbing, new electrical, new commercial kitchen. We lifted the whole structure and fixed the caving foundation by putting in a whole new basement. A geo-thermal heat system was installed, and we're giving all the bedrooms upstairs ensuite bathrooms. I'm sure you've noticed the new deck and the new wing of hotel rooms?"

"Yeah. Looks like you've been busy. What's left to do?"

"We're finishing the renovations to the upstairs bedrooms and bathrooms right now. The conference center that we're building for weddings, conventions and things like that is completely unfinished on the inside, including the owners' apartment upstairs on the second floor. We're mostly finished the new guest wing, only the last few rooms to complete. In the spring, there'll be quite a bit of landscaping to do, including repaving the parking lot. Ethan is supervising the completion of the renovation and my brother Glenn is heading up my crew. I want to spend as much time as I can with Abby." He got to his feet. "I'm going to take off now, if that's all right with you, Harper."

"Of course. We'll talk to Glenn if we have any questions."

"You know how to reach me if you need me." He laid his hand on Luke's shoulder as he walked by. "I'll see you later, son."

"You will. Thanks, Reese."

Ethan walked Reese to the door. Harper resumed her summary. "Last month, we hosted our first wedding. It went pretty well considering we were mostly under construction."

Scarlet jumped in. "I got a call from a bride in distress. The venue for her wedding was flooded and she couldn't find anywhere else to have it. We all pulled together to make it happen. Cameron finished two of the cottages so we could put some of the guests there, and Reese's crew finished the kitchen and most of the rooms in the new wing. Maggie created a fabulous dinner, and Harper and Ethan made sure all the rooms were equipped and our guests were comfortable."

Ethan returned and sat beside Harper once more. "It was crazy, but I'm proud we were able to pull it off."

Scarlet nodded. "It definitely was crazy, but the bride was happy. I'm sure our next event is going to be even better. We have a couple of small weddings booked in early spring that we'll host here in the dining room, and one outdoor wedding in late May."

Cam kissed Scarlet's hand once more. "Aren't you forgetting something? Like *our* wedding?"

She laughed. "Of course I'm not forgetting. I was talking about paying customers."

"Our wedding will be small, mostly family and a few good friends. We're having it here in December," Cam told him.

"Congratulations." Luke stole a glance at Maggie, who smiled at her future brother-in-law. "Your wedding will be a good test run for the lodge. We'll have a chance to see if everything is working properly. Do you have a reservation system in place?"

"No, nothing," Harper said. "Back in the day, I took reservations over the phone and wrote them by hand onto a calendar. I'm hoping you can help me set up all those modern details."

"Of course. That's why I'm here."

She nodded in relief. "I'm so glad."

"How long before the renovations on the lodge are completely done?"

"Reese figured construction on the rooms upstairs should be completed mid-January. Then we have to get the rooms ready with furnishings, so maybe the beginning of February. The event center won't be ready until late summer."

"What about the cottages, Cam? Will they all be ready by February?"

"We could get another two, or possibly three cottages ready by then. Why? What do you have in mind?"

"Well, it occurs to me that even though all of you have been working very hard to reopen the lodge, your target audience may not know you exist. I think if we host a well-advertised grand opening event, we could get the word out and generate some excitement. We'd want to do it mid to late winter, so we can get bookings for the spring and summer."

"That's a great idea," Scarlet said, leaning forward in her chair. "It's exactly what we need. Like I said, I've got a couple of weddings booked for the spring, but we're not going to survive unless we have a full house year-round."

"If we have a grand opening in February, it will give us a chance to try out different winter activities and see what's most popular," Ethan said.

"I think it's a fabulous idea," Harper said. "The reopening of Solace Lake Lodge is not only a big deal for us, but for our community as well. We should be celebrating."

Luke turned to Maggie, who'd said little since he arrived. "What do you think, Maggie?"

"A grand opening sounds like a nice idea."

He waited a beat for her to continue. She didn't. "I have a feeling there's a but attached to that statement. Come on, Mags. Tell me what you really think."

Her eyes flashed in annoyance at the use of one of his old nicknames for her. "I think it's all well and good to have a splashy grand opening but if we're not well prepared, we'll end up looking like foolish amateurs."

"What do you mean?" Harper asked.

"We've got to have staff in place, well-trained staff. We managed to cater the wedding in October with a couple of temporary staff because we kept the food simple and served buffet style. And we only offered two meals, the wedding buffet in the evening and a breakfast buffet the next morning. If we open the restaurant, at a minimum we're going to need a sous chef for each shift plus line cooks, wait staff and bar staff." She clasped her hands in her lap and looked down at them. "I'm sorry. I don't mean to sound like a Debbie Downer, but I think we have to be realistic."

"Maggie's right," Luke said. Maggie lifted her head and stared at him, and Luke got the impression she was surprised he'd agree with her. "The kitchen has to be prepared but so does the front desk and housekeeping. Recreational facilities need to be in place. We'll need to start hiring right away if we're going to make a grand opening successful. And of course, we have to make sure we have rooms ready for guests. It's going to be a lot of hard work, so I want you to think it over carefully before you commit."

"I don't have to think it over," Harper said. "This is what I've wanted from the beginning. I'm ready to get started."

Ethan linked his fingers through hers. "I'm in, too."

Scarlet nodded. "We've come this far and worked so hard. I say let's take it all the way."

"Agreed," Cam said.

Luke turned to Maggie. Her hands were palm down on top of the table, her body tensely coiled as if she were getting ready to jump up and run. "Maggie, what about you? Are you ready to take the lodge to the next step?"

She glanced up at him, and something that looked like fear flashed briefly in her eyes, surprising him once again. The Maggie he'd known wasn't afraid of anything. He wondered what had happened in the years they'd been apart to cause her to lose her fierce determination.

After expelling a breath, she lifted her chin in an almost defiant gesture and he caught a glimpse of the old Maggie. "I'm in."

He smiled at her. "Ladies and gentlemen, it's official. In three and a half months, we're going to hold the biggest and best Grand Opening Minnewasta has ever seen."

"God help us," Maggie murmured.

Chapter Four

LUKE SIPPED HIS TEA and grimaced. He didn't like the stuff any more today than he had two days ago. Bracing himself, he took another cautious swallow.

"If you don't like it, you don't have to drink it."

He eyed his mother skeptically. "Really?"

"Of course. You're not a five-year-old that I have to force to drink his milk." Abby smiled ruefully. "I appreciate that you're drinking tea as a concession to me, but if you don't like it, and it's pretty obvious you don't, don't drink it to try to please the sick woman 'cause it's not working."

Luke put down his teacup. He should have known he couldn't fool his mother. She'd always been able to read him and her illness obviously hadn't impaired that ability. "Do you have coffee?"

"In the pantry. Reese drinks it every morning."

He found a can of coffee grounds in the pantry and made himself a half pot in the coffeemaker. He sighed in pleasure as the rich aroma of coffee filled the kitchen. He may as well admit he was addicted to the stuff. Smelling the brew made him think of the little shop down the street from his condo in Napa that roasted their own beans and served the best coffee this side of Nirvana.

He stared out the window over the sink at the brown grass and the bare limbs of the poplar tree in the back yard. He was a long way from Nirvana.

As soon as the coffee finished brewing, he poured himself a cup, added a splash of milk, and rejoined her at the kitchen table. With the first few sips, a pleasant caffeine buzz flowed through his system.

Abby grinned at him. "Feel better?"

"Much."

"Good. Honey, I wanted to ask you. Have you had a chance to talk to Maggie? Do you think she'll come to visit me?"

This was the second time she'd asked about Maggie. He didn't know why seeing her was so important, but he'd make damn sure it happened. "I haven't talked to her about it yet, but I will. She'll come to see you soon. I promise."

She nodded, relief showing on her face. "That's good. Thanks, honey."

"No problem."

"At the risk of sounding like a nagging mother, have you given any thought to the other promise you made to me?"

His mother was nothing if not tenacious. He saluted her with his coffee cup. "After I leave here, I'm going to see Jerry."

"Good. Have you called him?"

"No. I thought I'd drop in." He wanted to see what kind of reaction he'd get if he showed up unannounced. In a perverse way, he wanted to disprove his mother and grandmother's belief that Jerry had changed.

Once a deadbeat, always a deadbeat.

"I understand he works at home so he should be around. Jerry told me he got married a few years ago, so don't be surprised if a woman answers the door."

"Who'd he marry?"

"A local woman, but I don't know her. Apparently, she's several years younger than Jerry."

He didn't welcome the news. Luke didn't like the idea of an audience for his meeting with his birth father.

"I want to come clean about something." Abby stared at her teacup as she gripped the delicate porcelain handle, her knuckles turning white from the pressure. "Your father not being in your life, that wasn't entirely his fault."

"Mom, don't take the blame for him."

She looked up at him. "I'm not. I'm taking responsibility for my own actions, something I should have done long ago."

"What are you talking about?"

She paused to drink some tea, her hand shaking slightly. "Jerry and I went to high school together. We never dated back then or were particularly good friends. As soon as he graduated, he joined the military and left Minnewasta. I stayed here and started working in the bank.

"About five years later, he came home on leave to visit his mother. She had cancer, I think, and wasn't doing very well. Jerry and I met, and I think we...needed each other. You were conceived as a result."

"I know the end to this story already, Mom. Jerry left and you never heard from him again."

"That's where you're wrong. Three months later, his mother died and he came home to bury her. About then, I found out I was pregnant with you. I told him, not because

I wanted anything from him, but because I thought he had the right to know. But Jerry astonished me by asking me to marry him."

The news shocked Luke. "He asked you to marry him?"

"He did. I turned him down. I didn't love him, and he didn't love me. He was asking because he wanted to do the right thing, but marriage would have been a disaster for both of us. So, once he settled his mother's affairs, he went back to the military base overseas where he'd been serving. And I had you."

He was almost afraid to ask his next question. "Did you ever hear from him again?"

Abby nodded. "He sent me a card with his contact information during my pregnancy. He wanted me to let him know as soon as you were born. So I did."

She stopped once again to drink her tea. Luke tamped down his impatience, resisting the urge to drum his fingers. He had to let her tell this story in her own way.

"He started sending money for you. Not a lot, but it certainly helped. I sent him a few pictures of you in return. But then when you were five and about to start school, he moved to an army base in Texas. He started talking about coming to Minnesota to see you. But I said no."

Another surprise. "Why?"

Abby's face crumbled. "I told him his sporadic visits would only confuse you. You needed someone who was with you for the long haul, not just when the mood struck him. But in truth, I was afraid. You were all I had, and I couldn't bear the thought of losing you."

"Losing me? Why would you lose me?"

She wiped at a tear that streaked down her face. "I didn't say I was being rational. I guess I was afraid if you got to know Jerry, you'd want to be with him. That you'd want your father. I was afraid to let that happen."

"Did Jerry argue with you about seeing me? Did he ever actually come to Minnesota?"

"No. He didn't push and I didn't offer. And together we were both guilty of depriving you of knowing your father. Me most of all."

Luke got to his feet, too restless to sit any longer. All these years he'd blamed Jerry, calling him a deadbeat and a deserter.

"I should have told you this years ago," Abby said. "But I was afraid you'd be angry with me. And you'd have every right to be. I'm sorry, Luke."

Her face was drawn and thin, the skin pulled tight over her cheekbones. Whatever she did, she did for love, misguided though it might have been. He thought back to his childhood. His mother had never once said a disparaging word about his father. Every Christmas, a gift from his father was under the tree, though he'd always known Abby had purchased it. She always said he sent her the money and asked her to buy him something he really wanted. When he got older and asked why all the other kids had fathers and he didn't, she'd taken him in her arms and told him she loved him enough for a mother and a father.

No matter what she'd kept from him, he couldn't be angry with her, especially now. He knelt beside her chair. "Like you said, he didn't fight you to see me. You have nothing to be sorry about. You were the best mother ever. You still are."

Abby stroked his hair. "And you're the best son a mother could ever want. I love you, Luke."

He swallowed back tears. "I love you, too."

A PROMISE WAS A PROMISE.

Luke repeated the phrase to himself as he parked in front of the house Jerry Fields used for his business and his home. A modest bungalow that appeared well cared for, it had what looked like a recent paint job and a well-tended yard. A sign on the fence circling the front yard announced the name of Jerry's business, Fields Digital Solutions. Luke had done some checking and discovered that Jerry's business, which specialized in setting up computer networks and security systems for businesses, was well thought of and very successful. Apparently, his services were in demand across the state and beyond.

Too bad he hadn't set up this business years ago. Maybe they would have had a chance for a relationship.

Luke huffed out a breath. He hated that all these years later Jerry's absence from his life still mattered. But after what his mother had told him, he supposed he wasn't entirely to blame.

But he wished his father had cared enough to fight for him.

He slid out of the rental car and slammed the door with a little more force than was necessary. As he walked to the front door, he blew out a breath to calm himself. Just because he'd been manipulated into this visit didn't mean he had to cop an attitude. He rang the doorbell.

A few moments later, a tall, lean man in his fifties wearing wire framed glasses answered the door. His thick hair curled around the collar of his denim shirt. It must have been dark brown once, like Luke's, but was now liberally streaked with grey. Eyes, the same grey-green color as his, stared at him first in shock, and then in welcome.

He smiled broadly. "Luke. It's good to see you. Come in out of the cold."

Luke stepped over the threshold into the front hallway of the house. To the left, the living room featured gleaming hardwood floors and tasteful modern furniture. In fact, the furniture looked a lot like the stuff he'd purchased for his condo in Napa. The idea that he and Jerry shared the same taste in décor annoyed the hell out of him.

"Please, take off your coat. Would you like some coffee?"

"Sure."

Jerry hung his coat in the closet next to the front door, then led the way to kitchen. The room was modern, yet warm and homey. Jerry busied himself making coffee. "This is a nice surprise. I appreciate you coming to see me. I'd heard you were back in town."

"I didn't think you'd recognize me," Luke said.

"Your mother gave me some recent pictures. I'm sorry she's so sick. Abby is the best person. She doesn't deserve this."

"No. She doesn't." Luke cleared his throat, not wanting to go there. He stood next to the table, shuffling from foot to foot. "I should tell you upfront, coming here wasn't my idea. It was hers."

Jerry placed two cups of coffee on the table, then went to the fridge for milk. "I expected so. It's not like I've given you a lot of reasons to want to see me. Why don't you sit down?"

Luke lowered himself onto one of the chairs. Jerry returned to the pantry and came back to the table with a bowl of sugar. "Did you get the letter I sent to you a few months ago?"

"I got it. I didn't open it." Once he'd seen Jerry's name on the return address, he'd fired the envelope straight into the garbage, just as he'd done with Jerry's other letters over the years.

"I got your new address from your mother. I wanted to connect with you, to explain, for a long time. I let you down when you were a child. If I could go back, I'd change a lot of things I did. I'm sorry for not being a real father to you."

Luke stared into his coffee cup, not trusting himself to meet Jerry's eyes. "I think you're about twenty-eight years too late with that apology."

"I know." Jerry sat in the seat across from him. "But it's all I've got."

Luke said nothing, and Jerry continued. "I thought by sending money to your mother while you were growing up I was doing the right thing, the responsible thing. It didn't occur to me till a few years ago that being a father is much more than throwing money at a kid. You have to be there, and I wasn't."

"No, you weren't."

"I know it doesn't excuse my behavior, but I had no idea what a father was supposed to do. I grew up without a father, too. My biological father walked out on my mother and me when I was a baby. I grew up poor, looked down on by everyone in town. I swore if I ever had a kid, I'd provide for him, so for a lot of years I thought I'd done right by you by sending money. I was wrong. A father is there every day, helping, teaching, soothing."

Despite himself, Luke's curiosity got the best of him. "If things were so bad for you here in Minnewasta, why did you come back?"

Jerry sipped his coffee. "I hadn't planned to. Once I left this place, I never wanted to see it again. And then, a few years ago, I was shocked to discover my no-good, dead-beat dad left me some property here. I came back, intending to sell it and get the hell back to Texas. And then I meet my wife."

He took another sip of his coffee. Luke sensed there was much more to this story, and he was curious, but he didn't want to appear too interested in Jerry's life.

He couldn't stop himself from asking one last question, though. "What made you realize what a father is supposed to be?"

Before Jerry could answer, he heard the front door crash open. A moment later, a small child bolted into the kitchen. "Daddy, Daddy, Daddy!"

The child ran to Jerry and he lifted her in his arms and kissed her cheek. At least, Luke assumed the child was a her. The pink snowsuit was a pretty big clue.

"Daddy, we got books from the library! Can you read them to me?"

"I will later, sweetheart. Right now, there's someone here I'd like you to meet. Luke, this is my daughter Emily. She'll be five next spring. Emily, Luke is my son. He's your brother."

She studied him with grey-green eyes. "No, Daddy. He can't be my brother. He's big."

"It's the truth, Em."

A heavily pregnant woman entered the kitchen. She was blonde and blue-eyed and probably in her thirties, which made her about twenty years younger than Jerry. She smiled in welcome and held out her hand. Luke got to his feet.

"Luke, how wonderful to meet you! I'm Denise."

"My wife," Jerry said proudly.

Luke shook her hand. "It's nice to meet you, Denise."

"I think I would have known you anywhere, even if I hadn't seen your picture. You look so much like your father."

He was taken aback by her statement, but when he glanced at Jerry, he couldn't deny the truth of her words. He'd never considered having anything in common with him before, including his looks.

"Jerry told me about your mother's illness. I'm truly sorry."

He believed her. Denise Fields struck him as the kind of person who meant what she said. "Thank you."

"Why don't you stay for dinner? We'd love to have you."

Something like panic made his heart hammer. "Thank you, I appreciate the offer, but I need to get back to the lodge." He gave them a brief account of the temporary work he was doing there.

Denise nodded. "It's good you can be here in Minnewasta. I'm sure it means a lot to your mother."

Luke's throat closed and for a moment, all he could do was nod. He cleared his throat and struggled to get himself under control. "I should be going."

He headed to the front door, anxious to make his escape. Jerry set Emily on her feet and retrieved Luke's coat from the closet. Emily grabbed Denise's hand and they watched him put on his coat. The little girl stared at him as she leaned against her mother's side.

Jerry pulled a coat from the closet and slipped it on. "I'll walk you to your car."

"Goodbye, Luke," Denise said. "I hope we can have you over for dinner soon."

"Thank you." He didn't know what else to say. Until ten minutes ago, he hadn't known a family existed aside from a wife. It was too much to take in.

Luke followed Jerry down the front walk. Once he reached his car, he opened the driver's side door. "Thanks for coffee."

"You're welcome. I'm glad you dropped by. I hope you know Denise's offer was genuine. We'd both love to have you over and get to know you."

"I'll think about it."

Jerry nodded. "You asked me what made me change my attitude about being a father. It was Denise, and then Emily. They're the ones who taught me what a father should be. I'm sorry I missed your growing up. I cheated you, and I cheated me."

It had never occurred to him that Jerry had missed out by not being in his life. He'd only thought about what he'd lost.

"We could use some expertise setting up the computer systems at the lodge. Would you be available?" The words flew out of his mouth, surprising him.

"Name a date and I'll be there." Jerry fished a business card from the inside pocket of his jacket. "Give me a call and let me know what you need."

Luke accepted the card, uncertain why he'd asked for his help. "I'll be in touch."

He got in the car and turned the ignition. As he drove away, he saw his father lift his hand in a wave. Without thinking, he waved back.

For most of his life he'd seen his parents in clear black and white terms. But now his world looked a whole lot greyer.

Chapter Five

THE NEXT DAY, LUKE buried himself in work, not wanting to think about his parents for a while. But despite everything he needed to do, he couldn't concentrate. He'd discovered Jerry wasn't a villain; he was simply a man who'd made mistakes. Making mistakes was something he could relate to. Lord knew, he'd made plenty. The biggest had changed his life.

Good grief. He had an almost fiver-year-old half-sister and another sibling on the way. As an only child, the idea blew him away. Especially since his half-siblings were young enough to be his own children.

A picture of Maggie with a baby in her arms popped into his mind. *My baby.*

Luke pushed the idea away, staggered by its intensity and the direction his mind had taken. He hadn't let himself dwell on thoughts like this for a long time and he couldn't start now.

If he'd stayed in Minnewasta, they might have had children by now. At one time he'd thought he'd spend his life with her, have children with her. But he'd thrown it all away. The pain of that loss came hard and fast. Followed swiftly by guilt.

Enough. He'd done what he had to do.

He forced his attention back to work and sifted through the resumes the lodge had received so far in response to the online ads for help he'd posted. Many applications were from locals, but some, especially those applying for the sous-chef positions, came from applicants living all over the country. He shook his head at one application from South Carolina. Did this person have any idea what a Minnesota winter was like?

He shivered at the thought. The November days were getting colder, and the worst was yet to come. For a moment, he longed for California and his sunny patio overlooking a hillside vineyard. Then he shut down that line of thinking completely. Right now his family needed him here, and so did the lodge.

With a sigh, he printed copies of the applications of those people he intended to interview. The job was massive. Kitchen and wait staff, housekeepers and front desk staff. Luke made a note on his phone to speak to Ethan about hiring some people to help him with all the recreational activities he planned for the lodge. And in the spring, they'd probably need grounds keepers...

Would Mom be alive in the spring?

Luke closed his eyes, steadying himself with a deep breath. He couldn't dwell on it. He had to focus on the present and the job at hand, or he wouldn't be any good to anyone, including himself.

"Luke?"

He looked up in surprise at Maggie. She set a tray with a coffee cup and a plate of cookies on the table in the dining room that he'd been using as a desk.

"Sorry. I guess I zoned out for a minute."

"I thought you might need a break." The aroma of a well-brewed cup of coffee tempted his senses as she passed him the cup. "Do you still take milk and sugar?"

He was amazed she remembered. "Just milk now. Everybody in California is trying to reduce carbs. If I was a real Californian, I probably wouldn't consume dairy either."

"Lucky for you, Minnesotans have no qualms about dairy products. Or at least, none of the Minnesotans at this lodge."

She passed him a small pitcher of milk and he added some to his coffee. He gestured to the plate of cookies. "If all of these are for me, I'm really going to blow my diet."

Maggie grinned as she pulled a chair closer to his table and sat. "Sorry about that. Actually, I wanted your opinion. I thought it might be a nice gesture to offer a container of fresh cookies in each guestroom as they check in. Or perhaps only in the cottages. What do you think?"

Luke reached for one of the cookies and took a bite. The taste of ginger and sugar exploded in his mouth as he bit into the chewy goodness. The taste was very familiar. "These taste like my grandmother's gingerbread cookies."

"They should. I'm using her recipe."

"Really? I thought she guarded all her recipes like the gold in Fort Knox. She wouldn't give it to me."

Maggie's lips quirked. "Maybe you didn't ask her nicely."

"And you did?"

"I suppose I did. I was visiting your mother a few weeks after my grandmother died, and Phyllis set a plate of these in front of me. I asked her for the recipe but instead, she insisted we make a batch together in the kitchen. I wrote down the recipe from memory the minute I got home." She gave a rueful smile. "She probably felt sorry for me."

Knowing his grandmother, she probably had, but he wasn't going to tell her so. Maggie and her grandmother had clashed over many things, especially her relationship with him, but she'd loved her fiercely. She'd been the only mother she'd ever known. He could imagine how intensely she must have grieved.

Another wave of guilt swept over him. He hadn't been there for her when she'd needed him most.

"These are as good as hers. Maybe better. Don't tell her I said that."

Maggie laughed. "I wouldn't dream of it."

The sound of Maggie's laughter transported him back ten years. Back then, she laughed easily and often. Her smiles were harder to come by these days.

Or maybe that was only when she was with him.

He cleared his throat. "I think it's a great idea to leave cookies for the guests. I think we'd probably only offer them to guests planning an extended stay in one of the cottages, though."

"That makes sense. If someone is only staying overnight, they likely wouldn't have time to eat all the cookies even if they wanted to."

"Right." He shuffled through the papers on his table until he found what he wanted. "Which reminds me, Harper emailed me this copy of your preliminary menu. I want to talk to you about it."

Her expression turned wary and her posture stiffened. "Do you have a problem with it?"

Her defensiveness took him aback. "No, of course not. I like the idea that the restaurant will aim to serve locally grown organic food as much as possible. I'm concerned about the fish dishes you're proposing. Are we going to have a steady supply we can count on all year long?"

"I wouldn't have put it on the menu if I hadn't considered that. I spoke to the owners of a local fish market. They sell fish brought in fresh everyday by commercial fishers including the walleye, lake trout and whitefish we plan to serve on the menu. All the fish are from Minnesota lakes. They assure me they will have the consistent supply we'll need."

He nodded. "Good."

"And before you ask, I've sourced local suppliers for most of our ingredients. The greens are going to come from a greenhouse outside of Brainerd. They can offer supply all year long, too."

"You've done your homework. It looks like you've got everything well in hand."

Her confused expression told him she'd been preparing herself for a reprimand. "Okay. Thank you."

"You're welcome. You're doing a good job, Maggie."

She blinked at him, then quickly rose to her feet. "I should go and let you get back to work."

He caught her hand before she could escape. "I could use your help interviewing the kitchen staff. They're first on my list to hire."

"Yes, of course. I want to be in on the hiring."

He held on to her hand as she tried to move away. "There's something else. My mother asked to see you. It seems really important to her that you do. Will you come with me tomorrow to visit her?"

He watched for her response. She closed her eyes and it seemed her breathing quickened. Finally, she nodded and lifted her gaze to meet his. "Yes, of course. I'll come with you."

Luke nodded, relieved. "Good. I'm leaving for Minneapolis in a few minutes to take back my rental car and find something used I can drive while I'm here, but I should be back by noon tomorrow. We'll go about one o'clock. She gets too tired later in the afternoon for visitors."

"I'll be ready."

She tugged on her hand, but he held firm. "You *are* doing a great job, Maggie. Don't doubt it."

She gave a brief nod, and he reluctantly released her. She turned and quickly fled the dining room.

He wondered again what had happened to destroy her confidence. Would she be able to handle the stress of a busy kitchen?

Luke hoped so. The restaurant was the centerpiece of the new lodge. If it didn't pan out, the future of the lodge would be in question. And so would Maggie's future as a chef.

LATER THAT EVENING, alone in her cottage, Maggie rummaged through the shelf of her closet, setting aside boxes and bags until she found what she was looking for. The blue cardboard box had been pushed to the back where she wouldn't be able to see it. She didn't want to open her closet every day and be reminded of the past, but she hadn't quite been able to make herself throw the box away either. So it remained on her shelf. In limbo.

Maggie brought down the box, sat on the edge of her bed and opened it. Mr. Jingles the Teddy Bear smiled up at her. Maggie caressed his soft fur, then lifted him from the box and gave him a quick hug before setting him on the bed. There was another box inside the first one. She removed the lid and carefully unwrapped the layers and layers of tissue paper protecting the delicate object inside. Finally, she pushed aside one last layer of tissue paper to reveal the glass unicorn.

She lifted the unicorn from the box and examined it. It had been a while since she'd opened the box, but the little unicorn was as pretty as she remembered. At about five inches in height and four in length, the unicorn was small and delicate. She fingered the tiny horn, marvelling at its fragility. How amazing it had survived unscathed considering the number of times she'd moved.

She didn't know why she'd kept it all these years.

That was a lie. She knew the answer. *Because Luke gave it to me.*

He'd told her it had reminded him of her – beautiful and unique. No gift she'd received before or since had meant as much.

She stared at the little unicorn in her hands. She'd almost discarded it when she packed up her apartment in Minneapolis to move to the lodge. At the last minute, she'd rescued it from the pile of stuff she was donating to a woman's shelter, unable to part with it. Her attachment to the unicorn was ridiculous, considering the thing was only a chunk of glass.

But, try as she might, she couldn't make herself believe it meant nothing.

Carefully, she wrapped the unicorn in its layers of tissue paper once more, laid it in the first box, then set that box into the blue one. Placing Mr. Jingles back inside and closing the lid, she returned the box to its spot on the shelf at the back of her closet.

Out of sight, out of mind. If only that were true.

SHORTLY BEFORE ONE o'clock the next day, an unfamiliar blue half-ton truck pulled up in front of the lodge. From what Maggie could tell, the truck, a domestic American model, wasn't new, but was in reasonably good shape. She stepped out onto the porch as Luke slid out of the driver's side. He let the truck idle as he came toward her.

"What do you think of my new wheels?" he asked.

"I didn't figure you for a truck guy. I thought you were more into luxury cars like the rental you were driving. You being a California boy, and all."

"I love trucks, remember? Besides, a truck seemed like a more practical option here." One side of his mouth turned up in a grin. "And for the record, the luxury car was the only vehicle I could rent on short notice. I drive an ordinary Ford SUV in California."

Maggie raised an eyebrow but said nothing. A memory flashed through her mind. Luke driving an ancient, mostly rusty Ford pickup to the lodge that summer. He'd worked odd jobs summers and after school for three years to buy it and keep it running. The old Ford had been his pride and joy.

Every chance they got, they'd sneak off in the Ford and park somewhere secluded. They'd been in that truck the first time Luke had kissed her. He'd pulled her toward him and covered her mouth with his, and she'd sworn she'd heard angels singing. And then, her body had gone up in flames in a very unangel-like way. As the summer went on, they'd grown bolder in their explorations. Harper had given her 'the lecture' on sex, but she hadn't prepared her for the way her body would react to Luke's kisses, or his touch. Like the way her nipples would harden as he caressed her breasts, and the way her panties would dampen. And when he'd reached inside her panties and inserted a finger inside her—

"Are you ready?"

Maggie stared at Luke in incomprehension. And then the present returned with forceful fury. Heat infused her cold cheeks. They were on their way to see his sick mother. Her thoughts shamed her.

She reminded herself that Luke had left her once and would do so again. The heat and her vivid memory dissipated.

"Yeah, let's go."

She followed him to the truck and hopped in the passenger side. As they pulled out of the parking lot and headed to Minnewasta, a light dusting of snow began to fall. The weather had turned cold, signalling the true beginning of winter. Though she knew a lot of people hated winter and would think she was crazy, winter had always been Maggie's favorite season. She loved the crisp, new snow that blanketed the landscape and hid imperfections with its tranquil beauty.

Luke turned up the heater. "Damn. Even inside the truck it's cold."

"You'll get used to it again," Maggie said.

"I don't know about that."

She tipped her chin toward his puffy blue jacket. "Nice parka. Is it new?"

"Yeah. I haven't worn a parka since I left Minnesota. Can't say I missed it."

She couldn't help smiling at the disgust in his voice. Luke had never been a winter person. That summer, he'd talked about his dream of moving to California so he'd never have to face another Minnesota winter again. But he'd said he didn't have the money to make it to California, and he wouldn't take anything from his mother or grandmother. She'd always wondered where the money had come from for him to travel to the west coast and go to school there. Perhaps, in his eagerness to get away, he'd taken money from his mother after all.

A lump of guilt formed in her throat at the thought of Abby. She should have visited her weeks ago instead of letting old resentments stop her. Now, her time with Abby would be limited. She hoped she wouldn't cry and upset her. Maggie's fingers tightened around the plastic container in her lap. The last thing Abby needed was a messy emotional display.

"You okay?"

Maggie blinked and looked at Luke. "Yeah, sure. I'm fine."

He glanced at her quickly before turning his attention back to the road. "I know you're nervous about visiting Mom," he said. "So was I. Reese warned me that she'd lost weight and that she had little energy. I was afraid of what I'd find when I saw her again. But even though she looks a little different physically, she's still my mom. She's still Abby."

Maggie gulped in a breath to steady herself. "Being Abby is pretty awesome."

He flashed her a quick smile. "Yeah, it is."

They drove in silence the rest of the way. Luke parked the truck on the street in front of Abby's house. They got out and walked to the front door. Luke knocked before opening the door and walking inside.

"Hi, Mom. We're here."

"Hello, hello!"

Abby sat in an armchair in the living room, a red and black plaid blanket covering her lap. Maggie couldn't believe how thin and frail she looked, as if the wind blowing into the house with them could knock her over. But the wide smile on her face was the one Maggie remembered.

"Maggie, it's so good to see you."

Maggie walked into Abby's open arms, stooping to hug her. She inhaled Abby's perfume, Chanel Number Five if she remembered correctly. The scent brought back old memories. Abby's kindness and the love she'd always received from her rushed back and in that minute, the years fell away as if they hadn't been apart a single day.

"It's good to see you, too. I've missed you." Maggie struggled to keep the tears at bay.

"I've missed you, too, dear girl."

Abby held her in a surprisingly strong grip, considering how much frailer she looked since she saw her in June. At last she let her go. “Let me look at you. I wanted to tell you at Harper’s wedding what a beautiful young woman you've become, but we never got a chance to talk. And I love your hair that way!”

Maggie lifted a self-conscious hand to the back of her neck and stroked the ends of her hair. “I cut it a few years ago. The long hair was too hot and heavy in the kitchen, and it kept getting in my way.”

“Don’t apologize. It suits you perfectly. You look gorgeous.” Abby gestured to the sofa next to her chair. “Sit down beside me. Luke, would you mind putting on the kettle for tea? You can make yourself some coffee, if you like.”

“Sure, Mom.”

He tossed his parka onto a chair and headed to the kitchen. Maggie handed Abby the plastic container she’d been holding before taking off her jacket. “I made you brownies. You always said they were your favorite.”

“Oh, they are. Thank you. We’ll have some with tea.” Abby set the container on her lap and rested her hands on top. “Tell me all about your adventures as a chef.”

“There’s not much to tell.” The last thing she wanted to do was to talk about her sordid work history, especially with Luke listening in the next room. She sat on the sofa near Abby. “I went to culinary school, I worked in some kitchens in Minneapolis learning the ropes, and now I’ve been given the opportunity to head up my own kitchen at the lodge. I’m very grateful.”

"I know you'll be a success. People will travel for miles for your food."

Maggie tightly clasped her hands together in her lap. "I hope so."

Abby tilted her head, regarding her. "You sound worried."

"There's lot at stake. If the restaurant isn't a success, the lodge will suffer."

"I've known since you were a child that you were a talented cook. You can do this. You just have to believe in yourself."

Maggie reached over and grasped Abby's hand. "Yeah. I suppose I should."

Abby covered her hand with her own. "It's going to be all right, sweetheart."

Her heart filled with love. Abby could always make her believe anything was possible. But Maggie wondered if her words held another meaning. Maybe she was trying to tell her that she'd be okay after she died. Her heart stuttered at the thought of Abby no longer in the world.

Maggie searched for something to talk about aside from Abby's health. Her gaze fell on the necklace at Abby's throat. "That's a beautiful necklace. It's a *Fleur-de-lis*, isn't it?"

Abby smiled as she touched the delicate silver chain. "It is. Harper gave it to me. She brought it back from her honeymoon in Paris."

"Harper had a lot of fun buying gifts."

"I'm happy she's found such a generous, loving husband. She seems very happy."

Thinking of Harper and Ethan together made Maggie smile. "She is. And now Scarlet and Cam are together, too. My sisters both found the loves of their lives. I'm happy for them."

"Your time will come too, sweetheart."

Maggie opened her mouth to protest, but closed it as Luke entered the living room carrying a tray. He placed his tray on the coffee table and poured tea from a pot into two cups.

"Are you going to share some of those brownies, or are you hogging them all?" He set up a folding table beside Abby's chair and placed one of the teacups on it.

Abby winked at Maggie. "Be a good boy and I'll share with you."

He went back to the kitchen and returned with three small plates and forks along with some paper napkins and a cup of coffee for himself. Abby handed him the container and he opened the lid and placed one brownie on a plate for each of them. He passed plates to her and Abby before taking one and sitting next to Maggie on the sofa.

Abby carefully sipped the hot tea. "Luke tells me you're planning a grand opening celebration around Valentine's Day. I hope you're going to serve your marvellous brownies."

"I'm not sure what we're going to serve. We haven't talked about it yet." She turned to Luke. "Did you have any ideas?"

He bit into his brownie and swallowed before answering. "I think a grand opening cake and free hot chocolate sounds good."

"That would be a nice touch after a cold sleigh ride. We'll have to make sure there's a fire burning in the hearth. What about food? Are we going to offer any kind of dinner?"

"What did you have in mind?"

She thought for a moment. "What if we have a special dinner? We can offer some dishes that don't appear on the regular menu."

He nodded. "Good idea. We can sell tickets in advance so we know whether there's enough interest."

Possibilities danced through her imagination. She turned to face him, folding one leg beneath her. "We could offer an array of winter comfort foods, like chilis and soups and hot desserts, like apple crumble. Instead of plate service or a buffet, how about we go with family style service?"

"What's family style service?" Abby asked.

"You place bowls of food on the table and let people help themselves, like at a family dinner," Maggie explained. "I think it makes for a fun and welcoming setting."

"That's a great idea," Luke said. "It'll be like inviting friends into your home. That's the vibe we should be going for. Warm and welcoming. Especially in the winter."

For once, dread didn't overwhelm her at the prospect of the upcoming Grand Opening. "Yes, exactly."

"Brunches are always popular with families. We could hold them for special occasions all year long, like Mother's Day and Father's Day." Luke tapped his finger against his thigh.

"For St. Patrick's Day we could serve green pea soup and spinach lasagne." Ideas exploded in her head. She could picture all the dishes she could make for each occasion. An enthusiasm she hadn't experienced since she'd arrived at the lodge made her giddy with excitement.

"We'll probably want to come up with at least one special dinner per month in the winter. We could do a weekly trivia night in the bar, or form a darts league. Things will likely be slow, so we'll want to give people a reason to drive out to the lodge."

Maggie put her hand on Luke's forearm. "What if we have an activity to go along with each special dinner? Like a costume contest at Halloween, and an Easter egg hunt for the kids at Easter."

"Yeah, that's perfect. We'll put our heads together with the rest of the group and come up with a list of activities to pair with dinners for an entire year."

"This is going to be fun, isn't it?"

Luke grinned at her. "You sound surprised."

She shrugged and let go of his arm. "Yeah, I am."

"My goodness," Abby said, with a laugh. "It all sounds so exciting."

Without warning, Abby's laughter turned to coughing, her body shaking with the violence of her coughs. Luke ran to the kitchen and returned with a glass of water. Maggie watched helplessly as she tried to drink between coughs.

Finally, the coughing subsided, but Maggie could see it left Abby drained. She leaned against the back of her armchair and wearily closed her eyes. When she reopened them and looked at her, they were filled with resignation. "I'm sorry, Maggie. I so wanted to visit with you this afternoon, but I think I need to rest for a while. Do you think you can come back again sometime soon?"

Maggie glanced at Luke, who stood at his mother's elbow, his face taut with stress. She could tell he was holding a torrent of emotions inside. "If you want me to, of course I will."

She sighed. "Good. There's so much I want to tell you..." Abby's voice trailed off and she closed her eyes in exhaustion.

What did she want to tell her? She'd been her mother's best friend. Possibly, she wanted to share stories about her. Maggie had been a baby when her mother Miranda died, so she had no memories of her. All her life, she'd clung to the remembrances her grandparents, sisters and her mother's friends had of her. But she could see only a reflection in a shattered mirror. There were many hazy pieces, but no complete picture. Miranda had been a puzzle to Maggie all her life.

Together, she and Luke helped Abby to her bedroom. Maggie pulled back the covers and Luke lifted her onto the mattress, lowering her head to the pillow with infinite care. Maggie slipped off Abby's shoes and tugged the blankets up to her chin.

"We'll stay until Reese comes home," Luke said.

"There's no need." Abby's voice was weak and she didn't open her eyes. "I'm fine."

"Don't argue with me. We're staying."

"Fine. Be stubborn." Abby gave an exhausted sigh. "Reese shouldn't be long. He was interviewing home-care nurses. I told him not to waste his money, but he thinks we need one."

"Look who's being stubborn now. Of course, you do."

Her mouth turned up at one corner, but she didn't say anything further. In a few moments, she was asleep. Luke nodded his head toward the door and they left the room, closing the door quietly behind them.

"Would you like more coffee, Luke?" Restlessness made her itchy with discomfort. She needed something to do, even if it was only filling the coffeemaker.

"No, thanks." He paced the living room, obviously as restless as she was. "I hope we hear back from the specialist in California soon. We sent her medical files to him and a technician came to the house for a blood sample yesterday. But she's getting so weak. I'm afraid even if she's accepted for the new treatment, it might be too late."

"You've done everything you can, Luke."

He made a scoffing sound and shook his head. Maggie turned her face away, a lump forming in her throat. That was the Luke she remembered. The selfless boy who loved his mother and would do anything for her.

She closed the lid on the brownie container, then gathered the cups and plates and washed them in the sink. As she placed them in the drain board, Luke dried them with a dishtowel. Neither of them said anything as they worked.

If the doctor in California couldn't do anything for Abby, Luke would be devastated.

Maggie prayed this doctor could help Abby, but she was afraid there was nothing anyone could do.

Chapter Six

REESE RETURNED TO THE house shortly before three. Maggie thought he looked tired and harried, and years older than he had only a few weeks ago.

"How's your mother?" he asked Luke.

"She started coughing and it tired her out, so we put her to bed. She's been sleeping for almost an hour."

Reese turned to Maggie. "Did you have a chance to talk?"

"Not much," she said. "But I promised Abby I'd come back soon. She wants to talk, and I'm happy to listen."

"That's good."

Though he nodded, his expression told a different story. Disappointment was etched into the lines of his handsome, weathered face.

Maggie wondered at his reaction, but then admonished herself. Of course he was disappointed, his wife was gravely ill. He was entitled to a whole gamut of negative emotions.

"Were you able to arrange a nurse for Mom?" Luke asked.

"Yeah. I talked to a private home-care agency. For now, they're going to provide nurses for two shifts a day, one for overnight and one for afternoons. That way, I can check in on the worksite at the lodge in the afternoons and be with

Abby in the mornings and evenings. Eventually, we'll have to go with round the clock care. I don't want her to be alone..." His throat worked and he closed his eyes before turning away to compose himself.

Luke put his hand on Reese's shoulder. "That sounds like a good plan. Maggie and I should get back to the lodge. Call me if you need anything. You've got my number."

"I'll call." He shifted his attention to Maggie. "You'll come see Abby again?"

"I will. I promise."

On impulse, she leaned in to hug Reese, to offer him whatever comfort she could. His arms came around her and, for a brief moment, he clung to her, his grief wrapping around her like a living thing. She understood what it was like to be left behind. Abby shouldn't have to suffer, and neither should he.

Reese let her go and she gave him a wobbly smile before following Luke to the door. They climbed into the truck cab and drove out of town, neither of them saying anything. There was nothing to say. Despite what Luke believed, Abby was very ill and was likely dying.

Abby was dying. The words hit her as if their meaning had only now became clear. Seeing her today, witnessing her frailty, meant she could no longer pretend everything would be fine. Abby had been her friend, her confidante. No matter how many years had passed, she was still her friend. And Maggie loved her.

She couldn't hold back the tears. She turned her face away, not wanting to further upset Luke. She swiped at the tears running down her cheeks with angry fingers. Tears solved nothing.

Maggie wasn't aware they'd pulled off the main road until the truck came to a stop. When she looked up, she saw they were on a side road lined with tall pines.

"I'm sorry, Maggie," Luke said. "I should have realized seeing Mom so sick would upset you."

She reached into her handbag for a tissue. "There's no need for you to apologize. I'll be fine."

"Will you?"

He sounded as if he were searching for hope, not only for her but for himself. She wanted to reassure him. The last thing Luke needed was to feel responsible for her.

"No, not really. At least, not right away." After her grandmother's death, and then her grandfather's, she'd learned that eventually life went on. With time, the sharp sting of grief softened to a place where she could remember them with more affection than pain.

Her relationship with Grandma Dorothy had been a complicated mix of love and resentment and guilt. The guilt haunted her. If she hadn't been so stubborn, so headstrong, perhaps Grandma would have lived longer.

Luke stared out the windshield, his fingers gripping the steering wheel. "Right now, all I feel is anger. Why is this happening to my mother? She never hurt anyone in her life. Why does she have to be sick?"

"I'm so sorry, Luke."

Maggie reached across the truck's console to cup his cheek. The years fell away like autumn leaves in a stiff breeze. All the emotions of that summer – the love, the excitement, the tenderness and especially the lightning attraction – rushed back, swamping her.

Luke must have felt it, too. He reached for her, wrapping his hand around the back of her neck as he leaned toward her. The minute his lips touched hers, fire ignited low in her belly. Her body remembered his kiss, remembered the shape of his lips and the way they fit so perfectly against hers. But the kiss was new as well. This wasn't Luke the shy, inexperienced boy. This was Luke the man and his kiss commanded, making her want more, so much more. His tongue ravaged her mouth until she wanted to cry out with the pleasure of it. He demanded an emotional response, and she gave it to him, pouring all her desire and all the love she'd once had for him into her kiss.

And then he abruptly pulled away, breathing heavily, his eyes wide with shock. He turned away, avoiding her eyes. "I shouldn't have done that. I'm sorry."

She needed a moment to grasp what he was saying. He was sorry he'd kissed her. Like he'd been sorry ten years ago when he'd taken her virginity and then left her.

Embarrassment flooded her. She'd known this was going to happen. She'd told herself to keep her distance. How foolish she was for letting her emotions run away. How stupid to let her body respond to his kiss as if she were still a damn fourteen-year-old.

She slid away from him and readjusted her seat belt while Luke put the truck into gear and turned it around. Soon, they were back on the main road heading to the lodge. As if the last few moments had never happened.

Maggie wished she could convince her body and her heart they hadn't.

AS SOON AS LUKE PARKED in front of the lodge, Maggie jumped out of the truck without saying a word. She was angry, and he didn't blame her.

He never should have kissed her. But one touch and he couldn't stop himself. She was soft and warm, and the remembered taste of her was intoxicating, like the finest California Syrah.

But then the guilt hit him. His stay in Minnesota was temporary, and he had no business starting something with Maggie. He'd hurt her by leaving before, and he'd be damned if he'd do it again.

Leaving Maggie ten years ago had been more difficult and painful than he cared to admit. It had taken him a long time to get over her. But he'd had no choice except to leave. At least, that's what he believed.

The jagged edge of guilt had eventually dulled to a bearable ache. He told himself they'd been kids, too young for any kind of lasting relationship. She'd only been fourteen, for God's sake. Her grandfather had been right to be worried about her.

But that didn't mean Luke's feelings for her that summer hadn't been real.

With a sigh, he turned off the ignition and made his way into the lodge. Better get to work.

As he stepped inside the lodge, he met Ethan and Cam in the entryway. Ethan raised one eyebrow. "You look like a guy who could use a beer. Come on, I've got some cold ones in our cottage."

Luke shook his head and checked his watch. Three thirty-nine. "Isn't it a little early for happy hour?"

"Fine. You can call it a business meeting if it makes you feel better. I'll show you the progress we've made on the new cottages in the last week." Cam clapped a hand on his shoulder. "Ethan and I watched our mother struggle with cancer. We know how tough it is. I'm sorry."

Luke lowered his head and stared at his shoes before lifting his gaze back to Cam. "Thanks. I appreciate that."

Ethan grabbed a jacket from the coat tree near the door. "Come on. Let's go."

They walked the quarter mile up a small hill to the new cottages. Luke was glad for the fresh air and exercise. The cold wind blew some of the anger and resentment from his head and eased his guilt regarding Maggie. At least a little of it.

The two cottages Cam's crew were working on were in the drywall stage. Once mudding and taping was complete, painting could begin. Finishing work could then take place – the flooring, tiling, cupboards and countertops, baseboards and mouldings. Soon, it would start to look like a place guests could enjoy staying at.

"How long will it take to finish these two cottages?"

"A couple of weeks, give or take. We're installing a solar electric system in all the cottages with a backup to the power grid if we need it. That could take some extra time," Cam said. "I wasn't a fan in the beginning because of the extra cost in the installation stage, but I think solar's going to save money in the long run."

"Harper's vision for the lodge was to be environmentally sensitive and sustainable, and I think we've achieved that," Ethan said. "And that concludes the business portion of this meeting."

They walked back to the first cottage, the one they'd passed on the way to the construction site. Luke stopped for a moment and examined the façade. "Is it my imagination, or does this cottage have a different vibe from the ones currently under construction?"

"It does," Ethan said. "Harper built this one and the one next door a couple of summers ago, hoping she could attract guests with something a little more modern than what was available at the lodge. Unfortunately, it didn't work out the way she'd planned."

"She purchased the plans online," Cam said. "They're nice, but generic. I changed the siding to match the other cottages so we'd have a more cohesive look."

"They look good," Luke said. He turned to Ethan. "So you and Harper are living in this cottage?"

"Yeah, for now, anyway. Maggie's in the one next door."

"If the grand opening attracts as many visitors as I'm hoping, we may need these cottages to accommodate them."

"Yeah, I know," Ethan said as he opened the front door. "We've been looking for someplace to rent or buy around Minnewasta, but there's not much available. Eventually we want to build a house, either on property the lodge owns or somewhere nearby. I'm waiting for Cam to finish the cottages so he can design something for us."

Cam laughed as he pulled out two cans of beer and a soda from the fridge. He handed the beer to Ethan and Luke. "So you're serious about me designing a house for you?"

Ethan accepted the can of beer and opened it with a pop. "Who else would I trust to build it?"

"I'm building it, too?"

"Naturally."

"I'll be happy to design your house. But I'd like to see the property first."

"You'll see it as soon as we do. We've spoken to a real estate agent. She's keeping an eye out for us."

"What about you, Cam?" Luke popped the lid on his can. "Where are you living?"

"Me and Scarlet and my daughter Tessa are living on a small acreage a mile and a half outside of Minnewasta. We're renting it right now, but we're in the process of buying. The house is a basic three-bedroom bungalow, but it's got a great workshop and a fair bit of land. If I ever finish all my projects for Ethan, I'll either add on to the house, or build a new one."

"I can see from the cottages that you're a talented builder."

"Thanks."

"He's also a talented furniture designer. He makes items from reclaimed wood. We used headboards he made in the two completed cottages. You'll have to get him to show you his workshop."

"I'd like that," Luke said. He nodded at the soda in Cam's hand. "I thought you said it was happy hour. You're not keeping up."

"I don't drink – anymore," Cam said. "I'm in AA."

Luke wanted to kick himself for his careless statement. "I'm sorry. I didn't mean—"

"Don't worry about it. Joining AA was the smartest thing I've ever done, aside from asking Scarlet to marry me. Besides, some of the best people in Minnewasta go to AA. Just ask Reese."

Luke set his can on the counter a little harder than he'd intended. "Reese is in AA?"

The grin left Cam's face. "I'm sorry. I assumed you knew. I wouldn't have said anything otherwise."

"No, Mom's never mentioned it."

Thinking back, he remembered that whenever Reese and his mother were in California and he offered them wine, Reese would always decline, saying he wasn't a wine drinker. He hadn't thought anything of it. Why wouldn't his mother mention something as important as her husband's alcoholism?

"Reese is a great guy. He's helped me through some rough patches. I don't know where I'd be without him."

"I've never seen him drink, ever," Ethan said. "I gather he's had his drinking under control for years."

If his mom died, would Reese turn to alcohol again? One more thing to worry about.

"I have nothing but respect for Reese. We grew up with an alcoholic father who never accepted any responsibility for his alcoholism. He blamed everyone but himself for his problems. Our father was a mean, angry drunk. He was especially hard on Cam," Ethan said.

"I was angry with him for a lot of years, but I've recently come to terms with my feelings," Cam said with a sigh.

"When my daughter was born, I swore I wouldn't make her life the hell my father had made mine, so I went to AA. She saved my life."

"I hope that when Harper and I have kids I can be as good a father as you," Ethan said.

Cam clapped him on the shoulder. "Thanks, E."

Luke's respect for Cam grew. Overcoming an obstacle like alcoholism was an amazing accomplishment. And ending the cycle of abuse was even more amazing.

He wondered which was worse – growing up without a father or growing up with an abusive, alcoholic one. He was certain both left scars.

"My father didn't care enough to stick around. Maybe you know him. He's back in Minnewasta now. Jerry Fields." He told them about his encounter with Jerry and his family.

"Yeah, I've met him. We joined the local Chamber of Commerce around the same time. He seems like a good guy but then, he's not my dad." Ethan paused to sip his beer. "I can't begin to explain why Jerry wasn't around while you were growing up. You can't change anything about the past, but you get to choose what your connection with him is going to be in the future."

Ethan had a point. Luke could choose to ignore Jerry for the rest of his life, or he could salvage some kind of relationship with him.

Jerry Fields hadn't been part of his growing up, but he'd helped his mother financially and he seemed eager to get to know him now. He supposed he had to give him some credit. But that didn't mean he was going to give him a prize for father of the year. Not even close.

Besides, he had more important things on his mind right now, like getting the lodge in shape for the grand opening.

And dealing with his mother's illness.

He pushed that thought from his mind, not wanting to think about the cancer that was ravaging her body. He lifted his beer can. "I propose a toast. To fathers and sons."

"And fathers and daughters," Cam added.

Cam and Ethan clinked their cans against his. As nasty as their father might have been, at least they'd known him. He'd never been given that opportunity.

He downed his beer and wondered if the chance for a father-son reunion had already passed.

Chapter Seven

MAGGIE HID OUT IN THE kitchen, needing the comforting surroundings to soothe her bruised heart. She heard Luke leave the lodge with Cam and Ethan and sighed in relief. For a little while, at least, she wouldn't have to hear how sorry he was that he'd kissed her.

To hell with his apologies and to hell with him.

She pulled cookie sheets and bowls from her cupboards, preparing to indulge in her favorite form of stress relief – baking cookies. Lots and lots of cookies. Everything but gingerbread.

She rolled her eyes, knowing that omitting Luke's favorite cookie was childish. He probably wouldn't even notice. *Damn it.*

After gathering her ingredients from the fridge and the pantry, she threw butter and sugar into the mixer and pulsed until a ball of buttercream formed. As she added vanilla and eggs for the chocolate chip cookies, some of the tension eased from her shoulders. There was something therapeutic in the simple act of baking.

Scarlet entered the kitchen and sat at the counter. "Hey. What are you making?"

Maggie stifled a pinch of annoyance. She'd needed to be alone for a few minutes, until she could process her feelings. Apparently, that had been too much to hope for. "Cookies."

Scarlet waited a beat, as if she expected her to say more. Maggie was sure she heard her sister sigh before she spoke again. "Cameron and I have finalized our guest list. There'll be forty people for dinner, including the bridal party. Did I tell you Cameron asked his nephew Drew to be a groomsman? He's going to be paired with you."

Maggie wanted to groan. Drew had made his interest in her crystal clear last summer at Harper and Ethan's wedding. But it was an interest she didn't return. "Wonderful."

"Come on, be nice. Drew's a good guy, and he has a big crush on you."

"He's too young for me."

"Only by three years."

Maggie removed the bowl from the mixer and added chocolate chips. Sometimes she felt a hundred and four instead of twenty-four. "In boy years that's at least twelve years of maturity."

Scarlet laughed. "Drew's a nice young man from a good family. You could do worse."

Maggie stopped folding in the chocolate chips to give her sister the evil eye. "Did you come into my kitchen to pimp me out or is there another point to your visit?"

Scarlet put up her hands in surrender. "Okay, I get it. No more trying to fix you up. But you and Drew are still going to be together in the wedding party."

Maggie rolled her eyes. "Fine."

"I actually wanted to talk to you about the dinner. You're in the wedding party. You shouldn't have to cook as well. I was thinking we should get Miller's Golf Resort to cater."

"Over my dead body." She slapped her spoon onto the stainless-steel countertop, splattering cookie dough over the pristine surface. "I managed the food for Harper's wedding. Wasn't it good enough for you?"

Scarlet blinked at her. "I didn't want you to feel obligated to make all the food again. But hey, if you want to be a martyr, be my guest."

"I can handle it." She gritted her teeth, trying to tamp down her anger and frustration. "Even if you don't believe in me."

"I never said that. What the hell is the matter with you?"

Harper entered the kitchen. "What's going on? I could hear the shouting from my office."

Scarlet pointed at Maggie. "She's being ridiculous. You talk to her."

Harper picked up the spoon, swiped a bit of the dough from the counter with her finger and stuck it into her mouth. "Making cookies?"

"Brilliant deduction, Sherlock." Maggie used a small scoop to slap small lumps of dough onto the sheet.

"How did your visit with Abby go?"

Maggie's hand stilled over the cookie sheet. "It was..."

Her throat closed with tears, and sorrow washed over her, not only for Abby, but for the tangled mess her relationship with Luke had become. How had a bond once so beautiful turned into something to be sorry about? Fresh humiliation swamped her.

"Oh, honey, I'm sorry." Scarlet circled the counter and wrapped her arms around her. "I forgot you went to see Abby today. Forgive me."

She sniffed against Scarlet's shoulder. "Nothing to forgive. I'm sorry, too."

Harper silently rubbed her back while she drew comfort from Scarlet's embrace. She blew her nose with the tissue Harper offered her.

"What if we plan the dinner together and buy the food?" Maggie dabbed at her eyes. "I can prepare as much as possible in advance, and then Miller's staff can put the finishing touches on the meal and serve. It's basically what I did for Harper's wedding."

Scarlet brushed a tear from her cheek. "That would be perfect. I want you to have some fun, too."

"Thank you." Fresh tears threatened, but she pushed them back. Her sisters were the two people in the world she could most count on. She'd let herself forget that for far too long.

"I was thinking," Harper said. "We need to decorate the lodge for the wedding."

"The lodge is pretty already. It doesn't need anything, other than some flowers," Scarlet said.

"Remember how pretty the tent was for your wedding, Harper, with the lights and the flowers and the gauzy ribbons? Scarlet did all that." Maggie made herself smile for them. "We can't let her show us up. We have to do something spectacular for her wedding."

"You got that right."

"You two aren't competitive at all, are you?" Scarlet grumbled, but her grin told them she really didn't mind.

"The wedding is three weeks before Christmas. What does every house need at Christmas?"

"A Christmas tree?" Maggie said.

"Right," Harper said with a nod. "I haven't had a Christmas tree since Grampa died, but this year I want a great big, huge pine from our property that we cut down ourselves."

"We can decorate it with Grandma's old ornaments. You said you boxed them up, didn't you?" Scarlet asked.

"Yeah, they're in the spare bedroom of our cottage along with the boxes of Mom's and Grandma's photo albums. I'll get Ethan to bring them to the lodge," Harper said. "I haven't gone through all the Christmas ornaments or the albums. To tell you the truth, I've been afraid to. Too many memories."

Scarlet nodded. "We'll tackle them together. It won't be so hard that way. And let's get some new things for the tree, too. We've been looking back for too long. Let's look forward for a change."

Maggie silently agreed. New ornaments, new future. Exactly what they all needed.

If only the past could be changed as easily. Though Luke's betrayal had happened years ago, she couldn't forget it. Or forgive. She was afraid forgiveness was something she wasn't capable of.

THE NEXT AFTERNOON, Luke left the lodge shortly before one. He wanted to visit his mother before she got too tired, but he also wanted to talk to her in private, before Reese came home. Luke had some questions that needed answers, and he didn't want an audience.

He let himself into his mother's house and found her in her favorite armchair, wrapped in a couple of colorful blankets.

"Hi, honey. I was hoping to see you today."

"I need to talk to you."

Abby tilted her head. "That sounds serious. What did you want to talk about?"

"Reese. Why didn't you tell me he's in AA? Didn't you think it was important to tell me your husband is an alcoholic?"

"A recovering alcoholic. He's been sober a long time." She expelled a long breath, then leaned her head against the back of the chair. "You're right. I should have told you. In the beginning, I didn't want you to form any judgements about him before you got to know him."

"Okay, I get that, but you've been together for years and I know Reese now. Why couldn't you have trusted me enough to tell me the truth?"

"He wanted to tell you. He doesn't like secrets. But I wanted you to respect him, and I didn't know if you would if you'd known his history. The alcohol is in his past. It has no bearing on the man he is today."

"You didn't think I could respect him if I'd known he was a recovering alcoholic? Come on, Mom. You raised me better than that."

Her eyes filled with tears. "You're right. I shouldn't have kept this from you, just as I shouldn't have kept the information about your father from you. You're not a child I have to protect. You're a grown man. A wonderful man. I'm so proud of you, Luke."

He nodded, not trusting himself to speak. Abby grasped his hand. "I'm very...protective of Reese. He means the world to me."

"I understand."

"I'm not sure you do. He's had a lot of adversity in his life. What I want most of all is for him to be happy. Promise me you'll support Reese and be his friend after I'm gone, that you won't abandon him."

"Mom, you're going to get better."

She gripped his hand. "Luke, promise me."

Luke closed his eyes against the pain. It hurt too much to imagine a world without his mother. But she needed his promise. "I promise I'll always be Reese's friend."

Chapter Eight

"HEY."

Maggie glanced over her shoulder, tensing as Luke walked into the kitchen. "Hey."

"Do you have a few minutes? I'd like to talk to you about the dessert menu."

Maggie couldn't look at him. They'd barely spoken since he kissed her two days ago and despite telling herself his rejection didn't matter, anger continued to swirl in her gut. Like ten years ago, he kissed her and then tossed her aside.

What made her even angrier was that she kept falling for it.

"What's wrong with the dessert menu?"

"Nothing's wrong with it. But it's limited. Why only three items? And why did you choose the ones you did?"

"Because we're trying to use locally grown products, remember? I chose the rhubarb crumble, the blueberry cobbler and the strawberry trifle because they're locally grown fruits that I can freeze and use all winter. In the summer, I can create a new menu using fresh fruit."

He leaned one hip against the counter next to the sink and folded his arms across his chest. "Okay, I get that, but why only three? There are dozens of other things you can make with those fruits. Why limit yourself? And surely we can offer at least one dessert with ingredients that come from more than a hundred miles away. Our guests will expect it." Maggie's hands shook as she peeled potatoes. "I'm trying to stay true to Harper's vision."

"I know you are, and you're doing a good job, but I feel like you're holding back." He touched her arm and though his voice was barely above a whisper, she heard the pleading note in it. "I know you have a lot more creativity in you. Come on, Maggie Cat. Don't settle. I know you can do better."

Her whole body vibrated with anger. She pushed his hand away. "Don't ever call me that again. You lost the right a long time ago."

"Maggie—"

"Don't Maggie me. Don't think you can kiss me and I'll do exactly what you want. Don't assume you can manipulate me like you did when I was a kid. I've grown up, but you haven't changed a bit in ten years. You're the same self-centered user you were back then."

His eyes turned a stormy, Arctic gray. "That's not fair."

"Isn't it?" She whirled to face him, the potato peeler clutched in her right hand. "Why are you even here, Luke? Why have you bothered to come back?"

"You know why. For my mother."

"If you were such a good son, why did you wait until your mother was dying before you came home to see her?" Even as the words spewed from her mouth she knew she'd gone too far.

Luke flinched as if she'd hit him.

"Luke, I'm—"

He held up his hands. “You’re right. A good son wouldn’t have let old fears keep him from doing right by his family. I should have been here when my mother and my grandmother needed me. But I wasn’t and that’s inexcusable.”

He turned and left the kitchen. Maggie swore and banged her fist on her stainless-steel counter, flinching as pain shot up her arm. She’d let her insecurities get the better of her. What she’d said to Luke...

She squeezed her eyes shut and let the shame wash over her.

She had to apologize. Maggie ripped off her apron and hurried out the door.

She found him in the dining room, standing near one of the French doors, staring out at the frozen lake. His despondency reached out to her from across the room, and she knew she was responsible.

He turned to her as she approached, his expression unreadable. “Coming back for round two?”

“I don’t want to fight with you anymore. Those things I said—”

“You don’t have to apologize for pointing out the truth.”

He turned toward the lake once more, his jaw clenched. His pain hit Maggie like a physical blow. She reached for his hand and squeezed it between hers, needing to soothe, to make up for the terrible things she’d said in anger and fear. “Luke, I—”

“Don’t, Maggie, please. Don’t apologize. I should have been here for them. I’ve let them down. I’ve always let them down.”

"That's not true! You know that's not true."

He simply shook his head and closed his eyes. Maggie looked at their joined hands, her much smaller one dwarfed by his. The summer they were together, she'd loved holding hands with him. Though his fingers had been callused from work, he had always touched her with tenderness.

His cell phone rang, jarring her out of her memories.

Luke reached for his phone. "It's the cancer specialist from California. I have to take this."

"Of course."

Maggie backed away, intending to give him privacy to take his call, but he held firmly to her hand. In a flash of understanding, she recognized he was afraid of what the doctor was about to tell him.

"Dr. Healey, hello. Do you have some news?"

Luke bent his head, listening intently, his gaze averted. Then, his body stiffened and he threw back his head in an anguished gesture, his eyes shut tightly. A sick feeling formed in Maggie's stomach. The news wasn't good.

"Isn't there anything you can do?" he asked.

His fingers tightened their hold on hers and she knew the answer was no.

Luke let out a breath. "I appreciate your time, Dr. Healey. Yes, I'm sorry, too."

He hit the off button and stuck his phone back in his pocket. "My mother's cancer isn't one that responds well to his new treatment. He says that even if it would respond, the cancer is too advanced."

"I'm sorry, Luke."

"Mom humored me. She knew I wouldn't accept her diagnosis until I had no choice."

Even though she'd seen for herself how sick Abby was, Maggie had been holding out hope for the new treatment almost as much as Luke. But now that last, faint hope was extinguished.

He dropped her hand, his gaze aimed at a point over her left shoulder. "I have to go. I have to talk to Mom."

"Yeah."

He lifted his gaze to hers and she read the pain in his eyes. "I haven't been here for her the last ten years, but I'm here now. I'll be here till...until she doesn't need me anymore."

Maggie nodded, unable to speak. Luke hurried out of the dining room, and she heard the front door open and close.

She bowed her head and wept.

LUKE HADN'T TAKEN OFF his jacket before his mother spoke.

"You heard from the cancer specialist in California, didn't you?"

He imagined his face told the whole story. He couldn't think. Sorrow and grief filled his heart and his thoughts. A leaden weight had settled on his chest, robbing him of breath and making it nearly impossible to speak. "Yeah."

"I'm guessing he said there was nothing he could do, that the cancer was too advanced."

Luke nodded, no longer able to form words.

Abby held out her arms. Luke went to her chair and dropped to the floor beside her, laying his head in her lap. Tears came hard and fast, the grief raw and unbearable. She smoothed her hand over his hair and whispered soothing words.

Later, exhausted and spent, he lifted his head. Abby brushed his hair from his face. "It's going to be all right, Luke. It really is."

He shook his head. How could anything be all right if she was gone?

She put her hand on his shoulder. "I can only imagine how you feel. I know I'd be devastated if my mother was dying. But I've made my peace with death, and I know it's my time to go. My only concern is for the people I'm leaving behind. I need you to promise me you'll live the rest of your life with love and forgiveness. Don't waste a minute on regret or guilt or anger. Be happy, Luke."

He nodded, though he wasn't certain he could keep his promise.

Chapter Nine

MAGGIE WAS SURPRISED by Luke's arrival at the lodge the next morning while they were having breakfast. After the news he'd received, she thought he might take the day off to be with Abby.

Harper approached him first, wordlessly putting her arms around him. Maggie had told her sisters about the specialist's diagnosis. She couldn't get her head around the idea that Abby would soon be gone.

But Luke didn't need her tears or her regrets right now.

"Have you eaten?" she asked.

He shook his head, and she nodded. "I'll make you a couple of eggs. Over easy with whole wheat toast, right?"

He gave her a small grin. "Right. You have an amazing memory, Mags."

She hurried to the safety of the kitchen and grabbed a carton of eggs from the cooler. Her memory was indeed amazing. She remembered every detail of their ill-fated summer together. How he'd raved over the eggs she'd made for him as if they were some sort of exotic dish. She remembered the heat of his skin and way the sun shone on his dark hair, bringing out the auburn highlights. She remembered the first time he entered her body, both the pain and the ecstasy. And she remembered his tenderness and how he held her like she was precious to him.

She wished she could forget.

For months following Luke's departure, she thought about him every minute of every day. She remembered the magic of the summer, but mostly she agonized over why he'd left her so abruptly and so cruelly. Fretted over what she'd done wrong. Eventually, she came to believe he grew tired of her and that her grandmother had been right in saying he'd used her.

But that hadn't stopped her from thinking about him, or comparing every man she met to him despite her best efforts to forget.

Maggie slid the eggs onto a plate and added the toast. Taking a deep breath, she picked up the plate and returned to the dining room. Luke gave her a grateful smile as she set it in front of him.

They finished eating in silence. Finally, Ethan spoke. "We heard about the specialist, Luke. If you want to take a few days—"

"No. I want to work. There's plenty to do before the grand opening, and I...I need to keep busy."

She should have known he'd want to bury himself in work because she used the same tactic. Whenever she didn't want to deal with reality, she headed to her kitchen.

Ethan nodded. "Okay. Whatever you want."

Luke got to his feet. "Thank you all for being so supportive. If you'll excuse me, I've got some resumes to go through."

Maggie watched him leave. There was a slump in his shoulders that hadn't been there before. Despite the hurt that had simmered in her heart for the past ten years, she didn't want to be angry with Luke any longer. Life was too short for anger, and she hated feeling that way.

But she wasn't sure she could forgive. Or trust. At least, not the way she once had.

LUKE GAVE THE WRENCH a quarter turn to tighten the drainpipe before crawling out from beneath his grandmother's kitchen sink. He turned the cold-water faucet on full and bent to see if the drain was still leaking. A steady stream of water told him he hadn't fixed the problem.

He turned off the tap. "Damn."

"I told you I could call the plumber. He lives right down the street."

"I can do this, Grandma."

"I'm sure you can," Phyllis said with a nod. "But you don't have to. You didn't need to clean out my garage either. This busy work of yours isn't going to change anything. Nothing will."

He wriggled his shoulders into the tight confines of the wet sink cabinet once more. "I can't sit around."

"Your mother says you haven't been to see her in a couple of days."

The wrench slipped and clanked against the copper pipe. He had no answer for her. The truth was he'd been hiding, either at the lodge or with chores at his grandmother's house. He couldn't make himself go to her.

"I know it hurts. I know you feel powerless because I feel that way myself. And I'm angry, angrier than I've ever been in my life. I'm so angry that Abby is leaving me that I want to spit. I want to hit someone. I want to break something. It's not supposed to be this way."

Luke's heart thumped painfully in his chest. He didn't want to hear about his grandmother's pain. His own grief tore at him like a wild animal, consuming him piece by piece. He couldn't deal with her grief as well. He fitted the wrench carefully on the pipe once more.

"But you know what, Luke? Every day I put on my big girl panties, and I suck it up to walk the two blocks to my daughter's house. I help her wash her hair or take a bath, and I make tea and chat. Whatever she needs. But I always make sure I share a laugh with her. Because right now, it's not about me and my suffering. It's about Abby."

He twisted the wrench with both hands, using every ounce of his remaining strength. He was rewarded with a tiny movement. What he needed to do was to get his ass out of this cupboard, turn on the taps, and see if he'd fixed the leak. Instead, he closed his eyes and rested his head against the wet cupboard floor, too exhausted to move.

His grandmother must have lowered herself to the floor because a moment later she touched his knee. "Stop punishing yourself, Luke. It's not your fault. It's not anybody's fault."

Was that what he'd been doing the last couple of days? Punishing himself? Throwing himself a little pity party? His grandmother was right, none of that would help his mother.

"Now, if you're finished under there, help me to my feet. I'm like a turtle who got flipped onto her back. I can't get up."

Luke scrambled up, then reached out his arms and gently helped her to her feet. He put his arms around her in a hug. "I'm sorry, Grandma."

"I know, baby. I know."

She patted his back with a soothing stroke, much like she'd done when he was a kid and he'd skinned his knees. He allowed himself a few moments of comfort before stepping back. "I'll clean up this mess and then walk over to Mom and Reese's place."

Phyllis nodded. "That's a good idea."

What would happen to her once his mother was gone? She didn't drive and had to depend on friends and Reese for rides to the grocery store or to her doctor. Phyllis was well into her seventies. She shouldn't have to worry about mowing the grass in the summer and shoveling snow in winter. And he was too far away to be of any help.

Time he stepped up.

He turned on the faucet once more. To his relief, the leak had stopped. "Grandma, have you given any thought to where you're going to go, when Mom...is gone?"

Her brow wrinkled. "I'm not going anywhere. I'm staying right here, of course. Where would I go?"

"You could come with me to California. I've got a decent-sized condo."

"Condo?"

Her horrified expression made him laugh. "Come on. You'd think I threatened to send you out on an ice flow. California is a nice place."

"Yes, it is, and it's very kind of you to offer, but my life is here in Minnewasta. I wouldn't know what to do with myself out there."

"You can do whatever you like. You wouldn't have to deal with the snow and cold, and I've got a patio where you can garden all year long. It would be good to have you with me."

She reached for his hand and linked his fingers with hers. Her palm was soft and warm, and her smile sad. "It's sweet of you to offer, but you're a young man. You need your own space. Anyway, this is my home and it's where I belong. All my friends are here. I know practically everyone in town. If I need something, a friend is only a phone call away." She gave his hand a little squeeze. "Besides, after Abby is gone, Reese is going to need me."

He nodded. She was probably right about that.

Phyllis bowed her head, her shoulders slumping. "It's a very sad thing, you know, for your child to die before you do. It's not supposed to happen that way."

"I'm sorry, Grandma."

He worried about how Reese and his grandmother would cope when his mother was gone.

But mostly he wondered how he would cope.

THE SOFT FOOTFALL ALERTED Luke to a visitor. He looked up from his desk to see Maggie standing at the open door of the office, a tray of coffee and baked goods in her hands.

"Can I come in?"

Her face was unsmiling and tense. He gestured to the chair in front of the desk. "Yes, of course."

She set the tray on the desk, but remained standing. "Would you like coffee?"

"Sure."

He watched while she poured coffee from a carafe. She had beautiful hands, petite yet elegant, with slim, tapered fingers and neat fingernails. He remembered how soft her hands had been as they'd touched his bare skin...

Don't go there.

Using tongs, she placed a shell-shaped confection onto a dessert plate and then pouring from a small jug, swirled a bit of creamy yellow sauce around the cake. "Would you like to try one of these?"

He accepted the plate from her. "What are they?"

"They're called Madeleines, my grandmother's recipe. These are blueberry-lemon and the sauce is a lemon curd. I'm developing some recipes that I thought we could use for afternoon Sunday teas. I figure not everybody is going to want to mush a dog sled or skate around the lake."

Breaking off a small piece with the fork Maggie handed him, Luke dipped the cake into the sauce and popped it into his mouth. The Madeleine was light and fluffy, and the blueberries and lemon curd combined to create an explosion of fresh flavors, like a little taste of spring.

"It's wonderful. I'm sure guests will love it."

"Thank you."

She fidgeted with the coffee carafe, picking it up and then setting it down again. "Do you mind if I close the door for a moment?"

Luke tensed, but nodded his assent. "Go ahead."

She closed the office door with a soft click, then turned to face him, her hands clutched in front of her. She lifted her gaze to his. "I know you said you didn't want me to apologize, but I can't let it go. What I said to you about...about not coming home until your mother was dying, it was a horrible thing to say and I'm sorry. You didn't deserve it."

"But you were right. I haven't been around for my mother or my grandmother."

Maggie sat in the chair on the other side of the desk. "You're here now. That's all that matters."

He nodded, even though guilt clawed at him. He couldn't make up for lost time, no matter how much he might want to.

She looked down at her clenched hands, the knuckles white with strain. "I lashed out at you because you hit on a sore point. I'm scared. I went with the three desserts because I've been preparing them for years and know I can do them well. I was afraid to try something more ambitious because if I fail, the restaurant fails. I can't let Harper and Ethan down."

"You never used to be afraid to try anything. What happened, Maggie?"

"Life happened. Turns out I'm not the hot stuff I thought I was." She looked away. "I'm not even the decent person I thought I was."

Luke leaned forward, his heart stuttering. Someone had hurt her badly. It suddenly occurred to him that he didn't know her anymore and the realization saddened him. Once, he would have said he knew her better than he knew himself. "I'm sure neither of those statements are true."

She frowned and gave a negligent shrug, dismissing his words. "I want to do the best job I can for the lodge, and I need to work with you to make that happen. Can you forgive me?"

Lines of tension had formed around her mouth, as if she was afraid the things she'd said were beyond forgiveness.

He couldn't let her believe that. Luke got to his feet and extended his hand across the desk. "Apology accepted."

She eyed his hand. "Just like that?"

"Just like that. Truce?"

Maggie rose and grasped his hand in a firm shake, her mouth unsmiling. Luke tried to ignore the awareness that shot through his body at her touch.

"Truce," she said.

SCARLET CRANED HER neck to see the back of the wedding dress in the three-way mirror. She frowned. "I don't know. All this stuff – the crystals, the train, the beading – feels like too much. We're having a simple wedding. I think I want a simpler dress."

"Of course," the saleslady said politely. Maggie was sure she heard disappointment in the woman's voice at the prospect of a smaller commission. "I'll search the racks again and come up with some simpler options. But I want to remind you that with your wedding being in a couple of weeks, it will have to be a sample dress that fits you well without a lot of alteration needed. That limits our selection somewhat."

"I understand. A dress I can take home with me today is exactly what I want."

Maggie and her sisters had taken the day off from preparations for the wedding and the grand opening to drive to Minneapolis to shop for Scarlet's wedding dress. She cherished this rare opportunity to spend time with them. With both her sisters finding love with the Hainstock brothers in the last few months, she'd become a fifth wheel, an outsider. Reconnecting with Harper and Scarlet made her happy, even if it was only for the day.

"This may not be your wedding dress, but I have to tell you, it looks beautiful on you," Harper said.

"What doesn't look beautiful on her?" Maggie said with a laugh. "The woman could wear a sack and look great."

With the three of them facing the mirror, Maggie marvelled at the dissimilarities in their physical appearances, as she had so often. Harper and Scarlet were tall and fair and lithe, and she was short and dark. As a child, she'd asked her grandmother why she didn't have blue eyes like her sisters. Grandma told her she resembled her own brothers and sisters who were short in stature and dark-haired, and she wasn't to worry about it. Maggie had never met any of these great-aunts and uncles so she couldn't judge for herself, but the answer satisfied her at the time.

Scarlet lifted the voluminous skirts of the wedding dress and followed the saleslady to the dressing room. "I'll be back," she said as she disappeared down a corridor.

"I don't think I've ever seen Scarlet so happy," Harper said. "She seems at peace."

"Yes, I think you're right. Cam makes her very happy. Just like Ethan makes you happy."

A dreamy smile spread across her sister's face. "Yes. Ethan makes me very happy."

Maggie wondered if happiness like that would ever come her way. A picture of Luke came to mind. Once, long ago, she'd been that happy. But she'd been far too young to understand how precious love like that was. It had ended quickly, and with a heart-breaking wrench, as did her next relationship. They'd both left such painful scars, she wasn't sure she even wanted to try again.

Maggie's breath caught in her throat as Scarlet re-appeared and stepped up on the pedestal in front of the big mirrors. Scarlet wore a full-length dress in a delicate ivory lace. From the front, the dress appeared relatively modest; an allusion neckline of sheer tulle and lace appliques covered her upper chest and shoulders and swept down her arms to form full-length sleeves. But the back of the dress was the true stunner. The same sheer material covered her entire back, giving the simultaneous impression of being both completely open and modestly covered. A simple lace train fell in soft folds and formed a half circle around Scarlet. The ivory color suited her red hair perfectly and made her fair skin look warm instead of washed out like the bright white had. The dress was deceptively simple, yet utterly stunning. Not to mention ridiculously sexy.

"I love the lace, and I think the color suits me. And it fits perfectly. No alteration necessary." Scarlet's eyes met Maggie's in the mirror. "I think this might be the one. What do you think?"

Maggie burst into tears, shocked at her emotional reaction. She was relieved to see tears streaming down Harper's cheeks as well. At least she wasn't the only one.

Scarlet laughed. "I'll take that as a yes."

She lifted her skirts and stepped off the pedestal, her arms open wide. Maggie and Harper stepped into them and, laughing and crying, they hugged each other.

"Oh, my God," Harper said through her tears. "Cam's going to lose his mind when he sees you in this dress."

Scarlet laughed. "If this is what the dress does to you, I can't wait to see his reaction."

"I'm thinking this means you'll take the dress," the saleslady said with a smile.

"You bet." Scarlet gave Maggie a wink. "Now all we have to do is find bridesmaid dresses for my sisters."

Maggie groaned. "More shopping?"

Scarlet threw her arm around her shoulders. "We're just getting started, sweetie."

Chapter Ten

LUKE LISTENED ATTENTIVELY as Anthony Bennett sat on a stool in Maggie's kitchen and spoke to her about his work experience. On paper, Anthony appeared to be the perfect candidate for sous-chef. He had experience in a couple of high-end Minneapolis restaurants, and he was able to start immediately because of the closure of his current restaurant. He'd even passed the test Luke used to weed out the lazy assholes. Every applicant was required to send a resume, at least three references, a cover letter stating why he wanted to work at Solace Lake Lodge, and a list of three chefs the applicant believed were changing the food world. If they couldn't be bothered to meet all Luke's requirements, the application went straight into the garbage. Anthony Bennett had provided all he asked for, proving he could follow instructions. Not to mention that he'd driven to the lodge today on short notice for this interview.

So why were alarm bells going off in his head?

Maybe because Anthony had been the head chef at his last position and sous-chef would be a step down, and likely a blow to his ego. Or maybe it had something to do with the way he'd caught him checking out Maggie's ass as she bent to retrieve a dish from the oven.

Of course, he couldn't blame the guy since he'd been doing the exact same thing. Still, it pissed him off.

He and Maggie asked questions about Anthony's training and education and then Luke gestured to the grill. "Let's get down to business. Make us each a burger, Anthony, including one for you. You should be able to find everything you'll need in the fridge."

"You want me to make you a burger?" Anthony sounded perplexed and more than a little disdainful. "I was under the impression this was to be a high-end dining room."

"It is. We'll serve a lot of high-end dinners at the lodge, but we'll also do a good business in what we'd typically consider fast food meals like burgers, fries, and sandwiches, especially at lunch. We're going to cater to a lot of families here and they're not always going to want *foie gras*."

Anthony dipped his head in a curt nod. "Of course. So the ingredients are in the refrigerator?"

"Yes," Maggie said, as she opened the refrigerator door. "We've got a choice of ground meats – beef, pork, and bison. Anything you need, but can't find, let me know. We've probably got it."

He nodded again, then began bringing out ingredients. Luke surreptitiously checked his watch, intending to time him. How fast was this guy? Would he get the job done quickly and efficiently or would he endlessly deliberate?

Fortunately, he jumped in quickly. Luke noted the skillful, quick movements Anthony used to dice the onion and mentally checked the "yes" box next to "knife skills". But it went downhill from there. Once he'd added the diced onion to the lean beef, he appeared totally unfamiliar with what else to include. He went with salt and pepper and some dried garlic, adding a beaten egg at the last minute as a sort of afterthought. He mixed the ingredients with a wooden spoon, then formed patties with his hands. Luke didn't miss the look of disgust on his face, as if he couldn't stand the idea of touching the meat.

Finally, he slapped the patties on the grill and turned them every couple of minutes. Removing three buns from the bag, he sliced them open with a bread knife and plated them. He squirted a bit of ketchup and mustard on the buns, and garnished each with a slice of dill pickle. Then, he slid the meat on the bottom half of the bun and covered it with the top.

"Okay." Beads of sweat dotted Anthony's upper lip. "There you go."

Luke handed one of the plates to Maggie and kept one for himself. He nodded at the remaining plate. "Try some of it. I'd like you to critique your own work."

Anthony shook his head. "Sorry, no. I'm vegan."

That would explain his apparent revulsion. He'd have no way of knowing if his food was any good if he never tasted it.

"Fine." Luke ate a mouthful of the burger. It was bland, with a dense texture, and dry. Once he'd managed to swallow, he turned to Maggie. "What do you think?"

He wanted to hear her honest opinion. If she was going to run this kitchen, she'd have to be tough. And she'd need the ability to figure out who would do the best job for the restaurant.

She swallowed her bite of hamburger and drank some water from her bottle before speaking. "I'm sorry, Anthony, but that was really dry. A burger should be juicy and flavorful, and I'm afraid yours wasn't."

He lifted his chin. "I'm more accustomed to working with vegetarian and vegan dishes, but I'm sure I could learn to work with meat. If I'd had more time—"

Maggie held up her hand. "I appreciate that but as Luke said, we expect to serve a lot of meals featuring burgers and other meats. We're opening soon, so we have to hit the ground running. I've created several vegetarian dishes, including a veggie burger, but I'm sure it will be only a portion of what we serve."

"I have impeccable references."

"Yes, that's why we called you for an interview." She picked up Anthony's resume. "I don't recall seeing any restrictions in your resume. Do you ever work with meats?"

"No." He cleared his throat. "Not since I became a vegan."

"Why didn't you mention that you only prepared vegan dishes?"

Anthony's face flushed. "I didn't think it mattered."

"I'm afraid it did. You don't need to love every item on my menu, but you shouldn't be repulsed by them either." She held out her hand. "Thank you for coming to Solace Lake Lodge, but I'm afraid we won't be able to offer you a position here."

Anthony ignored her hand and stared at her open-mouthed, clearly shocked. "You must be joking. You're dismissing *me*?"

"I'm afraid so." She lowered her hand, her tone kind but firm. "We aren't a good fit for you. I wish you good luck in your employment search."

"Just as well," he said, ripping off his borrowed apron. "This place won't last six months anyway."

He grabbed his jacket and stormed out the kitchen. When he was gone, Maggie blew out a breath, one hand over her stomach. "That went well, didn't it?"

Luke snorted, then laughed out loud. "Perfect, I'd say."

She rolled her eyes. "Oh, yeah? What was the best part, do you think? The part where I accused him of fudging his resume, or when I told an award-winning chef to hit the road?"

"Anthony Bennett is a prima donna and isn't a good fit for the restaurant. You knew that and you did what you had to do." Luke put his hand on her shoulder and gently squeezed. "You did the right thing, Maggie. Don't ever feel bad about doing the right thing."

She stared up at him with her large, dark eyes. He could drown in those eyes, the same way he had ten years ago. Her lips parted slightly and he fought the urge to kiss her, to take her in his arms and taste her sweetness once more. She trembled under his touch. He cupped her face with his hand as he closed the distance between them, ignoring the guilt screaming in his ear. If she knew the truth...

Maggie turned her head and stepped away. Luke's hand fell to his side.

She threw the remains of the burgers into the garbage and began cleaning the grill. "No, I won't feel bad about doing what I have to do."

Luke knew she wasn't talking about hiring staff.

JERRY FIELDS HIT A few keys on Luke's laptop and turned the screen toward him. "I've given you a temporary password to the network. The first time you log in, you'll need to change it to something else. Every month, the system will force you to change your password. Make sure you keep track of it and create a good, strong one."

"So, you'll come back later to finish once we get the rest of the computers in place?"

"Yeah, for sure. Then if you want, I'll periodically upgrade the security system. You always need to keep one step ahead of the hackers."

Luke was impressed with Jerry's knowledge and efficiency. He'd helped to set up some of their computers and had begun to put sophisticated security measures into place to prevent malcontents from hacking into their internal network. He really knew his stuff.

"Did you work with computers while you were in the military?" He simply wanted some background about the man who fathered him. He wasn't interested or anything.

Jerry grinned. "I could tell you, but then I'd have to kill you."

Luke grinned back. "So, top secret stuff?"

"Let's just say I worked in some sensitive areas."

Okay, then. "Mom said you were stationed in some bases overseas."

"I spent time in the Far East. Very interesting cultures."

Amazing how he could speak without revealing anything. The man certainly knew how to keep a secret. Maybe that was why he was so good at forgetting he'd had a son.

Luke flinched. *That was uncalled for, asshole.* Considering what his mother had told him about deliberately keeping him and his father apart, Jerry wasn't entirely to blame. But if he'd really wanted to know him, he would have fought harder for him. If Luke had had a child, it's what he would have done.

"When I was a kid, I pictured you as GI Joe, a hero. I even made up stories about you that I told kids at school. I told them you were away on a secret mission and that's why you didn't live with me and—"

Luke abruptly stopped. He'd revealed far more than he'd wanted to. But the truth was he'd longed for a father growing up, a man he could look up to, and emulate. All his friends had fathers.

Jerry fixed his gaze on a spot somewhere across the room. "I wish I could go back and change things. You can't imagine how often I've wished that. But I can't change the past. What I hope is that from this point forward, you and I can forge some kind of relationship. I know I'll never really be a father to you, but I hope we can be friends."

Friends? Luke didn't know how to respond to that. That might be the only option left open, but he wasn't sure it was enough.

LUKE CLICKED ON THE Zoom icon while Maggie pulled a stool up to the counter. A moment later, his laptop screen filled with Celeste Bishop's image. She was in her late twenties or early thirties, he guessed, with expressive dark eyes and *café au lait* colored skin.

"Hi, Celeste," he said after introducing himself and Maggie. "I'm glad to meet you."

Her smile had a nervous edge. "I appreciate your willingness to talk to me, even though I'm so far away in South Carolina."

Maggie answered before he could. "We're glad to do it. We're trying to find the best candidates for sous-chef, wherever they are."

"Why don't we begin? Did you get all the ingredients together for your burger?" Luke had emailed her and told her how they'd interviewed other prospective sous-chefs. It wouldn't be easy trying to assess her skills over the internet, but Maggie wanted to give her a shot. Celeste's resume was intriguing enough that he was willing to give it a try.

"Yes, I did." She adjusted her laptop so the camera pointed toward her kitchen counter.

"Tell us how you're going to make your burger," Maggie said.

Celeste disappeared from the screen for a moment, but they could hear her voice. "Before I start anything, I need to wash my hands and then I'll heat the grill on my stovetop to medium high. I like to start with medium ground hamburger because it tends to stay juicer than a lean ground."

They watched her set a bowl, a package of ground beef, and a carton of eggs on the table. She cracked one of the eggs, then whisked it with a fork.

"Next, I add my seasonings," Celeste continued. "A teaspoon mustard – I like Dijon best – a teaspoon Worcestershire sauce, about a half teaspoon salt and some pepper."

She disappeared from view again and returned with a small onion and a clove of garlic. Luke watched with approval as she finely diced the onion and efficiently crushed the garlic. The woman had good technique.

"I add the onion and garlic to my egg mixture, give it a bit of a stir and then crumble in the hamburger meat. Occasionally, at this point, I like to add a little something extra, like creamy Caesar salad dressing or chopped sundried tomatoes. It gives an extra kick of flavor." She opened the package of meat and then using her hands, gently crumbled the hamburger into the bowl. "I find the less I handle the meat, the juicer it stays. I only turn it once on the grill, and I never pierce it with a fork or all the juices run out."

She formed six patties and placed two on the grill. Luke heard the sizzle over the internet and swore he could almost smell it.

"So while the burgers are grilling, about six to eight minutes per side, I like to get the buns ready." Celeste disappeared from view and reappeared a moment later with a bag of hamburger buns. "I bought these buns at the supermarket. I'm guessing you would make your own in-house or get them from a bakery?"

Maggie answered. "Yes. I plan to purchase our breads from a local bakery. That may change in the future if it makes sense for us to bake our own."

While Maggie talked, Celeste sliced open two of the buns and placed them on the grill next to the burgers. "Personally, I like a nice warm toasted bun for my burger."

She flipped the burgers and couple of minutes later removed the buns, which were perfectly toasted. After slicing a tomato, she put one slice and a leaf of lettuce on one half of each bun.

"The fixings are to individual taste and we can add almost anything – cheese, bacon, pickle, relish – whatever. I like to keep it simple with the tomato and lettuce because I enjoy the fresh, cool taste of the vegetables right beside the hot meat."

A moment later, she slid the burgers onto the prepared buns. "And there you go. Lunch for my daughter when she gets home from school in a few minutes. My sister is walking her home today."

"How old is your daughter?" Maggie asked.

"She's six, in grade one." Celeste fidgeted with the plates, turning them around and around. Now that she was finished cooking, she appeared nervous again.

"Maggie, what did you think of Celeste's burgers?" Luke asked. He wanted her to take the lead as she'd done with the previous interviews. If she was going to be head chef, she'd be doing a lot of hiring and firing in her career, so she needed to get acquainted with the process and know what to look for.

"I think that if I was in Celeste's kitchen right now, I'd steal her lunch from her. Your burger looks delicious."

A brief, relieved smile crossed Celeste's face. "Thank you."

"You were quick, efficient and knowledgeable. You know your way around a burger."

Celeste's smile was more relaxed. "Well, I have flipped my share."

Maggie glanced at Celeste's resume. "I see you worked at a couple of well-known restaurants in the Myrtle Beach area in the past ten years, but I'm noticing a gap in your work experience. It looks like you haven't worked in a restaurant for over a year. What have you been doing?"

Celeste fiddled with the dishes on her counter once more, pushing the two plates with the burgers to one side. Luke knew a stalling tactic when he saw one.

An awkward moment of silence dragged on, making him fidget. Finally, Celeste replied. "I've begun a new business making birthday and wedding cakes."

"What made you leave the restaurant business?" Maggie persisted. "Why do you want to work for the Solace Lake Lodge? We're a long way from South Carolina."

Celeste sighed and closed her eyes, lowering her head before facing them once more, a resigned expression on her face. "I might as well tell you. I'm sure you'll find out anyway. At my last job at The Beachfront Bistro, the head chef became obsessed with me. He began making sexual advances at work and phoning constantly to harass me during my off hours. Occasionally, he followed me home, which was really scary. I told him repeatedly I wasn't interested, but he wouldn't stop. Finally, I got up the nerve to complain to the owners of the restaurant. All I asked was that they tell him to leave me alone and let me do my job. The head chef denied he'd ever harassed me. He turned the tables, saying I was the one who was harassing him. Who do you think they believed?"

"I'm guessing they went with the head chef," Maggie said. Luke heard the repressed anger in her voice.

Celeste nodded. "He was a star chef and I was a nobody. They fired me on the spot. But what was worse was that I was labeled a troublemaker. Nobody in this town has been willing to hire me. I've been making cakes out of my sister's kitchen the past year, but it's difficult to make a decent wage, especially since none of the restaurants will buy from me. My daughter and I had to move in with my sister and her family to make ends meet."

"I see." Maggie's face was devoid of expression. It made Luke uneasy not knowing what she was thinking. "Thank you for speaking to us, Celeste. We'll get back to you with our decision later today."

Celeste nodded, her expression tense. "Thank you for interviewing me. I appreciate your time." Her tone suggested she didn't expect to ever hear from them again.

"Goodbye."

Luke disconnected. "What do you think?"

"I want to hire her."

He blinked, totally taken aback. "Are you sure? Don't you think we should at least check with her last employer to get his side of the story?"

She folded her arms across her chest, her mouth unsmiling. "I can tell you exactly how that conversation would go. We'd ask about Celeste and the head chef would say she was nothing but trouble, and they had to fire her. Or perhaps he'd be more subtle than that. He might say there was a personality conflict in the kitchen and everyone agreed she'd be better off somewhere else. But he'd make sure we understood that Celeste was a bitch, a whiner and a troublemaker, and he was glad to be rid of her. Which is the message I'm sure he's given to every other prospective employer."

"This is more than idle speculation, isn't it? Have you had personal experience with sexual harassment?" The thought made him sick to his stomach.

She closed the lid of the laptop and slid off her stool. "Let's just say I understand what she's up against."

He grabbed her hand before she could run away. "What happened, Maggie?"

Pain and defiance shone in her eyes. "Nothing you want to hear."

She was scaring him. He gripped her hand a little tighter. "You're wrong. I want to know. I want to help if I can."

She tugged on her hand, and he let her go. "There's nothing you can do. It's ancient history. Can we drop this, please?"

Luke nodded, disappointed. He couldn't make her confide in him, and he certainly couldn't make her trust him. He'd burned those bridges.

Maggie tied her apron around her waist. "Celeste is in difficult position. I think she showed good skills and knowledge in her presentation. She could have made up some kind of story to explain the gap in her resume, but she told the truth. I believe she's an honest, hard-working woman who, through no fault of her own, fell into an impossible situation. But I don't want to hire her because I feel sorry for her. I want to hire her because I think she'll be an asset to our kitchen."

She stood completely motionless, her back straight, as if she was bracing herself for some kind of push back from him. But even though she expected to be overruled, she'd spoken her opinion bravely and honestly.

He'd never been prouder of her. "Okay. We'll hire her."

Maggie blinked. "We will?"

He couldn't help grinning at her surprise. "Yeah, we will. You've made a very compelling argument. I have one caveat. We hire her for a three-month probationary period. If we find that things aren't working out, we'll go our separate ways, no harm, no foul."

"Fair enough. Can we call her back right now and let her know?"

"Sure. Go ahead."

Her sudden smile transported him back to that summer so long ago, back to the beautiful, happy teenager she'd been. His breath caught in his throat. He wished he could make her smile like that more often. His heart squeezed at the thought of all he'd lost.

A few moments later, Celeste's picture popped up on the laptop screen once more. This time, she wasn't alone. A little girl with large dark eyes and curly pigtails stood at her side, munching on a hamburger.

"Hi, Celeste. I'm glad we caught you," Maggie said. "Who do you have with you?"

Celeste put a hand on her daughter's shoulder, as if trying to protect her from whatever was going to happen in the next few minutes. "This is my daughter Hope."

"Nice to meet you, Hope. How's your burger?"

The little girl smiled shyly. "It's good."

"I thought it would be," Maggie said. She turned her attention to Celeste. "We've talked it over, and we want to offer you the job as sous-chef at the Solace Lake Lodge."

Celeste simply stared, her eyes wide. Hope tugged at her arm. "Mama, Mama! You got a job!"

Luke told her about the probationary period and what they were prepared to pay. Still, Celeste said nothing. He and Maggie exchanged a concerned glance.

"I know the lodge is a long way from South Carolina, and I understand it would be a big adjustment for you and Hope. We'll give you a couple of days to think things over and get back to us," Maggie said. She sounded disappointed.

"No!" Celeste stretched her hand toward the screen as if she were trying to reach out and touch Maggie. "Don't go! Yes, I'll take the job. I didn't expect... I didn't think... after I told you about... I didn't think you'd want me."

"We do want you, Celeste. Very much," Maggie said, her smile warm and reassuring. "How soon can you get here?"

Celeste froze, her expression crestfallen. "I don't know. I don't have a car, and I don't have the money for airfare. I didn't think that far in advance when I sent in my resume. I'm sorry."

Maggie tapped her finger on the counter and bit her lower lip before turning to him. "I'm about to make an executive decision, Luke."

"Go for it." He was unbelievably proud of her.

She returned her attention to the screen. "We'll arrange and pay for your airfare to the lodge. You can pay us back over the next three months. Does that sound fair?"

"More than fair. Thank you." Celeste's brow wrinkled. "I almost hate to ask after everything you've done, but is there some place Hope and I will be able to stay? It doesn't have to be fancy."

Maggie turned to him again. "What do you think?"

"Well, the lodge isn't officially open yet, so we have several rooms in the new guest wing available. Celeste and Hope can stay in one of the double rooms until we can arrange something more permanent."

"Does that sound okay?" Maggie asked.

Celeste laughed and dabbed at her eyes with a tissue. "It sounds more than okay. I don't know how to thank you."

"You can thank me by being the hard-working, creative chef I believe you to be. I can't wait to meet you and start working together."

Celeste laughed while tears spilled down her cheeks. "I can't wait either."

Luke watched Maggie's face as she went over a few details with Celeste. Despite everything she'd been through, or maybe because of it, she was a strong, capable, compassionate woman. She was going to make a success of the restaurant, and her life.

Too bad he wasn't going to be around to see it happen.

His joy at seeing her excel, his pride at her strength and resilience, faltered at the thought.

Chapter Eleven

MAGGIE POURED TEA FOR Abby and placed the cup and saucer on the table next to her chair. She opened the plastic container she'd brought and held it out to Abby. "Can I tempt you with some cookies?"

Abby reached for an oatmeal raisin. "You know I've always loved your baking." She ate a small bite of the cookie and set the rest on a plate beside her teacup. "Tell me about your adventures at the lodge."

"Well, we've hired a sous-chef."

Maggie launched into the story about how they'd interviewed Celeste online. She even told her their newest employee had been harassed and unable to get a job in her community, knowing that Abby wouldn't share that information.

"So, she and her daughter will arrive here in a few days. Luke and I will drive to Minneapolis to pick them up at the airport."

"She has a daughter?"

"Yes. Hope is six. I imagine it's going to be a big change for them moving here. Starting with the weather."

She looked out the window at the heavy coating of snow covering Harper's truck, which she'd borrowed to visit Abby. "I hope it's not such a big adjustment that she leaves in a couple of weeks. I hope I haven't made a huge mistake in hiring Celeste."

"Trust your gut, Maggie. You have good instincts."

She smiled, amused by Abby's certainty. Her instincts had been off before. "You think so?"

"Absolutely. Always listen to that little voice in your head. It won't lead you astray."

"I'll try to remember that."

Abby was silent for a moment while she drank her tea. Then, she placed her cup on her saucer. "I'd like to tell you some stories about your mother. Would you like to hear them?"

Maggie sat up straighter. "Yes, of course. I'd love to hear them again."

When she was a teenager, Abby had told her stories about some of the things she and Miranda had done as girls. Like Miranda perming Abby's hair and leaving the solution in too long, resulting in frizzy mess that Abby had to endure for weeks until it grew out. Maggie had treasured those stories.

Abby shook her head. "I want to tell you some other stories about Miranda. You were too young before, but you're an adult now and I can tell you things I couldn't back then."

"What kind of things?" Maggie's interest was definitely piqued.

"About her life, and the person she was. The things that happened to her. The first time she fell in love."

"With my father?"

Abby hesitated. "With a boy from school. He was nearly five years older – eighteen and a half to her fourteen. He'd recently graduated high school and she'd finished ninth grade. As soon as her parents found out they were...together, they forbade her from seeing him."

Maggie's breath caught in her throat. "Like me and Luke."

"Yes. It must have been difficult for your grandparents to see you fall in love so young, like Miranda." She covered her mouth with a tissue as she coughed. After sipping some tea, she continued. "Things would have been so different if they could have accepted him."

"What happened?"

"Miranda and her boyfriend ran away together. But they didn't have much money and couldn't get far. Your grandfather caught them and brought Miranda home. He threatened to have the boy charged with rape and abduction if he didn't leave town. The boyfriend was scared and broke and believed he had no choice but to leave. Miranda was broken-hearted, but she was also angry with him for leaving. She had some adolescent romantic notion that if he really loved her, he would have stayed, no matter what."

Abby leaned back in her chair, as if telling her this much had exhausted her. Maggie didn't want to push, but she had so many questions, chief among them why Abby was telling her this story now. She curled her legs underneath her on the couch and leaned toward Abby. "What happened to the boy?"

Abby turned to look at her, resting her head against the back of her chair. “He went away, worked hard, and built a career and a life.”

“Did he ever come back to Minnewasta?”

“He wanted to—”

She stopped speaking and coughed again into the tissue. Maggie could see the tremor in her hands as she reached for her teacup and swallowed a few sips to quiet the cough. She wanted to jump up and do something, anything, to help Abby. But there was nothing she could do. The knowledge made her want to weep.

Finally, the coughing subsided. One side of Abby’s mouth turned up in a grin, but her face was a mask of exhaustion. “I’m afraid the answer to your question is a story for another day.”

Maggie tamped down her frustration and impatience. “You’re killing me, Abby.”

“Sorry, sweetheart. I don’t mean to tease, but I don’t have the energy to tell you the whole story all at once.” She winked at her then, reminding Maggie of the fun-loving woman she'd been. “Besides, if I stretch out the story, you’ll have to come back and bring me more cookies.”

Maggie chuckled. “You know I’d come back to see you even if you didn’t dangle this story like a carrot in front of my nose.”

Abby reached for her hand. “I know.”

“Can I ask one last question before I go?”

“Sure.”

“Why aren’t you telling this story to my sisters, too? Why only me?”

"Because it's your story, sweetheart. Someday you can share the story with them but for now, it's only yours."

That didn't make sense. A story about their mother should belong to all of them, not only her. But she wouldn't push Abby. She trusted her.

"Okay. I'll be back in a few days for the next installment. It might have to be a quick visit though. We're up to our eyeballs in preparations for Cam and Scarlet's wedding."

"I'm hoping to come, at least for the ceremony. I'd so love to see Scarlet get married."

"I'm thrilled for her. I've never seen her so happy."

"I'll make a special effort to get there. I'll even wear my best wig."

Maggie laughed as she rose to her feet and leaned over Abby to kiss her cheek, the scent of Chanel Number Five surrounding her. Abby's cheek was soft and smooth and paper thin under her lips. "I can't wait to see it."

LUKE STOOD WITH MAGGIE in the arrivals area at the Minneapolis airport holding two borrowed parkas. Coming from South Carolina, they'd been reasonably sure Celeste and Hope wouldn't have outerwear warm enough for a Minnesota winter, especially a blustery day such as this. Fortunately, the weather hadn't delayed their flight; the board told them the plane had arrived. Luke hoped they'd deplane soon and collect their luggage before the storm got any worse.

His hopes were answered a moment later. He recognized Celeste and her daughter as they approached the baggage carousels. Smiling, Maggie walked toward them.

"Hello! I'm so glad you made it."

Celeste smiled back with what looked like both relief and uncertainty as she shook Maggie's hand. Luke could understand her emotions. She was stepping into the unknown, away from family and everything that was familiar. It had to be scary, like jumping off a cliff and hoping for a soft landing.

Maggie was taking a similar leap of faith. For her sake and the lodge's, he hoped this arrangement worked.

Celeste put a protective hand around Hope, who clutched a stuffed rabbit and looked up at them with wary eyes. "Thank you. We're glad to be here."

"We brought you some winter coats. I hope they fit."

She handed a bright blue parka to Celeste. "I borrowed this one from my sister Scarlet. I think the two of you are about the same size. And this one's for you, Hope. My niece Tessa was excited to lend it to you. She's close to your age and can hardly wait to meet you. Can we try it on and see if it fits?"

Hope nodded wordlessly. Maggie took the stuffie from her and helped her remove her Dora the Explorer backpack. She handed both to Luke and he gave her the purple down-filled parka. Maggie helped Hope push her arms through the sleeves, then zipped it up to her chin.

"It fits!" Hope gave a gap-toothed smile.

"It's perfect. There's a hat and gloves in the pockets. You'll need them today. It's pretty cold."

Hope reached into a pocket and pulled out a lavender-colored knit hat with white pom-poms dangling from the top. She held it out to Celeste. "Isn't it pretty, Mama?"

"Yes, so pretty. It's so pretty..."

Celeste burst into tears. Luke blinked at her, stunned by her reaction. Passersby stared and made a wide berth around the weeping woman. He wished he could do the same. He had no idea what to do or say, or even why she was crying.

But Maggie seemed to understand. She pulled her into her arms. "It's all right. You and Hope are safe now. Everything's going to be okay."

Celeste soon got herself under control. Maggie handed her a tissue, and she wiped her eyes and blew her nose. Hope wrapped her arms around her mother's waist, her excitement of a moment ago forgotten.

"Why are you crying, Mama?" Her voice was filled with anxiety.

Celeste ran her hand over the top of her daughter's head. "Because Miss Maggie and Mr. Luke have been so kind to us. And I'm very happy to be here." She looked at Maggie and smiled tremulously.

Maggie smiled back. Looking at her made his heart expand in his chest. She was amazing. She was a person able to feel another person's pain and do something about it.

The carousel bearing the luggage from their flight came to life. Luke gestured toward it. "Let's get your things. I'd like to get on the road as quickly as possible."

Fortunately, their two suitcases were among the first to appear on the carousel. Soon, they were on the highway, making their way to the lodge.

"Mama, look at all the snow!"

"I've never seen so much snow, except on TV," Celeste said in wonder. "And I've never been so cold! I thought I was going to freeze into a popsicle when we stepped outside the airport terminal!"

"Welcome to Minnesota," Maggie said with a laugh.

Luke hoped the snow and cold wouldn't prove too much for their new sous-chef. He prayed she'd be able to tough it out.

"How far is it to the Solace Lake Lodge?" she asked.

"It's about a two-hour drive," Maggie said.

"I see."

Luke glanced in the rear-view mirror at Celeste's tense face. Aside from the weather, his biggest fear was that she'd find the lodge too isolated, and the nearby town of Minnewasta too small. If that happened, homesickness could drive her back to South Carolina.

He wanted to say something to reassure their new employee. "You're coming to the lodge at a great time. We're not officially open yet, so you'll have the opportunity to familiarize yourself with the kitchen and the menu before we get really busy. Our grand opening isn't set until the middle of February."

"That's true, but we do have one very important event coming up next weekend." Maggie turned in her seat to look at Celeste. "My sister Scarlet is getting married. We're holding a small reception at the lodge for about forty people."

She talked about the food choices for the wedding and the fact they were using servers from Miller's resort to look after the buffet and cleanup since they hadn't yet hired wait staff of their own.

Celeste nodded eagerly. "I'm excited to get to work. I can handle most of the preparations so you can be free to enjoy the wedding."

"That would be very nice," Maggie agreed.

"Did you make a wedding cake already?"

"No, I was going to make a chocolate sheet cake, but I haven't had a chance."

"I enjoy decorating cakes. I can take over that job from you, if you'd like. Do you think your sister would mind?"

"No, I'm sure she wouldn't mind at all, and I'd appreciate the help. I'll introduce you to Scarlet, and the two of you can talk about what she'd like."

"That's good. I want to be useful and do my share."

"Don't worry. You'll get your chance. Once the lodge officially opens, the kitchen is going to be very busy. Or so we hope. You're going to be a very big asset."

For Maggie's sake, Luke hoped that was true.

THE NEXT DAY MAGGIE stole away from the lodge to visit Abby. As she'd hoped, Celeste was talented and efficient, and she had no worries about leaving her in charge of the kitchen for a few hours. She borrowed Harper's truck again and drove to town, anxious to hear more of Abby's stories of her mother.

Reese answered her knock on the door. His smile was tired, but welcoming.

"Come in, come in." She handed her coat to him and he hung it in the closet. "I'm afraid Abby is sleeping. She wanted to see you, but she had a bad night and didn't get much rest."

"Oh." She couldn't keep the disappointment out of her voice. She so wanted to learn more about her mother. "I can come back another day."

"Why don't you stay a few minutes? Abby made me promise to keep you for a little while. It was the only way I could get her to lie down. If she wakes up soon, you could have a visit."

Maggie hesitated. She had a lot to do at the lodge to get ready for the wedding. But she could spare a few minutes, even if she didn't get to see Abby. "All right."

Reese looked pleased and a little relieved. "Good. Would you like some tea?"

"Sure."

He busied himself in the kitchen while she restlessly prowled the living room examining knick-knacks. A picture of Luke on the fireplace mantle caught her eye and she picked it up. He was about ten and dressed in his Boy Scout uniform. His impish grin made her smile.

Reese brought in a tray with the tea and set it on the coffee table. "That's Abby's favorite picture of Luke. He'd just earned a badge for canoeing and he was feeling pretty proud of himself."

"I can see why it's her favorite. He's adorable."

"Abby told me the two of you fell in love as teenagers." He poured tea into two cups and sat on the sofa. "Do you still feel that way about him?"

Maggie carefully set the picture back on the mantle, avoiding his eyes. "That was long ago."

"Sometimes those feelings linger."

"Until a few weeks ago, we hadn't seen each other in ten years. We barely know each other anymore."

Maggie moved to the sofa and sat next to him. Reese stared into his teacup. "Abby and I hadn't seen each other for about ten years either, but as soon as we did, the years melted away as if we'd never been apart."

"Were you two sweethearts in high school?" Maggie reached for her own teacup.

"No. We were friends, sort of. I was a few years older, so I didn't hang around with her much in those days, but I knew who she was. Even back then, she was bright and funny."

She knew what he meant. She'd always remember Abby as a ray of sunshine. "So what happened when you met again all those years later?"

A smile curled one corner of his mouth. "For once, I really saw her. I'd been blind before, but finally the scales fell from my eyes."

Maggie waited for him to elaborate, but he remained silent, sipping his tea in quiet contemplation as if lost in memories. She sat wordlessly, not wanting to intrude.

Finally, he roused himself. "Perhaps you and Luke can recapture what you once had."

"It was a long time ago and we were very young. Besides, Luke isn't staying. He'll go back to California when—"

She flinched. Abby's impending death was the last thing she wanted to remind Reese about. To her amazement, he smiled at her.

"Maybe for the right reason, he'd stay."

"I don't think I'm that reason."

"Don't sell yourself short, Maggie. And don't ever pass up a chance to love. Those opportunities are very rare."

Maggie tilted her head as she studied him. "That almost sounds like a warning."

He shrugged. "I guess it is. I almost let Abby slip from my life, and it would have been the biggest mistake I'd ever made."

She lifted her gaze to his. "Even knowing what you know now, about how it will end?"

"Absolutely. Loving Abby is even worth the pain of losing her."

Reese smiled again but said nothing further on the subject. They chatted about Scarlet's upcoming wedding and how easily Celeste was fitting in as they finished their tea.

Finally, he set down his cup and got to his feet. "I'll see if Abby is still sleeping."

"Please don't wake her on my account."

He nodded. "I won't, but I know how much she wanted to see you."

With that, he quietly walked down the hallway to the bedroom. A few moments later he returned, his face solemn. "She's sleeping soundly, and I hate to disturb her."

Maggie rose from the sofa. "Of course not. Please tell her I'll stop by again, probably after the wedding."

"I will."

He removed her coat from the closet and held it for her it while she slipped it on. "Drive safely, Maggie."

"I will. I'll see you at the wedding, I hope."

"If Abby's feeling up to it, we'll be there."

She mulled over her conversation with Reese all the way back to the lodge. He believed Luke would stay if she asked him to. And he'd implied a relationship with him would be worth the risk, even if it ended badly.

After barely surviving Luke's last rejection, she wasn't as sure.

Chapter Twelve

CAM'S SISTER AND HER family arrived at the lodge the day before the wedding. His nephew Drew pulled Maggie into a hug as soon as he saw her in the front entry of the lodge. "Good to see you again, Maggie."

He let her go as soon as she pulled out of his embrace, though he continued to hold her hand. "It's been too long. Thank goodness your sisters keep marrying my uncles."

His smile told her he wanted to be more than partners in the wedding party. A shiver of unease trickled up her spine, but she made herself smile. "Well, this is the end, I'm afraid. I'm fresh out of sisters."

"Ditto for me. No more uncles." He leaned in close to whisper in her ear. "It would be great if the next time we meet it would be on a date."

Maggie stared at him, not knowing what to say. She liked Drew. He was Cam and Ethan's nephew, and he was a nice boy. But that was the problem. She thought of him as a boy, not as a potential partner. Somehow, she had to let him know she wasn't interested in him romantically. She gently tugged on her hand and he released his grip immediately.

"Drew, that's not going to happen. I live too far from Minneapolis for us to date. Not to mention, I'm nearly four years older than you."

"Neither of those things matter. Not to me anyway."

"Drew—"

"Give me a chance, Maggie. That's all I'm asking. If at the end of this weekend you still don't want to go out with me, I won't bother you again."

She really didn't want to hurt his feelings. "I don't think the weekend is going to matter. I'm not going to change my mind."

His smile was quick and full of youthful confidence. "Never say never, Maggie. I have amazing powers of persuasion. You'll see."

She couldn't help laughing at that. "You're full of yourself, aren't you?"

"It's part of my charm." He clasped her hand again, his expression growing serious. "I really like you, Maggie. I think you'd like me, too, if you'd let yourself."

She stared up at him. For one crazy minute, she wished she could be attracted to someone like Drew, someone uncomplicated and fun. Someone she didn't share a complex, painful history with.

Like Luke.

Where things were going with Luke, if they were going anywhere, she didn't know. But she did know she couldn't manufacture feelings for Drew that didn't exist.

Once more, she pulled her hand from his. "It's been nice seeing you again, Drew, but duty calls. I need to check on dinner. I'm sure we'll talk later."

"We will. Count on it."

Maggie inwardly groaned as she hurried to the kitchen. How the hell was she supposed to handle Drew?

How the hell was she supposed to understand her feelings for Luke?

She ducked into the relative safety of the kitchen, glad to have an excuse to hide out for a while. She grabbed her white chef's jacket from a peg near the door and slipped it on. At least in the kitchen she'd been able to regain a sense of control, and for that she was profoundly grateful. She'd gained more confidence in her abilities as a chef in the last few weeks than she had in the last couple of years.

Because of Luke. He'd praised her efforts, pushed her to believe in herself the way she had when she was younger.

But right now, she didn't want to deal with her complicated, mixed-up emotions where Luke was concerned.

"Maggie, hi." Celeste looked up from the pot she was stirring. "I thought you were visiting with your guests."

"They're more my sisters' guests than mine. Cam and Ethan's sister and her family and some relatives from Wisconsin. I did the polite thing and said hello, and now I thought I'd work on dessert."

With Luke's encouragement, she'd begun working on a more sophisticated dessert menu. For this dinner, she'd prepared the pastry for *tarte au citron*, a French lemon pie. The pastry had rested in the fridge for a couple of hours and would now be firm enough to roll out.

"It's done. I assumed you wanted me to finish the *tarte*. It's chilling in the fridge. I didn't mean to be pushy."

"You're not being pushy, just efficient. Have you peeled potatoes?"

Celeste pointed to the pot on the stove. "Yes."

"The prime rib's in the oven?"

"Yes."

Desperate, Maggie asked, "What's left to do?"

"I was about to get the vegetables ready to steam."

"I'll peel the carrots."

"Let me do it," Celeste said. "You've done so much for me. I want to do something for you."

Maggie decided to trust Celeste. "I know you can handle things on your own. But I don't want to go out to the dining room yet. Cam's nephew Drew has a bit of a crush on me, and he's made it clear he wants to be more than friends."

Celeste's eyes widened in alarm. "Is he harassing you?"

Maggie put her hand on Celeste's arm. "No, no nothing like that. But I don't feel the same way, and I don't want him to think I'm making time for him."

"Well, of course not. You're already involved with Luke."

She abruptly withdrew her hand. "Involved? No! What made you think something like that?"

"I thought...the way you look at each other... I'm sorry."

Maggie shook her head, embarrassed by her reaction to Celeste's innocent statement. "No, I'm the one who's sorry. I didn't mean to jump all over you. Whatever Luke and I had is long in the past, and there's no future. He's only here at the lodge temporarily." Maggie told her about Abby. "We were...close once. But that was ten years ago. I was a kid."

"If you genuinely care for someone, it doesn't matter how old you are." Celeste pushed herself away from the counter and pulled a bag of carrots from the fridge. "Come on. You can hide out with me while we get the vegetables ready."

They worked in compatible silence at the sink, peeling carrots and stripping the outside leaves from Brussel sprouts. Thankfully, Celeste didn't ask any more uncomfortable questions.

The way you look at each other. When Luke looked at her, what did he see? A girl he'd once loved? Or a bullet he'd managed to dodge?

And how did she see him?

She sliced a carrot in half with a ruthless stab and pushed the thought away, unable and unwilling to answer her own question.

AFTER DINNER, THE HUGE pine tree Harper had selected from their forest and had cut herself the previous day was dragged into the dining room. It required the strength of five men – Ethan, Cam, Luke, Drew, and Drew's father Graham – to hoist the tree into a huge tub of wet sand and set it into place near the fireplace. The tree soared toward the ceiling and filled the room with its fresh, outdoor scent. A rush of memories sent Maggie back to childhood Christmases when similar trees stood in the same spot.

Harper carried a scarred and battered cardboard box into the dining room, followed by Ethan and Cam who carried similar boxes. Maggie recognized Grandma Dorothy's scrawling handwriting on the sides of the boxes, the words "Christmas Decorations" written with permanent marker. Scarlet followed with a couple of large plastic shopping bags displaying the name of a hardware store in Brainerd.

Harper set her box near the tree. "These are Grandma's old decorations I told you about." She sliced open the tape sealing the box with a utility knife but turned to Maggie and Scarlet before opening the flaps. "Are you ready to see what's in here?"

Scarlet nodded. Taking a deep breath, Maggie did the same. They were only old Christmas ornaments. Seeing them again shouldn't make her uneasy, but somehow, they did.

Harper lifted the first tissue-wrapped bundle from the box and peeled back the paper to reveal a delicate, clear glass ball. A snowflake covered in glitter sparkled inside.

"I remember these snowflakes," Scarlet said. "Mainly because I broke one when I was ten and Grandma never let me forget it."

"That was dear old Grandma, wasn't it?" Harper said with shake of her head. "Grampa once told me that possessions meant so much to her because she'd grown up dirt poor."

Maggie took the glass ball from Harper. "I didn't know that."

It made sense. She'd often thought Grandma's fine bone china meant more to her than she did. She'd treated the flowery china as if it were priceless beyond measure. Heaven help you if you chipped a piece or, God forbid, broke one. If Grandma had known she'd pawned her mother's antique diamond earrings, the ones she'd passed down to her on her fourteenth birthday, she would have gone ballistic.

A pang of deep regret struck her over the loss of the earrings. She swept it aside, knowing regret changed nothing. She'd done what she'd had to do to survive. End of story.

Ethan brought a stepladder into the dining room and set it up near the tree. Harper handed him a large, glittering star and he secured it to the top branch. Luke and the others strung the new lights and garlands that Scarlet had purchased. The tree was beginning to make the place feel like Christmas.

Christmas had been her favorite holiday as a child. Not only because of the presents she received, but because of everything surrounding Christmas – the carols, the concerts at school and church, the special baked treats and meals only made once a year. But mostly she loved it because of the time spent with her family. The lodge would always be closed to guests between Christmas and New Year's, and the five of them spent those days together skating on the lake or playing board games next to the fire. Those Christmases were her happiest childhood memories.

Maggie shook herself out of the past. She used Harper's utility knife to open the last of Grandma's boxes. Pushing back the flaps, she carefully removed tissue wrapped bundles and set them on the floor. Scarlet knelt beside her and unwrapped the first one, a glass angel with the words "Baby's First Christmas" written in gold script. Beneath those words was the year of Maggie's birth. Maggie couldn't remember ever seeing it before.

Scarlet held the angel up to the light. "Harper, do you remember this?"

Harper knelt beside her, taking the angel from her. "Yeah. Mom bought this the year Maggie was born. I remember it on our tree in Minneapolis. I think that was our last Christmas there with Mom and Dad."

Maggie's breath caught in her throat. She wished she could remember that Christmas, wished she could remember *them*.

Harper began digging in the box. "These must be Mom's decorations. There should be two more angels."

Scarlet pulled out ornament after ornament from the box. "I remember a lot of these. If Grandma saved them, why didn't she ever put them on the tree when we were kids?"

Instinctively, Maggie knew. "Because it was too painful for her." Despite all their differences, she'd always known how profoundly their mother's death had affected Grandma Dorothy. She'd been destroyed, mentally and physically, growing more cynical and bitter with each passing year. When their father killed their mother, he'd killed her, too. It had just taken her longer to die.

Scarlet uncovered two more glass angels, identical to the first, the only difference the dates printed on the bottom – one for Harper's birth year and the other for Scarlet's.

Cam gently lifted one of the delicate ornaments from Scarlet's hands. "We're definitely putting them on the tree this year."

He handed Scarlet's angel to his sister Lydia and she placed it, along with the other two, in a little circle at the front of the tree. "A place of honor," she said. "You'll be able to see them whenever you look at the tree."

Maggie watched as tears filled Scarlet's eyes. Cam pulled her into his arms and she rested her head against his broad shoulder. For a fleeting minute, Maggie wished for that kind of safe harbor, for someone who would hold her as she cried, and make everything bad go away.

Her gaze collided with Luke's. Did he ever think about what might have been if he'd stayed in Minnewasta? She had. Too often.

With an effort, she returned her attention to the box in front of her. There was something at the bottom, another smaller box with a lid. She pulled it out and laid it on the floor, then removed the lid. Her breath caught in her throat at what she found.

A framed picture of her parents on their wedding day. They looked so young, so happy, their fresh faces showing no hint of the tragedy to come. Maggie traced the lines of her father's face. She'd never seen their wedding picture before and had only seen a few candid pictures of her father that Abby had shown her. Grandma had removed all traces of him from their lives. Maggie had assumed she'd destroyed all the pictures she'd had of him.

But she'd kept this one. She may have planned to give it to them one day. They'd never know.

"I wish I remembered him," she said. "He was very handsome, wasn't he?"

"Yeah, he was."

She didn't realize she was crying until Luke sat beside her on the floor and put his arm around her. For a moment she leaned into him, letting herself remember the happiness of being in his arms. All these years later, her body hadn't forgotten how safe he made her feel.

How loved.

Too soon, he pulled away. He gently removed the picture from her hands and offered her a tissue. She dabbed her eyes with it and tried to get her emotions under control.

Luke handed the picture to Harper and Scarlet, and they wordlessly stared at the photo together. Then, Harper handed the picture to Ethan. "Would you put this on the mantle? I'd like to keep it there, at least until after Christmas."

"Of course."

No one spoke as Ethan set the picture on the mantle. Finally, Lydia broke the silence. "For whatever reason, your grandmother saved these mementos but hid them away. I think finding them again is cause for celebration, don't you?"

Scarlet wiped a tear from her cheek. "Yes, you're right. We should celebrate. Maggie, why don't we make some hot chocolate? And what about some Christmas music?"

"I'll take care of the music," Harper said. She held out her hand and Ethan helped her to her feet and held her close.

Maggie got to her feet and pulled Scarlet up. Scarlet put her arm around Maggie's shoulders as they walked to the kitchen. She needed to start fresh, like the lodge, to take the good things from the past and let everything else go. Time for joy again.

She glanced over her shoulder and saw Luke watching her. Their gazes connected and he smiled. Maggie returned his smile with a tremulous one of her own. *Time for joy again.*

Turning, she wrapped her arm around Scarlet's waist. "Celeste made some sugar cookies this morning. Would you like some?"

Scarlet hugged her shoulder. "Absolutely."

LUKE TURNED UP THE heat in his truck and sipped the hot coffee he'd purchased at the airport, while the three women in the back seat laughed and talked amongst themselves. The good news was that Cam and Scarlet's wedding day dawned bright and sunny with little wind. The bad news was that the temperature had dropped to minus twenty Fahrenheit overnight. Since he'd volunteered to drive to the airport in Minneapolis to pick up Scarlet's friends from Chicago, he was grateful he didn't have to contend with a snowstorm. But he could live without the cold.

He glanced in the rear-view mirror and saw that one of the women – did she say her name was Jill? – was staring back at him. He'd seen that look often enough to know she was interested, and it made him uncomfortable. He really didn't want to deal with any unwanted attention right now.

"So, you said you work at Scarlet's lodge?" she asked.

"Yes, temporarily. I'm the hotel and restaurant manager. I'm helping to get the lodge established and launched into the market."

"Why only temporarily?"

He hated talking about his mother's imminent death. "I grew up with Scarlet and her sisters. My mother's been ill so when the job at the lodge came up, I applied for it. Scarlet's family was willing to hire me temporarily so I can be with her. I took a leave of absence from my job at a resort in the Napa Valley. I'll go back there in a few months." He didn't add, 'after she dies.' It was too hard to say the words and besides, he didn't want their pity.

"You're a good friend. And a good son."

He shifted in his seat, knowing he was undeserving of the praise. As Maggie had reminded him, a good son wouldn't have waited until his mother was dying before coming home. And a good friend wouldn't take advantage of friendship to get a job. Maggie's family was doing an enormous favor for him.

And a good friend wouldn't fantasize about sleeping with Maggie the way you've been doing for the past couple of weeks.

To his relief, the women chatted amongst themselves the rest of the way to the lodge, though he sensed Jill's gaze on him often. He'd employ the tact he'd used on other occasions to ward off the attention of female guests. Total professionalism and a firm but polite decline of any offered invitations. He pulled in front of the lodge and unloaded the luggage while Scarlet's friends got out of the truck.

Harper opened the front door. "Come on in! It's too cold to be standing around outside for long!"

She ushered them inside, and Luke closed the door behind them.

"We're so happy you could come for Scarlet's wedding. She'll be thrilled to see you."

"Scarlet's a wonderful person. We really miss her, but we're happy she's happy."

"I'll show you to your rooms and then you can meet us in the dining room for lunch."

Jill turned to Luke. "Thanks for picking us up and getting us here safely."

He gave a polite nod. "You're very welcome. I hope you enjoy your stay."

The other two women followed Harper toward the new wing of guestrooms, but Jill hung back. Once the others were out of earshot, she touched his arm. "Will you be here at the inn this evening?"

"Yes."

"We could meet later, in my room."

She was an attractive woman and at one time, he might have taken her up on her offer. But to his surprise, he found he wasn't interested. He gently pulled back his arm.

"I'm sorry. I can't." He stepped back. "Enjoy your stay."

He beat a path to the privacy of the office, expelling a relieved breath once he was safely inside with the door firmly closed. He leaned against the door and wondered what the hell he was doing. His relationship with Maggie, such as it was, wasn't going anywhere, especially to the bedroom, so why say no to an attractive woman who was obviously interested.

He didn't have any answers, only the gut feeling he'd done the right thing.

Chapter Thirteen

LUKE HELPED THE TEMPORARY wait staff move the dining room tables to the edges of the room to create an open area in front of the fireplace where Scarlet and Cam would exchange their vows. Rows of chairs were then set up for the guests. Following the ceremony, the chairs would be cleared away to make room for dancing.

Half an hour before the ceremony was to begin, Luke examined the room to make sure everything was in place. The Christmas tree was lit and sparkling with decorations, the scent of pine sweet in the air. A fire burned in the hearth, lending a soft, warm glow to the room. The tables were covered with white tablecloths, pots of red poinsettias serving as centerpieces. Dozens more red and white poinsettias decorated the dining room, giving a classic Christmas vibe to the place.

Satisfied everything was ready, he went to the kitchen. Celeste bustled from station to station, directing the two line cooks they'd borrowed from Miller's on what needed to be done. Though everyone was busy, there was no panic, only calm efficiency. It looked like Celeste had everything well in hand. Maggie had been totally right in putting her faith in her.

"Anything I can help you with?" he asked.

"I think we've got everything covered, thanks," she said. "Everything's nearly ready for the buffet."

"Good." Their first major test of the kitchen with its new staff appeared to be going well. He spied Celeste's daughter Hope lying on her stomach in a corner of the kitchen, coloring in a book in desultory fashion. She looked bored, and Luke decided she needed rescuing.

"Hope, would you like to help me greet guests as they arrive?"

She sat up and gave him a gap-toothed grin. "Yes!" She looked beseechingly at her mother. "Can I, Mama?"

Celeste cocked her head at him. "You're sure?"

"Absolutely."

"Okay, then. Pick up your crayons first and then you can go with Mr. Luke."

Hope stuffed the crayons back in the box. He held out his hand, and she jumped to her feet and grabbed it.

"Be a good girl for Mr. Luke," Celeste said as they left the kitchen. Hope turned to wave at her mother, then skipped along beside him. Luke smiled. She had sunny, cheerful disposition. Thankfully, Celeste had been able to shield her from the ugliness of the sexual harassment that had driven them from their home.

When they reached the front entrance, he pointed to the small table he'd set up near the door. An open book, a pen and a wicker basket sat on the table. "This is the guest book, Hope. Cam and Scarlet would like all their guests to sign as they come in."

"Why do people have to sign, Mr. Luke?"

"I guess so that years from now, they can look at the book and remember who came to their wedding."

She seemed satisfied with the answer. "Okay."

"Can you sit here and ask everyone to sign the book?"

"I can do that," she said gravely.

"Once you do that, you can hand everyone one of these leaflets. It tells people who's in the wedding party. And if they have a card for the couple, you can tell them to put it in this basket. Gifts go on the table behind you."

Again, she nodded. "I can do that, too."

He smiled and tugged on one of her pigtails. She was a great kid. Perhaps he related with her so strongly because he knew what growing up without a father was like. "I knew you could. Did I tell you how pretty you look today?"

She made a little twirl. "I got this brand-new dress for Christmas. Mama gave it to me early so I could wear it today."

The ivory lace of the dress was a lovely contrast against her dark skin. The red velvet ribbons in her pigtails bobbed as she moved. "It's a very nice present. Very pretty."

The front door opened and he helped Hope into her chair behind the table, giving her an encouraging smile. He moved forward to greet the arriving guests. He shook hands with members of Cam's crew and their spouses while they signed the guest book. Hope solemnly handed them a program and then he led them into the dining room and offered them seats. When he got back to Hope's table, she was handing programs to Jill and her friends.

Luke smiled politely and held out his arm. "Hello, ladies. May I escort you to your seats?"

Jill laid her hand on his arm, looking up at him with a warm smile. "That would be lovely, Luke."

He found them three seats and Jill's friends sat down. Jill squeezed his arm and smiled once again. "Be sure to save me a dance later."

He gave a noncommittal smile as she took her seat. Obviously, she hadn't given up. He'd have to tread carefully. He had no desire to sleep with Jill, but he didn't want to offend her either, especially since she was a friend of Scarlet's. The last thing he wanted was to create some kind of scene on Scarlet's wedding day.

He returned to the foyer as Reese came through the front door.

"Luke, can you hold the door open for your mother?"

"Sure."

While Luke held the door, his grandmother walked in, followed by Reese pushing his mother in a wheelchair. He should have known she'd have to use the chair today, but for some reason Luke's heart gave an unexpected lurch to see her in it. She smiled up at him, her face even thinner than it had been only a day or two ago.

"Hi, honey."

He forced a smile to hide his distress. "Hi, Mom. I'm glad you could make it."

He bent to kiss her and his heart thumped with pain. She was so small and delicate, like a tiny sparrow with a broken wing. He had to swallow and make himself smile again before lifting his head.

"Would you please sign the guest book for the bride and groom?" Hope said.

"Of course, we will," Abby said. "What's your name, sweetheart?"

"It's Hope."

"Hope is Celeste's daughter. She's our new sous-chef," Luke explained.

"We flew all the way from South Carolina. I've never been on a plane before."

"You've come a very long way, Hope. I'm glad to meet you."

"Hope, this is my mother Abby, her husband Reese and my grandma Phyllis."

Hope shook hands with them. "Hello."

Phyllis signed the guest book and then turned to him. "You must thank Scarlet and her new husband for inviting me. I was so pleased to get their invitation."

Scarlet had told him that because she had so few relatives, only her sisters, she was happy to borrow a few from her friends. Luke was simply glad his grandmother had been included.

He kissed her soft cheek, inhaling the floral scent of her perfume. "You're looking very chic this evening, Grandma."

She blushed as she looked down at her pantsuit. "Thank you, Luke. I would have preferred to wear a dress, but it was far too cold today. This way, I can wear my long johns."

She lifted her pant leg above her ankle length boot to reveal pink, flowered, thermal underwear. Luke laughed in genuine amusement. Thank God for his grandmother.

"Good thinking."

The door opened again to admit more guests and Abby shivered. “Could we move away from the door, Luke? It’s so cold.”

He should have thought of it himself. “Let’s get you out of here.”

He wheeled his mother into the dining room while Reese and his grandmother followed. A spot near the front was open, so he sat them there, removing a chair so he could fit in the wheelchair. “The wedding will start soon. I should go back to the front door and make sure Hope is okay. I’ll see you later.”

He turned away before his mother could see the anxiety on his face. He had to get over his shock about seeing her in the wheelchair. Logically, he knew she was using it because it made it easier for her to get around and helped to reserve what little strength she had left. But to see his once vibrant, energetic mother confined to the chair, her body wracked by disease, hurt to the core of his marrow. Not since he had arrived back in Minnewasta had anything shown him with such complete clarity that his mother was about to die.

He concentrated on collecting himself before meeting more guests. Fortunately, Hope was instructing newcomers to sign the guestbook and passing out programs. Luke was grateful he didn’t have to make small talk.

A few moments later, Cam’s sister and her husband and daughter came through the door from the new wing of guestrooms where they were staying. They signed the guestbook at Hope’s request, and Luke escorted them to their reserved seats at the front of the room. When he returned to the front entrance, Cam, Ethan and Drew were in the entry. Luke took their heavy winter coats and hung them on the coat racks they'd set up for that purpose.

"Looking good, gentlemen."

They each wore elegant dark grey suits and crisp white shirts, their ties in various patterns of red and black. Luke reached for the box of boutonnieres Scarlet had left him in charge of and pinned a red rose bud to Cam's lapel. When he finished, he shook his hand. "Congratulations, Cam. Make her happy."

"I will," he said solemnly. Luke had no doubt he would.

Once Luke pinned matching boutonnieres to Ethan and Drew's lapels, Cam wordlessly clapped his nephew on the shoulder in an unspoken signal to head into the dining room. Ethan followed Drew, and Cam brought up the rear. Luke held out his hand to Hope.

"Come on, sweetie. Our job here is done. Let's go watch the wedding."

Hope eagerly reached for his hand, her eyes wide with excitement. They stood at the back of the dining room, which gave them a view of the fireplace where the groom and his attendants now stood. They also had an excellent view of the staircase the bride and her bridesmaids would soon descend. Luke lifted Hope into his arms so she could see over the adults sitting in front of her.

The organist began to play Pachelbel's Canon in D, signaling the bride's imminent arrival. All eyes turned to the staircase. Cam's daughter Tessa led the bridal party. She wore a red lace dress and carried a basket of flowers in one hand.

Following Tessa, Maggie began a slow descent down the stairs, one hand on the railing and the other holding a bouquet of white roses. All the air rushed from Luke's lungs. Her full length, lace dress in dark red fit her perfectly. The low bodice that skimmed the sweet swell of her breasts nearly undid him. Her dark hair shone in the glow from the fireplace, her smile wide and happy.

When her gaze connected with his, his heart squeezed with unexpected longing. He swallowed, his mouth suddenly dry, his heart hammering. Maggie's smile faltered. She quickly turned her attention to the men standing in front of the fireplace. She walked toward them, taking her place on the bride's side, opposite Drew, her smile firmly in place once more. Only the slight trembling of the ribbons cascading from her bouquet hinted at any nervousness.

He was aware that Harper and Scarlet had descended the stairs and now stood with the others in front of the fireplace. He was sure they were both lovely, but he couldn't take his eyes off Maggie. In her chef's whites, her face pink with the heat of the stove and her hair dampened with perspiration, she was beautiful. Always had been.

But today, she was stunning. He'd never seen her more exquisite.

The ceremony went by in a blur. Scarlet and Cam exchanged vows and wedding rings, and sealed their union with a lingering kiss. They looked at each other as if they were the only two people in the room. The bond between them, the sense they knew without question they belonged together, and would always be together was profound. No matter what life threw at them, they would endure, as long as they stood side by side.

I want that, Luke realized with a start. He wanted to be with a woman who truly understood him, loved him. Someone to share his dreams, his hopes, his fears. His gaze drifted to Maggie once again. They'd had that once, that special bond, but they'd been far too young to appreciate it. Or at least he had.

When such a bond was broken, could it ever be mended? If Maggie knew the truth...

He pushed the guilt away. Tonight, he wanted to forget.

As soon as the justice of the peace pronounced Cam and Scarlet husband and wife, a cheer went up from the assembled group. Cam picked up Tessa and settled her into the crook of his arm and, with one hand holding Scarlet's, he addressed their guests.

"Thank you all for coming. It means a lot to us to have our family and friends here to share the happiest day of our lives." He lifted Scarlet's hand to his lips for a kiss before turning back to the crowd, his smile conveying his joy. "Now, let's party!"

Luke set Hope on her feet and she ran off to see Tessa. He helped Ethan and Drew move chairs to the side of the room. When they were done, he looked around for Maggie. She was talking to his mother and Reese, holding Abby's hand and laughing. Even from this distance, he could see the lines of fatigue on his mother's face, and his heart squeezed with pain. This outing was likely too much for her.

Luke walked across the floor to join them. "How are you doing, Mom? Are you getting tired?"

Abby brushed off his concern with a wave of her hand. “Oh, I’m fine. I’m enjoying seeing everyone. Wasn’t it a lovely wedding?”

Luke glanced at Maggie before answering. “Yeah. Beautiful. Don’t overdo, okay?”

Abby grasped his hand with surprising strength. “I’m fine, Luke. Really. The nice thing about being a lady of leisure is that I can sleep all day tomorrow if I want to.”

Luke wanted to cry at her feeble attempt at humor but instead, he made himself smile. “Be sure you do, or you’ll have me to answer to.”

“Spoil sport,” Abby said with a grin. “Now, if you’ll excuse us, I’d like to congratulate the bride and groom. Reese, would you mind wheeling me over?”

“Of course.”

Reese’s gaze met his and in that split second, he read his stepfather’s anguish. And also his resignation. The woman he loved was dying, and there wasn’t a damn thing he could do about it.

There wasn’t a damn thing Luke could do about it either.

They left to speak to Cam and Scarlet who were talking with other guests across the room. Maggie laid her hand on his arm. “I know it’s a shock for you to see Abby in the chair. It was for me, too.”

Luke bowed his head. “I hope I didn’t upset her. I can’t...” He couldn’t finish, couldn’t put into words the grief squeezing his heart so hard he could barely breathe.

“I know. Every time I see her she looks a little more ill, a little closer to leaving us. I’m not ready. I’ll never be ready.”

"Yeah." He lifted his head and looked into her beautiful dark eyes. He should have known she'd understand. "I don't want to spoil Scarlet's wedding. Is it obvious I'm upset?"

"Only to me."

Luke struggled with the urge to pull her into his arms and kiss her. *God, I need her.* But Maggie wouldn't thank him for making such a statement in front of her family and friends.

As if she could read is mind, she let go of his arm. "I should check on the food, see if Celeste needs help."

He was sure Celeste had everything well in hand, but obviously Maggie needed an excuse to escape. "You'd better go then."

"Yeah." But she didn't move. "I'm so sorry, Luke."

He didn't know if she meant she was sorry about his mother's impending death, or if she was trying to tell him they could never return to the easy relationship they'd once had.

Perhaps, she was sorry about both.

Luke nodded and Maggie stepped away. He watched as she wove her way through the crowd and disappeared behind the doors to the kitchen.

"You look like a guy who could use one of these."

Luke turned to see Jill holding out a flute of champagne. "Thanks." He accepted it from her, being careful not to touch her hand.

Jill smiled knowingly, easily reading his actions. "You don't have to worry. I know when I'm beat."

"Excuse me?"

"Please, don't pretend you don't understand. Short of taking out a billboard in flashing neon, I've done everything I can think of to let you know I'm interested. But I've seen that besotted look on a man's face before. You're in love with her, aren't you?"

He didn't want to spill his guts to a woman he barely knew. "We're old friends. We've known each other since high school."

"And you loved her back then, didn't you?"

Luke sipped some of the champagne, letting the bubbles dance across his tongue. He couldn't deny it. Jill sighed, and he turned to look at her.

She gave him a rueful smile. "First love is a powerful thing, very difficult to leave behind. Even if you want to."

Her words echoed those of his mother. *I can tell you that first love is a powerful thing. It stays with you all your life.*

"You sound like you're speaking from experience."

"Perhaps." She touched her glass to his. "It's been nice meeting you, Luke. Enjoy the wedding."

"You, too. Maybe we can have that dance later."

She smiled. "I'd like that."

She walked over to one of the tables along the edge of the dance floor to join her friends. Luke finally understood what his mother had tried to tell him. He'd thought he'd gotten over Maggie years ago, but she'd always been there, whenever he reached for another woman. Without realizing, he'd been measuring other women against her, and they always came up short. Would he always want her? What if he gave in to desire and followed where it led? But that assumed Maggie felt the same desire.

He drank more champagne. Even if she did, once she discovered the truth about why he'd left Minnesota, nothing would be the same.

Chapter Fourteen

ONCE THE BUFFET HAD been served and the wedding cake eaten, the dishes were cleared away. The DJ hired for the evening set up in a corner of the room and began to spin some tunes. Scarlet had told Maggie she wanted everyone to dance, and have fun, and be as happy as she and Cam were. By the way they looked at each other, Maggie knew they were enjoying themselves. And they were deeply in love.

She was happy for them. She really was. But seeing them smile at each other, the look of love in their eyes, caused a dull ache to pound through her chest.

She pushed away the unwelcome jealousy. *Embrace the joy, Maggie.*

As Scarlet had hoped, the wedding dance was a lot of fun. Maggie danced with Drew and Cam and Ethan, jived very badly with Cam's brother-in-law Graham, and even polkaed with Cam's cousin from Wisconsin. She hadn't laughed so much in a very long time.

She danced with everyone but Luke. He never asked her.

She was keenly aware of him and everything he was doing, as if she had some sort of weird internal radar where he was concerned. Her heart melted to see him get his grandmother up to dance, and she nearly cried as he pushed his mother out on the dance floor, twirling Abby's chair in a slow circle. But when he danced a slow waltz with Scarlet's friend Jill from Chicago, white hot jealousy slammed into her gut, especially when he smiled down at her. Maggie had no right to feel that way. She and Luke had a history, and some unresolved feelings, at least on her part, but nothing more. Once again, she reminded herself of her vow to find the joy in life instead of focusing on the negative.

But even with the internal pep talk, she couldn't help wondering what Luke saw in Jill that he didn't see in her.

Maggie watched Reese push Abby's chair toward the front door with Phyllis and Luke closely behind. She followed them, wanting to say goodnight. By the time she caught up with them in the front entrance, Reese had already helped Abby into her winter coat, and Luke had gone outside to bring their car to the front door. Maggie helped Phyllis with her coat.

"Thank you so much for coming," Maggie said, taking Abby's hand as soon as she was settled in her chair once more. "I know it meant a lot to Scarlet and Cam to have you here tonight. It meant a lot to me, too."

"Darling girl," Abby said, giving her hand a light squeeze. She looked exhausted, her face grey with fatigue. But she hadn't stopped smiling all evening. She gave Maggie a tired smile. "You'll come see me soon? We can continue our story."

Abby's determination to tell her stories about her mother puzzled her. She wasn't sure why she insisted on devoting her dwindling time and energy on her, and she didn't understand why her sisters couldn't hear the story, but she was grateful for the gift. "Of course I will. Whenever you're ready."

"Good." Abby turned her attention to Luke when he returned from outside. "Goodnight, son."

He stooped to hug her. "Goodnight, Mom. I'll drop by tomorrow."

"That would be wonderful."

Luke shook hands with Reese. "I'll get Mom and Grandma into the car."

"I'll be right there, Luke," Reese said. "Just need to grab my coat."

He held the door open while Luke wheeled his mother to the waiting car. Maggie rubbed her bare arms against the cold blast of air that invaded the lodge. Reese firmly closed the door once Luke was through, then turned to Maggie. "I want to thank you for coming to see Abby. It means a lot to her, to both of us."

Maggie studied his face. His eyes were hooded and he looked almost as tired as Abby. Deep lines bracketed his mouth and she was sure more gray was mixed with his dark brown hair than when she'd first arrived in early June.

"I'm the one who's grateful. My mother has been like a mythical figure most of my life, someone not quite real. Abby told me stories about her when I was a kid, but these are different. She's making her come alive for me. Miranda feels like an actual person now."

"Abby will be happy to hear that."

"I'm looking forward to whatever else she has to tell me."

Reese nodded, his brows knitting together in a way that made Maggie think he wanted to say more on the subject. Instead, he shuffled through the coatrack and pulled out a grey parka. “I should go. Make sure you step away from the door. I don’t want you to catch a chill.”

“I will.”

Reese slipped on the parka and zipped it to his chin. Pulling a red knitted hat from his pocket, he twirled it in his hands, his gaze fixed on a point somewhere over her left shoulder. “Your mother was a wonderful person.”

“Harper told me you knew her.”

“Yeah, back in high school.” He shifted his gaze to look at her. Sadness flitted across his face, but he quickly covered it with a grin. “A million years ago.”

“Were you friends?”

“For a while.”

His short answers both frustrated and intrigued her. She’d known Reese, and had worked with him since she’d moved back to the lodge in the spring, but he’d never talked to her about her mother before. She wanted to know more. What was she like as a teenager? What was their relationship back then?

Reese’s throat moved. “I knew her well enough to tell you how proud she’d be of you. She’d be so proud of the hard-working, compassionate young woman you are today.”

Maggie stared at him, unable to speak past the lump that had formed in her throat. The last thing she’d expected this evening was a speech like this from Reese.

He shifted his gaze and stepped back, obviously uncomfortable with her silence. “I’m sorry, I shouldn’t have said that.”

She laid her hand on his arm, stopping him. "Reese, there's nothing you could have said that would have meant more to me. Thank you."

She put her arms around him in a hug. For a moment he held himself stiff, but then he relaxed and put his arms around her shoulders and held her tightly. His throat hummed with a sound somewhere between a groan and a sigh. For a moment, she thought he was crying. But when he pulled away, his eyes were dry.

He smiled at her, still holding her arms. "Thank you, Maggie."

She had no idea what he was thanking her for but before she could ask, the door opened and Luke stepped in along with a bitter gust of cold wind. Reese let her go and stepped away.

"I should get Abby and Phyllis home," he said, all formality once more. "Thank you for a wonderful evening. We all enjoyed it."

"I'm glad you could come."

Reese nodded, his hand on the doorknob. "Step back, Maggie. You're definitely not dressed for this cold."

Luke wordlessly removed his jacket and wrapped it around her shoulders. Maggie blinked up at him. The jacket was warm from the heat of his body and smelled like a combination of his aftershave and the clean, male scent unique to him. She swallowed, her mouth suddenly dry. Luke stared back at her, but she could read nothing in his enigmatic gaze.

Reese cleared his throat. "Goodnight, Luke."

"Goodnight."

He slipped through the door and closed it softly behind him. Maggie removed the jacket and handed it back to Luke, immediately feeling the chill lingering in the air. "Thank you."

"You're welcome." He tossed the jacket over his arm. "You looked like you were having a very intense conversation with Reese."

"Yeah, I guess we were. Did you know he knew my mother when they were young?"

"No, but that's hardly a surprise. Minnewasta is small town. Everybody knows everybody."

"Yeah, I guess that's true."

Even so, it had sounded as if Reese and Miranda's relationship had been more than small-town acquaintance. She'd have to ask Abby.

Luke let out a long sigh and stared at the door. "I hope tonight wasn't too much for Mom. I'm afraid she overtired herself. She's got so little time..."

Maggie's heart thumped painfully at the look of despair on his face. She wished there was something she could say that would make things easier for him but at this point, words meant little. "Abby was determined to come to the wedding. She wants to embrace every moment she has left."

His mouth unexpectedly turned up in a lop-sided grin. "That's Mom. Her whole life has been about embracing moments. I guess I shouldn't expect her to stop now."

Maggie smiled at his assessment. It perfectly described Abby. "I guess not."

"What about you? Are you having fun?" he asked.

"Yeah." Maggie picked at an imaginary piece of fluff on her dress. "I saw you dancing with Scarlet's friend. Did you enjoy yourself?"

"You mean Jill? I was being polite. I asked everyone to dance."

"You didn't ask me."

She sounded pissy, even to herself. Luke was consumed with the impending death of his mother and all she could talk about was her petty jealousy. Her face grew hot with embarrassment and shame.

"I wanted to dance with you but every time I was about to ask, you were already dancing, especially with Cam's nephew." His voice went low and quiet. "Is there something going on between you two?"

"With Drew? No, of course not. We were paired in the wedding party, that's all."

"He looked like he was into you."

She bit her lip. She was going to have to have another talk with Drew. A relationship between them wasn't in the cards. "I don't feel the same way."

Luke nodded and looked toward the dining room where couples were dancing to a slow waltz. "There's a few dances left," he said, taking her hand and intertwining her fingers with his. "We should take a page from Mom's book and embrace the moment. Would you like to dance?"

Despite all her misgivings about their past, her grief over Abby's impending death, even her worries about living up to her responsibilities of being head chef, happiness bubbled through her veins. Or maybe she'd had too much champagne.

"I'd like that a lot."

She followed him onto the dance floor and when he pulled her into his arms, they fit together like two pieces of a puzzle. Her body hummed with desire.

If she wasn't very careful, she could fall in love with Luke all over again. Maybe she already had.

And when he left, her heart would be broken for a second time.

She didn't want to think about that. Not now. *Embrace the moment.*

Luke bent close to whisper in her ear. "You're beautiful tonight, Maggie. I've never seen you more lovely."

"Thanks. You're pretty lovely yourself."

He chuckled at that, his laugh tickling her ear and making her laugh, too. How wonderful, how freeing, to laugh, to be happy, to have fun. It had been far too long.

Maggie gave herself over to the romance of the evening. She let herself sway to the beat of the music, loving the feel of Luke's hand on her hip and his body pressed close to hers. She stared up into his face, unable to look away. Every detail of his face was dear to her. His beautiful grey-green eyes with their ridiculously long lashes. The long, straight nose and elegantly shaped mouth. A mouth she wanted to kiss. Desperately.

She inhaled an unsteady breath as a shiver raced down her back. There was no doubt she wanted him, and she believed he wanted her, too. But even if they made love, he'd still leave.

Don't think about it, Maggie.

Instead, she smiled up at Luke as if neither of them were facing the imminent loss of someone they loved. Or the loss of each other.

And they danced. At least on the dance floor they could hold each other and pretend they'd never let go. At least she could touch him, and be touched. She longed to feel him skin to skin, to feel his hard muscles beneath her questing fingers. She wanted his weight on her, his body inside hers.

Dancing with Luke was an exquisite kind of torture. These perfect moments on the dance floor couldn't last. Reality would return soon enough.

And it did. Soon the DJ announced the last dance. Luke held her a little tighter as they moved around the floor. Maggie closed her eyes and listened to the steady beat of his heart. As the final notes of the song faded, he held her a minute longer before letting her go. The sudden chill made her shiver.

"Goodnight, Maggie." Though he smiled, she read the sadness on his face. She wanted to reach out to him, beg him to spend the night with her, make love with her. If only for a few hours, they could lose themselves in each other.

But it would change nothing. She returned his sad smile. "Goodnight, Luke."

Chapter Fifteen

THE NEXT MORNING, LUKE and his grandmother stopped at his mother's house before heading to the lodge for the wedding brunch. Reese answered their knock, his face drawn and tired. A sense of dread settled in Luke's stomach.

"We came to see if Mom felt up to the brunch, but I have a feeling the answer is no."

Reese scrubbed a hand over his face. "Abby had a bad night. She's finally sleeping now, so I'm going to stay with her in case she wakes up. Please give my regrets to Cam and Scarlet."

"I can stay with Abby," Phyllis said, setting her purse on a side table and unzipping her coat. "You go with Luke to the brunch, Reese."

Reese caught Phyllis' hand, stopping her from taking off her coat. "I'm not fit company for any kind of social occasion at the moment."

"But I want to look after her. I want to look after both of you."

The pain in his grandmother's voice punched Luke in the gut. He couldn't imagine losing a child, no matter how old they were.

"I know you do, Phyllis," Reese said quietly. "I can't tell you how much that means to me. I'll make you a deal. Later today, you can cook and clean and fuss over us as much as you want, but right now Abby and I both need some sleep."

Phyllis inhaled deeply and let her breath out slowly. She nodded and reached for her purse. "You're right. You should sleep. But I'm coming over this afternoon to cook. Don't think you can stop me."

Reese gave her a tired grin before kissing her cheek. "I wouldn't dream of it."

She nodded again, and Luke saw that her eyes were shiny with unshed tears. He put his arm around her small shoulders and led her to the door.

Reese followed them. "I nearly forgot. Abby wants you to ask Maggie to come see her tomorrow."

"Tomorrow? Is Mom going to be up for a visit?"

"I don't know, but she was adamant I give you the message."

Luke wasn't sure why his mother was so insistent about speaking to Maggie, but it seemed important to her and he wasn't about to argue. "I'll tell Maggie."

Reese nodded and closed the door behind them. Luke helped his grandmother into his truck, then reached across her to fasten her seatbelt. She scowled at him. "I'm not a child, Luke. I can do up my own seatbelt."

He was glad to see her feisty spirit re-emerge. "You're not the only one who wants to look after their family."

"No, I guess not." She sighed. "I wish it was me, Luke. I wish I could take her place, take away her pain. I've lived a long, happy life. I'd be happy to go if it meant Abby had more time."

Luke's chest ached with sorrow. He squeezed her hand. "I don't want to lose either of you, Grandma."

A tear ran down her wrinkled cheek. "I know, Luke. I know."

He closed her door and walked around the truck to the driver's side, trying to get his emotions under control. How could he leave his grandmother all alone?

MAGGIE ROSE EARLY TO help Celeste get the wedding brunch prepared. With the help of a couple of servers from Miller's, they set up the steam table with French toast, scrambled eggs, waffles and bacon. The cold food table was loaded with a variety of sliced fruits, cheeses and a selection of desserts, including delectable chocolate truffles, several kinds of cheesecake, and a red velvet cake topped with cream cheese, all made by Celeste. When the set-up was complete, and she was satisfied everything was in place, Maggie checked her watch. Guests would begin arriving very soon.

Drew entered the dining room alone, grinning as he walked toward her. Maggie tensed. She hated the idea of being cruel but, now more than ever, she had to tell him there could never be anything between them.

"Good morning." He swept out his arm to indicate the buffet tables. "Looks like you've been busy."

"Good morning, Drew." She untied her bibbed apron and pulled it over her head. "I can't take much of the credit. Our sous-chef, Celeste, prepared most of it. Is your family on their way to brunch?"

"They'll be here in a few minutes. I came early because I was hoping to talk to you."

"Oh, I see. Drew, you're very nice, but—"

He set his hand on her arm. "It's okay, Maggie. You don't have to let me down easy. I saw you dancing with Luke Carlsson last night. I could tell by the way you looked at him your heart is someplace else."

She couldn't deny it. "We have a history."

"Harper mentioned it. She said you were childhood sweethearts."

Maggie smiled at the innocent term. "Something like that."

"She also said Luke is going back to California."

"That's true."

Drew linked his fingers with hers, his eyes growing solemn. "Don't let him break your heart, Maggie. You're far too special."

She wished it was within her power to prevent a broken heart. "I'll do my best."

"If he gives you any trouble, say the word, and I'll kick his ass all the way back to Napa Valley."

That made her laugh. Standing on her tiptoes, she kissed his cheek. "I'm sure we won't need to resort to violence, but thanks for the offer."

"You deserve to be treated right."

His words caused a lump to form in her throat. "You're a wonderful person, Drew. Some day, some lucky girl is going to realize what a treasure you are, and she's never going to let you go."

He brought her hand to his mouth for a kiss, his lips lingering against the tender skin of her wrist for a moment before releasing her. "I wish that someone could be you. But I know it can't be."

"I'm sorry."

"Don't be. I wish you nothing but happiness, Maggie."

"I wish that for you, too."

He nodded, his expression more serious than she'd ever seen it. "I'm going back to check on my family, see if they're ready for brunch. I'll see you later."

With that, he headed out of the dining room. Maggie sighed. She hated hurting him, but it would have been far worse to let him think they could be more than friends. She hoped he found someone who would treat him right. He deserved that.

Soon, guests began filing into the dining room. Her sisters and their husbands arrived and mingled with wedding guests before lining up at the buffet tables for food. Maggie joined the line-up, keeping one eye on the door for Luke and his family, worried by their lateness.

Finally, at half past ten, Luke and his grandmother arrived. As soon as they entered the dining room, Maggie knew something was wrong. Both wore subdued expressions, and the solicitous way Luke held his grandmother's arm made her think he was trying to protect her. She went to greet them, bracing herself for bad news.

She held out her hands to Phyllis. "I'm glad you could make it. Will Reese and Abby be joining us?"

"No," Luke said. "Mom's resting right now. She didn't get a lot of sleep last night."

"I'm sorry," she said. He acknowledged her sympathy with a nod but avoided her gaze.

Phyllis squeezed Maggie's hand. "Reese said to tell you she wants to see you tomorrow."

"Tomorrow?" She'd thought she'd give Abby a few days to rest after the excitement of the wedding. Did this mean she believed her time was even more limited than they'd first believed? The thought made her stomach clench in pain. She glanced at Luke.

"It seems to mean a lot to her," Phyllis said.

"Then I'll go," Maggie said simply. She swallowed and gestured to the brunch buffet, pasting a smile on her face. "Please help yourself and then join us at our table. We've saved seats for you."

Luke nodded wordlessly and with a hand on Phyllis's back, he led her to the buffet table. Maggie hated to see him in pain like this. Last night, as they danced, he seemed to genuinely enjoy himself. She hoped she was part of the reason for that. It had been so good to be in his arms.

More than good, if she was honest with herself. Magical. The way he'd looked at her made her almost believe they had a future together.

But reality was never far away. Last night, they'd let themselves forget the reason he'd come to the lodge in the first place – Abby's illness. The morning reminded them her death was creeping ever closer.

Maggie returned to the table she was sharing with her sisters and their husbands, her appetite for the remains of her brunch now diminished. She sipped her coffee instead.

"Abby and Reese aren't coming?" Harper asked.

Maggie shook her head and relayed the information she'd received from Luke and Phyllis. A stricken look came over Harper's face, and the rest of the group went quiet and solemn.

"Please, let's try to stay upbeat for their sakes," Maggie whispered. "Abby wouldn't want to put a damper on your wedding, Scarlet."

"No, she wouldn't." Scarlet's attempted smile looked strained.

Luke and Phyllis brought their plates to the table and sat next to her. One of the servers brought coffee and filled their cups. Phyllis lifted hers in a toast. "Congratulations, Cam and Scarlet. May you have as lovely a married life as you had a wedding celebration. Thank you again for inviting me. I had a wonderful evening."

Scarlet's smile was completely genuine this time. "It meant a lot to us to have you at our wedding, Phyllis. I'm glad you enjoyed yourself."

Everyone resumed eating and conversation centered on the wedding the previous night, an appreciation for the food and a discussion of the weather. By mutual, unspoken consent, they steered away from the topic on everyone's mind. Luke stayed mostly silent, responding to questions, but otherwise keeping his thoughts to himself. Maggie wished there was something she could say that would make things better.

Tessa and Hope emerged from the kitchen, each carefully carrying a bowl. Their giggles provided a much-needed ray of sunshine in the room. They'd become fast friends since Hope's arrival at the lodge.

Cam took their bowls from them and placed them on the table before helping the girls into their seats.

"Where'd you get the ice cream?" he asked.

"From Hope's mom," Tessa said as she kneeled on her chair and reached for her spoon. "She said if we ate all our breakfast, we could have it."

"Good for you." Cam tucked a paper napkin into the neckline of Tessa's shirt.

Luke did the same for Hope, who gave him a charming gap-toothed smile. "Thank you, Mr. Luke."

"You're welcome, Miss Hope. I wouldn't want you to get chocolate ice cream on your pretty sweater."

She grinned at him and stuck a heaping spoonful into her mouth. Luke grinned back at her with genuine amusement and affection, and Maggie's heart melted a little. She was grateful Hope had accomplished what she'd been unable to.

Once she finished, Luke wiped the ice cream from Hope's face and lifted her down from the chair. Hand in hand, the girls ran to the kitchen, giggling all the way.

Phyllis smiled. "When I was kid, ice cream made me that happy, too."

If only a bowl of ice cream could alleviate the troubles of the world.

A man stood at the dining room entranceway, holding a parcel wrapped in brightly colored paper. Maggie didn't recognize Willy Eklund until he removed his cap. She hadn't seen him since he'd turned up drunk at Harper's wedding last June and made a scene. Her stomach clenched as she braced herself for more of the same.

"Harper," she whispered. "Willy is here."

Harper and Ethan both turned to watch him, the tension in Ethan's body telling Maggie he was ready to spring into action at the first sign of trouble. Willy scanned the room, then headed straight to their table. Maggie held her breath, but as he came closer, she was relieved to see that his gait was steady, his clothes clean, and his eyes clear. His grey hair had been pulled back into a neat ponytail. He stood beside Scarlet's chair and held out the package, the ribbons trembling slightly.

"I want to congratulate you on your wedding, Scarlet, and to offer you this as a wedding gift."

He handed the parcel to her, then stepped back as if preparing to leave. Scarlet set the parcel on the table and got to her feet, grasping Willy's hand before he could run away. "Thank you, Willy. That was very kind of you."

"I wish you much happiness, Scarlet. You deserve it."

She gave him a hug, then turned to Cam. "This is my husband, Cameron Hainstock. Willy is an old friend of the family."

Cam rose and shook Willy's hand. "We've met. Thanks for coming, Willy."

He nodded. "I've seen you with Reese at the AA meetings."

Maggie winced. Obviously, Willy didn't get the anonymous part of AA.

"You've been going to AA?" Harper asked.

"Yes," Willy said with another nod. "Been sober forty-five days now. And I have you to thank for it."

"Me?"

Willy twisted his cap in his hand. "When you washed your hands of me and said you wouldn't pick me up the next time I was too drunk to drive, I hit rock bottom. You were my last friend. I want to make you proud."

"Oh, Willy." Harper jumped to her feet and hugged him. "I am proud of you."

He squeezed his eyes shut and held onto her. When Harper pulled away, he pulled a small package wrapped in tissue paper from his pocket and handed it to her. "I didn't get you anything for your wedding. I'd like you to have this."

Harper unwrapped the package and held up a man's heavy, gold chain. "What's this?"

"Your mother gave that to me for my birthday, not long before she died."

She tried to hand it back to him. "This is yours. I can't take it from you."

Willy put his hands over hers. "I want you to have it. Miranda would want you to have it, too."

For a moment Harper looked like she would argue the point, but at last she nodded. "Thank you. This means a lot to me."

"Willy, why don't you grab a plate and sit down with us?" Maggie said. It seemed like the hospitable thing to do for an old friend, especially one who'd been working so hard to retain their friendship.

He gave her an appreciative smile. "I'd like that. Thank you."

Maggie helped him fill his plate and carried orange juice and coffee back to the table for him. The spot beside Luke where Hope had previously sat was cleared by one of the servers.

Once Willy got himself settled, Luke offered his hand. "I'm Luke Carlsson. I'm working temporarily at the lodge."

"I remember you." Willy shook his hand. "Grew up in Minnewasta, didn't you? Abby's boy."

Luke smiled. "That's right."

"I'm sorry she's so sick."

"Yeah. So am I."

"I see your dad around town. Have you talked to him since you've been home?"

"Yeah, I've seen him."

"Jerry's a good man. Got a nice family now, I hear. Have you met them?"

Luke fiddled with his cup. "Yeah, I've met them."

"You're lucky to have such a nice family, especially now, with Abby...you know."

Luke's expression closed down, his feelings concealed as if he'd pulled a shutter across his face. He grabbed his coffee cup and drank. Then stood up. "Excuse me. I need more coffee."

Maggie watched him go, feeling the anguish in every step. She hurt for him. Even if he were to make some kind of peace with his father, it could never make up for his mother's loss. No one could replace Abby.

Willy set down his knife and fork. "I'm sorry. I shouldn't have said anything."

"His father is a sensitive subject," Maggie said.

"Yeah, I can imagine. But he needs to forgive him, for his own good. Forgiveness frees you. Otherwise, that anger sits inside your soul forever."

Maggie glanced toward the buffet table where Luke was examining the contents of the steam table. He was stalling, most likely. She was afraid Willy might be right. Unless Luke could find a way to forgive his father, and come to terms with his mother's impending death, anger and despair would eat away at him.

Willy dug into another pocket of his jacket and pulled out a small package, this one wrapped in red tissue. "I have something for you, too. Something your mother gave me years ago."

He handed the package to her. Maggie held the little rectangular gift in her hand, hesitating. "Why are you giving me this, Willy? I'm not getting married."

"Because Miranda was special. I loved her very much." He added quickly, "As a friend. She was my best friend. Open it, Maggie. Please."

Nodding, Maggie ripped open the tissue paper to reveal a tiny framed picture of her mother as a teenager. She couldn't have been more than fifteen, and she was laughing as if sharing a secret with the picture taker.

"That's my favorite picture of her," Willy said. "It's how I want to remember her."

Maggie tried to give it back. "Then you should keep it."

He closed his hands over hers. "No. It belongs to you. *She* belongs to you. And I need to make amends. For AA."

With that, Willy picked up his fork and resumed eating. Maggie stared at the picture, not sure what to make of this gift, or of him. She wanted to ask him more about his relationship with her mother, but this wasn't the place. Still, she had questions. What kind of relationship had her mother and Willy really had?

Chapter Sixteen

ON THE DAY FOLLOWING the wedding brunch, the business of the lodge resumed top priority. Maggie sat with Luke, Ethan, and Harper around one of the tables in the dining room, and Celeste arrived a few minutes later with a carafe of coffee and mugs. Hope and Tessa played with dolls nearby. With Scarlet and Cam away on a short honeymoon, Tessa was staying with Ethan and Harper at their cottage. Shortly before the wedding, Cam and Scarlet received news that they would soon have sole custody of Tessa. The whole family rejoiced over the news and breathed a sign of relief.

Maggie poured mugs of coffee and passed them around. "I guess the biggest item on our agenda today is figuring out where we're all going to live. Celeste and Hope can't live in a hotel room forever. If we get as many bookings as we're hoping for during our grand opening, we're going to need the cottages we're living in as well."

"Well, there's the owner's suite above the event center," Harper said. "Reese says it can be finished by the middle of January if we need it. It's got two bedrooms, with a small living room and kitchen. It's a lovely space."

"Have you found a place to buy or rent, Harper?" Luke asked. "Ethan mentioned you've been looking."

"No, not yet, but our real estate agent found a rental house for us to look at. We're meeting with her later today to check it out. She seems excited about it so hopefully, it's the one."

"If you're not going to be living in the owner's suite, I think it makes sense for Celeste and Hope to move into it as soon as it's finished," Maggie said. "Celeste doesn't have a car, so if she lives on-site, she doesn't have to worry about commuting. The school bus can pick Hope up at the door."

"What about you?" Celeste asked. "Where are you going to live?"

Good question. What she really wanted was her own place again, but until the lodge started to make money and she could draw a salary, she couldn't afford one. Besides, she didn't have a car either. "I suppose I can stay in one of the smaller hotel rooms, at least for a while."

"I appreciate you giving us the owner's suite, Maggie, but you need a place to stay, too. You should have it. You're part owner. I'm only an employee."

"You're an integral part of the success of the lodge. I'll be fine. I'm sure I'll find something."

"You could stay with us. Hope and I don't mind sharing a bedroom," Celeste said.

"That's generous of you, but I think Hope deserves her own room, and so do you. I want you to feel comfortable, like it's really your home, not some temporary accommodation."

Celeste shook her head and smiled. "Now who's being generous?"

Maggie shrugged. "I've got ulterior motives. I want you to be happy here, so you'll stay with us. We need you."

"I'm not going anywhere, Maggie."

"I'm glad to hear it, but I'm still not sharing the suite with you. It's barely big enough for two."

Celeste blew out a breath. "Well, if you're determined," she glanced at the others. "And if it's okay with everyone else, then I'll accept. But you'll need to give the place a new name. We can't call it the owner's suite anymore."

"That's easy," Maggie said with a grin. "From now on we'll call the apartment Celeste's Place."

Celeste reached over to squeeze her hand, her eyes suspiciously bright. Maggie squeezed back, glad the matter was settled. It really was the best solution, for Celeste and Hope, and for the lodge.

"The place we're looking at renting today is a three-bedroom house in Baxter. There'll be plenty of space for you to stay with us," Harper said.

The last thing she wanted was to be a guest in Ethan and Harper's house. She'd feel like she was impinging on their privacy. Harper's offer was made with love, but she hoped she never had to take her up on it.

Before she could respond, Luke spoke. "Would you consider staying with my grandmother and me in town, at least for a while? I know she'd love the company. You'd be doing me a favor, too. I hate the idea of her rattling around that big old house all alone after I leave."

Abby would soon be gone and so would he. The thought of losing them both shattered her.

He lowered his gaze. "If you're not interested, it's okay."

He must have mistaken her silence for refusal. She forced a smile. "It's a good solution. I like your grandmother and I think she'd be a fun roommate, but I don't have a vehicle either. I need some way to get to work every day."

"If that's the only thing that's stopping you, I'll leave you my truck."

"I can't afford to buy your truck."

"I didn't say I wanted to sell it to you. I'm giving it to you."

She blinked at him, floored by his generosity. "You can't do that."

"Sure I can. I want to."

She didn't know what to say so she simply nodded her acceptance. And she knew as she looked into his eyes that she loved him, that she'd never stopped loving him.

Old fears crowded into her memory. He'd left her before, and he was planning to leave her again. Her love hadn't held him then, and it likely wouldn't be any different now.

Get a grip, Maggie. She pushed away the realization of her love for Luke, and her fear. She made herself smile again, not wanting him or anyone else to pick up on her feelings.

"If Phyllis is okay with the idea, then so am I. We can take care of each other for a while."

He smiled in relief. "Thank you. That means a lot to me."

Maggie looked deep into his eyes. The excitement and wonder of being in love was dulled by fear. How she wished she could declare her love, and rejoice with her sisters in her happiness, the way they'd rejoiced with her. Mostly, she wished Luke could return her love, that he'd stay with her, but that wasn't to be.

Ethan cleared his throat, and Maggie dragged her gaze from Luke to him.

"Now that we've settled on living arrangements, let's move on."

The discussion turned to other matters – the new reservation system, the purchase of recreational equipment and possibly a van to pick up guests at the airport – but Maggie barely listened. She imagined she and Phyllis trying to comfort each other once Abby was gone. And after he left.

But no amount of comfort would ease the pain of losing them.

Maggie squeezed her eyes shut. What was she going to do? He wouldn't stay, and she couldn't go. She'd made a commitment to the lodge and to her sisters that she couldn't, wouldn't go back on.

It didn't matter who stayed or who went. She might be in love with him, but he'd given her no indication his feelings ran the same way.

Once more, she was in this thing alone.

WHEN THE BUSINESS MEETING concluded, Luke refilled his coffee cup, knowing he needed to go back to work, but not quite ready to do so after the excitement of the last few days. The others must have felt the same way, because no one left the table. Harper sat back in her chair and looked around the room, a smile on her face. "I haven't seen the lodge decorated so beautifully for Christmas since I was a kid. Grandma loved dressing the place to the nines."

"I remember," Maggie said. "Next Christmas we should throw a party and show off the lodge while it's looking its best."

An idea began to brew in Luke's head. "Why wait till next Christmas? The dining room is already decorated. We wouldn't have to do anything elaborate. It could simply be a Christmas open house one afternoon for neighbors. We can show people around and let them see what we've done so far, and what we plan to do in the future. It would be a good opportunity to advertise our grand opening – like a kick-off to the grand opening."

Maggie leaned forward. She hadn't said much during the latter half of the meeting, but now her eyes shone with excitement. "That's a great idea. We'll keep things simple. We can serve coffee and hot chocolate and cookies. Maybe we can have games for the kids and some prizes."

"I love making Christmas cookies. Sugar cookies are my favorite," Celeste said. "What kind do y'all like?"

"Gingerbread," Luke and Maggie said together. They both laughed, as if they were sharing a secret. But it was only a cookie.

"So, what do the rest of you think? Are you onboard with this idea?" he asked.

Ethan looked at Harper. "I am. If we keep it simple, it'll be like inviting friends over for Christmas. What do you think, Harper?"

"I'm all for it. I think it'll be fun. And since Cam and Scarlet are away on their honeymoon, I'll vote yes for them, too," Harper said with a laugh.

"We might be slightly crazy to plan an open house along with everything else, but I say we go for it," Maggie said. "If we're going to get the lodge off the ground, we're going to have to take some chances."

Luke nodded at her. "Yes. We're going to have to take some chances."

She regarded him solemnly and returned his nod. He wasn't sure if he meant taking a chance with the lodge or with their hearts.

He was used to taking chances in business. He didn't know if he was brave enough to risk his heart.

MAGGIE ARRIVED AT ABOUT one in the afternoon, early enough so Abby wouldn't be too tired. She knocked on the door and when it opened, Maggie was surprised to see an unfamiliar woman on the other side.

"Hi. You must be Maggie."

"Yes, I am."

The woman stepped aside so she could enter. "Please, come in. I'm Paula Jenkins, Abby's nurse. She told me you were coming for a visit."

Maggie made herself smile. Of course, the nurse. Reese said he was going to have someone stay with Abby during the day. "Nice to meet you, Paula. Is Abby awake?"

Paula smiled. "She's in the living room waiting for you. She's been looking forward to your visit."

"I'm glad. I'm looking forward to it, too."

She followed Paula into the living room where Abby was in her wheelchair with the red and black plaid blanket once more covering her lap. Despite her tired appearance, her smile was radiant. "Maggie! I'm so glad you could come."

She reached for her hand. "I wouldn't miss it for the world."

A moment later, Paula brought in a tray with a pretty flowered teapot and two matching cups. After pouring the tea, she laid her hand on Abby's shoulder. "I'll leave you two ladies while I run some errands. Enjoy your visit." She put on her jacket and quietly left.

"She didn't have to leave on my account," Maggie said.

Abby delicately sipped her tea. "I asked her to give us some privacy. I want to continue the story about your mother."

"I'd like that."

Abby set down her teacup. "When we last spoke, I told you about Miranda's first love, a boy from high school who was five years older. Her parents disapproved and threatened to have him arrested for rape, so he went away. Miranda was heartbroken, but she was also very young and naïve. She believed if he really loved her he would have stayed and waited until she turned eighteen. And this is where we pick up the story."

"Did she meet him again?"

Abby smiled. "You're getting ahead of me. You have to be patient, Maggie."

"Sorry. Patience is not one of my virtues. Please, continue." She'd have to let Abby tell the story in her own way, as difficult as that was for her.

"Miranda continued high school. She was busy with different sports like track and volleyball and basketball, and all kinds of high school experiences and clubs. She was a popular girl, and very pretty. Everyone wanted to be her friend. She had a special light inside her that everyone wanted to be close to."

"Did she date much in high school?"

"Some, but never seriously. However much she wanted to fall in love with another boy, her heart belonged to her first boyfriend."

"How did she meet my father?"

"She met Robert at the University of Minnesota while she was pursuing a degree in interior design and he was at law school. He was immediately smitten with her. She once told me he fell in love with her the minute he spied her across the room at a sorority party."

"Did she fall in love with him at first sight, too?"

Abby's smile was sad. "No. She liked Robert, and I think eventually she came to love him, but she wasn't *in love* with him. He was handsome and smart, and he came from a prominent, wealthy family. He was the kind of man she thought she *should* marry, the kind of man she thought her parents would approve of. And he was crazy about her. So, when he asked her to marry him, she said yes."

The idea that her mother didn't love her father, at least not in the way a wife should love the man she was about to spend the rest of her life with, came as a shock. "I don't understand. Harper and Scarlet have happy memories of our family."

"They were happy, Maggie, for a lot of years. Miranda finished school and went to work for an interior design company, and Robert worked for a very prestigious law firm in Minneapolis. Harper came along in a couple of years and Scarlet two years after her. They were happy together and if Miranda wasn't passionately in love with her husband, that was all right with her. She'd been passionately in love once before and it had only brought her pain."

"When did things start to go wrong?"

"The summer Scarlet was five and Harper seven, Miranda was the lead designer on the renovation of a mansion in Minneapolis. Robert was working on a very important case, as he often was. This one took him to New York for the summer. Because they were both so busy, she brought the girls to the lodge to stay with her parents."

"And then?"

"Her old boyfriend came to work at the mansion. He was a carpenter now. Miranda found she was still madly, passionately in love with him, and he hadn't stopped loving her either. They were together every possible minute that summer."

Maggie sat back in her chair, stunned. "Scarlet was right. It was Miranda who cheated. Harper thought our father might have had an affair because he was away so often, but Scarlet heard them talking on the day they died." A thought occurred to her. "But Miranda must have gone back to Robert. They were still married when they died, even though they were on the verge of divorce. They must have patched things up, or at least tried, because they had me."

"Yes, they tried, but—"

A sudden coughing fit cut off her words. Her body shook as if she would break in half. Maggie jumped to her feet, terrified and unsure what to do. She ran to the kitchen to get a glass of water. By the time she returned Abby was gasping for breath, struggling to get air into her damaged lungs. She tried to drink the water Maggie gave her, but the cough wracking her body left her too shaky to even hold the glass. Desperate, Maggie patted her back. Should she call Reese? An ambulance?

She almost cried with relief when Paula entered the house with a couple of bags of groceries. She immediately set the bags on the floor and ran to Abby's bedroom, returning a moment later with a machine on a table with rolling wheels. Maggie stepped back. Paula plugged in the machine and turned it on, then put a mask over Abby's mouth and nose and gently encouraged her to breathe. "Let the nebulizer do its work, Abby, " Paula said quietly. She held the mask because Abby couldn't. Gradually, Abby's coughing subsided. She slumped in her chair, her head bowed.

"There, that's much better, isn't it?" Paula removed the mask from Abby's face, and Maggie was relieved when the coughing didn't resume. "Let's get you into your room so you can rest."

Abby lifted her head and looked up at Maggie, her eyes panicked, beseeching. She had to be frightened by what was happening to her. Maggie stuffed down her fear and anguish to smile at her. For Abby, she'd suck it up and do what needed to be done. "If you like, I can stay with you until you fall asleep."

Abby gave a faint nod and bowed her head once more. Paula rolled the wheelchair into the bedroom and, together, she and Maggie helped her out of the chair and settled her into the bed. Maggie sat in the chair next to the bed and held Abby's hand in hers.

"I'll be right here till you fall asleep," she whispered.

The panic entered Abby's eyes again. "But you'll come back, won't you?"

"Of course." She willed herself to smile and not to cry. "Whenever you want me to."

"Okay."

Abby relaxed and closed her eyes. In moments, her grip on Maggie's hand slackened and she was asleep. Maggie watched her face, watched the slight up and down movement of her chest that told her she was breathing. Her face was ashen, pale to the point of ghostliness. Skin stretched over sharp cheekbones, swooping down to hollow, gaunt cheeks. For Abby's sake, she wished she could have finished the story. It seemed to mean so much to her.

She set Abby's hand carefully on the bed, then leaned over to kiss her forehead. "Rest well, Abby," she whispered.

She and Paula left the room. Paula closed the bedroom door softly behind them and turned to her. "I'm so sorry. I shouldn't have left you two alone, but Abby was adamant she had to speak to you in private. I won't be leaving her alone again."

"Thank goodness you came home when you did."

"Was she able to tell you what was so important to her?"

"Partially, I think. But I believe there's more she didn't get a chance to say." It occurred to her that she didn't get an opportunity to ask how well Reese and her mother had known each other. But it didn't matter. With Abby's health so precarious, she wouldn't burden her with more questions.

"Come back in a day or two. I've found that my palliative patients need that final goodbye to say everything that needs to be said. It helps the people they love as much as it helps them. Perhaps more."

Maggie squeezed her eyes shut as tears threatened again. "Okay."

Whatever it took, she would hear what Abby needed to tell her.

Chapter Seventeen

THE WORK TO MAKE THE Christmas open house a reality began in earnest the next day. Maggie and Celeste baked four different kinds of cookies – sugar, chocolate chip, shortbread and of course, gingerbread. While Maggie mixed the batter for the chocolate chip, Celeste began decorating the sugar and gingerbread that had already cooled.

"Those look almost too cute to eat," Maggie said.

Celeste smiled as she piped an icing smile onto a gingerbread man's face. "Not too cute, I hope. Just cute enough. This is my favorite part."

"You're very good at it."

Actually, she was amazing at it. Each tiny Christmas tree was decorated with garlands and ornaments in a rainbow of colors. Each gingerbread man had a different collar and buttons down the front of his shirt. The candy canes were swirls of red and white goodness. Maggie wasn't sure she'd have the patience for such intricate work.

Hope and Tessa skipped into the kitchen and climbed onto the stools at the island. Celeste broke a candy cane cookie in two and gave them each a half. "We don't want you to get too full before lunch."

Maggie poured them some milk and smiled at their matching milk mustaches. Hope swallowed another mouthful and set down her glass. “Miss Maggie, did you know I’m going to go to school on the bus tomorrow?”

“Yes, and I heard you met your new teacher yesterday.”

She nodded, making her pigtails bob up and down. “Yes. Her name is Mrs. Andrews.”

“I know Mrs. Andrews,” Maggie said. “She was my teacher in kindergarten and grade one.”

Hope’s eyes widened. “She must be old!”

Both Maggie and Celeste laughed. Celeste admonished her gently. “Don’t you go calling Mrs. Andrews old to her face. That wouldn’t be very nice.”

“Mrs. Andrews was a brand-new teacher when I was in kindergarten. She was Miss Jones back then. She was one of my favorite teachers. I’m sure you’ll feel the same way.”

She’d probably been something of a handful in those days. Because she’d been the youngest, and motherless, her grandparents and her older sisters had spoiled and coddled and sheltered her. Once she started school, she was shocked to discover the world didn’t revolve around her. The other children all got their fair share of attention from Miss Jones, too. Her teacher had been patient and kind, even after Maggie had thrown a tantrum because she didn’t get her way in some game or other. Maggie remembered being taken aside and gently told that everyone deserved a turn. Her turn would come around again, she promised.

And it had. Maggie had been devoted to Miss Jones the two years she’d been her teacher. She’d taught her how to fit in with the other children and how to make friends, and she’d do the same for Hope.

“Mama says I’m going to have my own room soon.”

"I have my own room," Tessa said. "It's purple."

"That sounds very pretty." Maggie dropped spoonfuls of chocolate chip batter onto the cookie sheet. "What color do you want your room to be, Hope?"

"Pink," she said without hesitation. "It's my favorite color."

"Pink it is then." She'd make sure Hope's room was painted pink even if she had to do the job herself. "Pink's the perfect color for your room, the same way purple is the perfect color for Tessa's room."

"Are my Mommy and Daddy coming home soon?" Tessa asked.

Maggie's heart gave a little kick to hear her call Scarlet her mommy. "Yes, sweetheart. Two more sleeps and they'll be home."

She seemed satisfied with her answer. "Okay."

The girls finished their cookies and milk and slid off their stools, ready to find adventure elsewhere in the lodge. Celeste looked up from the cookie she was decorating. "Is Mrs. Andrews really as nice as you told Hope? We met her the other day, and she seemed all right, but it's hard to tell."

She understood Celeste's apprehension. Hope was starting a new school in a new state. She wouldn't know any other child except for Tessa, but because she was a year older, she was in another classroom. "I wasn't making that up for Hope's benefit, or yours. I really do remember Mrs. Andrews as a kind and patient teacher. Lucky for me she was. I was a brat."

"I can't imagine that." Celeste chuckled as she filled a piping bag with pink icing. "I don't know if I've ever properly thanked you for everything you've done for us. And I don't know if I've ever asked you why you've done so much."

"Your story resonated with me. Not so long ago, I was where you were – scared, broke, and a little desperate. My family gave me a chance to prove myself, and I want to give you that chance, too. I know it sounds crazy, but ever since I met you on that Zoom call, I've felt like we're kindred spirits."

Celeste didn't look up from her work, but her voice was husky with emotion as she spoke. "I can't tell you how much your faith has meant to me."

"My faith has already been justified."

They worked in silence for a while longer. Maggie filled two cookie sheets with dough and slipped them into the hot oven. She set the timer and turned to Celeste. "Can I help you with anything?"

"I'm running short of plain white icing. Could you whip up another batch?"

"Sure." Maggie gathered ingredients for the icing.

When she finished the cookie she'd been working on, Celeste set down her piping bag. "Can I ask you a question? A personal one?"

Maggie didn't make eye contact. "You can ask. I won't guarantee I'll answer."

"What's the story with you and Luke? You told me you were close as teenagers, but I get the feeling there's so much more to the story."

For the first time, Maggie found she wanted to speak, to tell someone she trusted about the love and the heartache she'd experienced that summer. She glanced up at Celeste. "He was my first love."

Celeste nodded with understanding, as if she'd expected her answer. "First love is hard to forget. It stays with you."

"Are you speaking from experience?"

"Hope's father was my first love, the love of my life." Celeste's smile held a tinge of sadness. "He died in a car accident when Hope was three."

"I'm so sorry."

"So am I." Celeste picked up her piping bag and gave her gingerbread man a wide grin. "What happened with Luke?"

She told Celeste how he'd come to work for her grandfather the summer she was fourteen. "I loved him, and he was my first sexual experience. But I was only a kid. I was young enough to believe we'd be together forever. Turned out, forever only lasted until the end of August."

"You don't believe he returned your feelings?"

Maggie shrugged. "I thought so, even though neither of us spoke the words.

But then, a few days after school started, I found him kissing another girl."

Even now, ten years later, her devastation at seeing him with Cheryl Bradley, along with the confusion and hurt, shattered her. And she remembered her shock at the coldness in his eyes.

Go home, Maggie. You've been making a nuisance of yourself all summer. Go play with your dolls and leave me alone.

"Then, he was gone. No note, no phone call, no explanations. Abby told me later he'd scraped the money together to go to school in California." Maggie measured icing sugar and butter and added them to the bowl. "She was the only person I'd told about Luke and me. My grandmother died unexpectedly the day Luke left, and I was a mess. Abby was the one I went to in late September when I thought I was pregnant."

Celeste looked up sharply. "Were you?"

"No." Her period had been two weeks late and when it had finally come, it had been unusually heavy. She'd always believed she'd had a miscarriage. Abby had told her it was for the best. She'd been an unmarried mother and knew how hard it could be. But at least Abby had been in her twenties when Luke was born. If she'd been pregnant, she would have had a baby at fifteen. How could she have coped? She would have been a baby having a baby.

Even so, she'd mourned the loss. And she'd mourned Luke, for a very long time.

"You've really never told your sisters any of this?"

"No. Only Abby, and now you."

"I'm honored, Maggie. I'm glad you felt you could trust me."

She looked up from the icing she was mixing and smiled at her. "I do."

"Are you still in love with him? I see the way you look at him."

She put down her spoon. "Please don't tell me I'm making cow eyes at him."

"You didn't answer my question."

"Just because I said we were kindred spirits doesn't mean you can get bossy."

Celeste simply smiled and waited. Maggie sighed. "In spite of everything, I do have feelings for him. I...I love him, which is crazy." She couldn't believe she'd said the words out loud. She glanced at the door to make sure no one else had overheard her confession.

"Why is it crazy?"

"Because it was so long ago, and I was a kid. I should be over it by now, over him. I thought I was. He didn't want me then. Why would he want me now?"

"His feelings might have changed. Or maybe things weren't as you thought they were back then."

"It hardly matters now. Once Abby dies, he'll go back to California and likely never give me a second thought."

Celeste made a guffawing sound in her throat. "I doubt that. Why don't you talk to him?"

The thought of putting her feelings into words, of laying open her heart and being vulnerable to Luke again, frightened her even more than the possibility of poverty and homelessness had. "I can't do that."

"I didn't think you were a coward," Celeste rebuked gently.

Maggie shook her head. There was no point in embarrassing Luke and making him uncomfortable. Abby's illness, and imminent death, was enough for him to deal with.

And the thought of facing his rejection once more made her heart fall into her shoes.

"You'd be amazed at what a chicken I am."

Chapter Eighteen

CAM AND SCARLET RETURNED from their short honeymoon, looking happy and relaxed and very much in love. Luke joined everyone in greeting them with handshakes and hugs. Tessa bounced with excitement as Cam and Scarlet enfolded her in their arms.

Luke watched Maggie embrace her sister and brother-in-law with genuine affection. But as they began unloading gifts from a large duffle bag, her face changed. They placed a mountain of Christmas presents under the already present-laden tree in the dining room. Harper and Ethan had been adding gifts to the tree ever since they put it up.

He didn't think anyone else noticed the subtle change in her demeanor. He only had because he was attuned to her every movement and emotion and facial expression. She made an excuse about needing to check on dinner and escaped into the kitchen. Luke followed her, concerned.

Maggie's back was turned to him as he entered the kitchen, her head bent and her hands covering her face. She looked vulnerable and small, and very, very sad. Luke's heart clenched. He put one hand on her shoulder, unable to stop himself from touching her. "Maggie, honey, what's wrong?"

She startled at his touch and stepped away, wiping her eyes as she put some distance between them. "Nothing. Something in my eye."

"Yeah, there is. They're called tears." He gently turned her to face him. "Tell me what's wrong. Maybe I can help."

She shook her head and looked away. "There's nothing you can do."

"Try me."

She briefly lifted her gaze to his before turning away again, but not before he saw the bleakness. He cupped her chin and gently forced her to look at him. Her dark eyes were huge and shiny with tears. She put her hand on his arm but didn't push him away.

"You can trust me, Maggie."

She raised her eyebrows at that, as if she didn't believe him. Her distrust stung, but he supposed he deserved it. "If you tell me what's wrong, I won't tell anyone. I promise."

She shook her head. "Celeste will be here soon."

"She won't be here for a while." He waited, holding his breath.

She stared into his eyes with a puzzled expression. "Why do you want to know?"

Because I care about you. Because when you hurt, I hurt. Because I hurt you once and I'll do anything, everything, to make up for it.

"Because I don't like to see you unhappy. C'mon. Maybe talking about it will help."

She closed her eyes. "It's stupid."

"No, it's not. Not if it's making you cry."

She opened her eyes once more, and he was relieved to see some of her old fire in them. "It *is* stupid. It's been hard enough to watch Harper and Ethan pile presents under the tree, but then Scarlet and Cam added their gifts...I saw all those presents, some of them for me, and it made me feel so completely... inadequate."

He brushed the soft skin of her cheek with the pad of his thumb to wipe away a tear. "Why?"

Her eyes were resigned, hopeless. "Because I can't return them. I don't have any money. Other than some candy I made, I have nothing to give." Her laugh was bitter. "Even the candy is made from ingredients I used from the lodge's kitchen."

He fought the urge to take her into his arms and hold her. "You don't have any money at all?"

"Actually, I'm in the negative. I owe about fifteen hundred dollars on my credit card. I've been making the minimum payments for the last few months to keep afloat, but as of this morning, my bank balance is one dollar and twenty-seven cents."

"How did you get into such a crunch?"

She looked away. "It's a long story."

"I've got time."

To his surprise, she smiled at that. But she shook her head. "No, you don't."

"Maggie, please."

This time, he couldn't stop himself from pulling her into his arms. She held herself stiff, and he held his breath, afraid she'd push away. But then with a sigh, she relaxed against him, her head against his chest and her arms loosely circling his waist.

"It started in culinary school," she began, her voice so quiet he had to strain to hear her. "One of my instructors took a special interest in me. He told me how talented I was, how good my ideas were. I was so flattered to be singled out like that."

Luke smoothed his hand over her hair, struggling not to reveal his growing unease. He could guess where this story was going but he said nothing, wanting her to tell it in her own way.

"We started a secret affair, or at least I thought it was secret. He was very handsome and charming and even though he was nearly fifteen years older than me, I thought we had something special."

"What happened?" he asked when she fell silent.

She clutched the material on the back of his shirt. "His wife contacted me. Seems he had a habit of having an affair with a new student every year. She told me he picked the neediest, most easily seduced girl."

He hugged her a little tighter. That didn't sound like the Maggie he'd known. Even as a girl, she'd been strong and able to stand up for herself. But she'd also been young and trusting, and no match for an accomplished liar and cheat.

"I was appalled. There's no way I would have slept with a married man if I'd known. Especially a married man with two kids. I broke it off immediately."

"Good for you."

"Yeah, good for me." She gave a choked laugh and pushed away from him. Reluctantly, he let her go. "He didn't it take it well. Apparently, he was used to being the one ending an affair. He started criticizing my work in front of my classmates, and marking my assignments harshly and unfairly. But I couldn't complain to the school because he said if I did, he'd flunk me and tell them I was the one who came on to him."

"Bastard." Luke could barely contain his rage.

"I thought about quitting, but I knew how much Harper had sacrificed so I could go to school. She was running the lodge and caring for Grampa single-handedly, and somehow she'd managed to pay my tuition. I couldn't bear to disappoint her.

"So, I toughed it out and graduated – barely. But every job I applied for in the kitchens of high-end restaurants, they'd call the culinary school and the instructor would tell them that not only was I a mediocre chef, I was difficult to work with. I got passed over again and again."

"Did you ever tell Harper or Scarlet what you were going through?"

"No. Grampa died soon after I graduated, and Harper had enough on her plate. And Scarlet had her own troubles. Around then, she called off her wedding, the second wedding she'd cancelled. She was going through a lot and I didn't want to burden her."

Luke didn't trust himself to speak. Her sisters would have done their best to help her if they'd known, no matter what was going on their lives. At the very least, they would have provided a shoulder to cry on. But Maggie had been too proud.

"I finally found a job as a head chef with a new restaurant because I was willing to accept a wage far lower than the industry standard, and the owners were willing to take a chance on a rookie chef. But I soon discovered this new venture was doomed from the start. They controlled purchasing and hiring of staff for the kitchen, and they created the menu. I had very little input."

From experience in the hotel industry, Luke knew the responsibilities of the head chef included purchasing food and creating his or her own unique menus. They also hired staff they believed would be a good fit in their kitchens. The arrangement she'd entered into was unusual.

"I worked hard, I really did. But the menu the owners created was uninspired and the portions small. We didn't have enough staff in the kitchen or servers in the restaurant, so service was impossibly slow. Word got around, and business fell off dramatically. And when it did, the owners blamed me. They said my food was the problem. The restaurant closed a few weeks later. Finding work was even harder then."

"What did you do?"

"I had no choice but to go to work in fast food restaurants, sometimes two or three at once. They weren't as choosy about who they hired."

"Fast food restaurants aren't known for their high wages."

"No, they aren't. I didn't make much more than minimum wage, but I managed. At least till I got sick."

His stomach dropped. "You were sick?"

"I got mononucleosis last winter. Even after I was feeling better, my employers wouldn't let me back in the kitchen because they thought I might still be contagious. I was off work for over eight weeks and maxed out my credit cards." Her chin wobbled but she held back her tears. "I had to sell my mother's antique diamond earrings to a pawn shop to make rent."

He wanted to shake her. If she'd reached out to her sisters, to his mother, to someone, they would have helped her. But she'd been too stubborn and too proud.

She must have been so alone and scared. And desperate. He remembered how much those earrings had meant to her. She'd worn them the first time they'd made love. They were made of gold and had several diamonds in the design. They were the only physical connection she'd had to her mother, and she wouldn't have parted with them unless it had been a last resort.

Luke didn't know if he could do anything about the earrings, but he could help with her current money situation. "I'm going to speak with Ethan and Harper as soon as possible, and we're going to start paying you a salary."

She grabbed her apron from a peg near the door, drying her eyes with one corner before slipping it on. "I'm a part owner, not an employee. I can't do that."

"Who says? You've been working hard for months and you deserve to be paid. Now that Harper and Scarlet are married, they've got financial support. You're the only one left to fend for herself."

She lifted her chin, a gesture he remembered from her youth. She was going to be stubborn. "If my sisters aren't taking a salary, neither am I."

"Fine. Then all three of you will start getting regular paychecks."

She stared at him, her lips parting slightly. "Where's the money supposed to come from? We haven't even opened yet."

"Ethan's putting up the seed money. He'll have to fork over a little more."

Maggie turned away and began taking bowls and utensils from the shelves. "No. I don't want them to know how bad things are for me financially. Or how I got to this point."

"We don't have to tell them. I'll say I think everyone should start taking a regular salary."

She said nothing as she pulled ingredients – flour, white sugar, brown sugar – from the pantry and set them on the stainless-steel island. After retrieving eggs and butter from the fridge and placing them beside the flour, she braced her hands on the island and looked up at him. "Do you think Harper and Ethan will go along with the idea?"

"I think I can make a good case."

"Without telling them the whole truth?"

"Would it be so awful if they knew?"

"Yes!" Her chin lifted at that stubborn angle once more. "I don't want them to know."

He put up his hands in surrender. "All right. I won't say a word. I'll stick to the line about it being time for the lodge to start paying the three of you."

Her shoulders visibly relaxed. "Okay. It would be nice to start drawing a salary again." She bit her lip, her gaze veering away from his. "When do you think I could get my first paycheck?"

Luke breathed a sigh of relief and did a few quick calculations in his head. "As long as I can add all your information to the payroll system in the next day or two, you'll be paid on the fifteenth of December."

Maggie blew out a breath, then offered him a smile. "I could do a little Christmas shopping."

Would she have said anything at all about her financial difficulties if not for wanting to buy Christmas gifts for her family? Whatever the reason, he was glad she'd confided in him. And he was happy he was able to help. "We can go into Brainerd together. I want to get a few gifts, too."

"I'd like that."

Her tremulous smile abruptly gave way to tears. He covered the distance between them in two strides, taking her into his arms and kissing away the salty tears from her cheeks. "It's okay, sweetheart. Don't cry."

She clutched at his shoulders. "I'm sorry."

"Shh. You have nothing to be sorry about."

He kissed her, his mouth finding her soft, sweet lips. He meant the kiss to be brief and comforting, a gesture to let her know he was on her side. That he was always on her side.

Something inside him snapped the instant he heard her soft moan, felt her arms slip around his neck. Desire roared in his ears, making him pull her hard against his body. She responded with a fervor of her own, moulding herself against him as if she wanted, needed to get closer, was desperate to join their bodies together. Her small hands caressed his shoulders, his back, his buttocks. His need for her spiralled out of control. He slid his hand inside her sweater and palmed her breast, reveling in the sweet weight of its perfection. The hard, puckered nipple declared she wanted him as much as he wanted her. She gasped and pushed herself into his hand, giving herself to him.

"Hi, Maggie—Oh!"

Maggie abruptly ended the kiss and pushed away from him, her mouth swollen and her eyes glazed. A stricken expression quickly replaced the passion in her eyes, as if she were embarrassed, or worse, ashamed. "Celeste, I—"

"I'm sorry. I'll come back later." Celeste left the kitchen and closed the door quietly behind her.

Maggie's breath was uneven, her frantic gaze landing everywhere but on him. He cupped her chin and made her look at him. "Why are you acting as if we've done something wrong?"

Her dark eyes flashed. "I'm not. We didn't."

"Damn right, we didn't." He dared to take a step closer. "We're grown up now."

"Yes, we are. But that doesn't mean that sleeping together for old times' sake is a good idea. You'll be leaving. Again."

"Yes." He tried to remember why going back to California was so important, but his brain was too full with thoughts of her in his arms.

"It... it hurt when you left before. I don't want to go there again."

He squeezed his eyes shut and let go of her chin. He wished he could tell her the truth, tell her why he left, but that would only hurt her more.

And make her hate him.

"Neither do I."

She let out a shaky breath. "I care for you, Luke. I probably always will. But my life is here now and yours is in California. It's no one's fault, just the way it is."

No one's fault but mine.

He turned and walked to the door. "I'll talk to Ethan and Harper about the payroll as soon as I can."

"Thank you."

Luke left the kitchen and grabbed his jacket from the closet near the front door before heading outside. He welcomed the strong gust of cold wind that stole his breath. Maybe the north wind could blow the guilt from his heart.

Because in ten years, nothing else had been able to accomplish that feat.

Chapter Nineteen

LUKE MADE COFFEE IN his mother's kitchen and waited for it to brew. The short wait gave him the opportunity to steel himself. Every time he visited his mother, he had to put on his protective armor. She grew thinner and more frail looking by the day, but she never complained. She always had a smile for him. Perhaps the smile was her armor.

When the coffee finished brewing, he poured himself a cup, added a little milk and brought it to the living room where his mother was seated in her wheelchair chatting quietly with her nurse Paula.

Paula rose as he came into the room. "I'll leave the two of you to visit. I'll be changing the sheets on your bed if you need me." With that, she disappeared down the hallway leading to his mother's bedroom.

"How are preparations for your Christmas open house going?" his mother asked.

"Good, I think. Maggie and Celeste have been baking up a storm. Ethan's clearing a spot on the lake for skating, and we've arranged for Jim Fisher to give hayrides with his heavy horse team. As long as we don't get forty below weather, we should be fine."

"Sounds lovely. I remember how Miranda's father used to clear snow from the lake so we could skate. We had so much fun."

"We're hoping people have fun skating during the open house." He cleared his throat. "Mom, do you remember a pair of antique earrings Miranda owned? I think they were gold, with diamonds. Maggie inherited them."

A brief smile flitted across Abby's face. "Yes, I remember them. Miranda received them as a gift when Maggie was born. That's why she inherited them."

"Would you happen to have a picture of them?"

His mother thought for a moment. "I think I do. Why do you need a picture of the earrings?"

He hesitated, but there was no way he could keep this from her if he wanted to find the earrings. "Maggie pawned them." He gave a brief account of how she'd had to sell them at a pawn shop.

Abby shook her head. "The poor, stubborn girl. Why didn't she come to me? Reese and I would have helped her."

"She's too proud, Mom. She didn't want anyone to know she was in trouble, and she still doesn't want anyone to know. She wouldn't be happy if she found out I told you."

"Then I won't say a word. What do you plan to do?"

"I'm hoping to get them back for her. I'll check pawn shops in Minneapolis and see if I can find them."

"And if you can't?"

Luke shrugged. "Then I guess they're lost forever. Don't tell Maggie I'm looking for them. It's a longshot at best, and I don't want to raise her hopes."

"All right." She pointed to a bookcase across the room. "There are some old photo albums on the bottom shelf of that bookcase. Can you bring them to me?"

He hauled six albums over to her and together they leafed through the pages until she found the picture she wanted. "That's the one. I was pretty sure Miranda was wearing the earrings in this picture."

She pointed to a studio picture of Miranda with a baby on her lap. "I think Maggie is about a year old in this picture. Isn't she a beautiful baby?"

Maggie was as beautiful then as she was now. Luke's throat constricted and all he could manage was a single syllable. "Yeah."

Abby turned the page of the album. There was another studio picture, this one with Miranda and all three of her daughters. Luke flipped to the first picture and then back again to the second. He pointed to the photo of Miranda and the three girls. "She's not wearing the earrings in this picture. Her dress is the same, and so is Maggie's, so obviously the photos were taken on the same day. Why would she take off the earrings?"

His mother shrugged one small shoulder "I couldn't say."

Luke looked at her sharply. Interesting choice of words. *I couldn't say.*

"I don't think the girls have ever seen these pictures. She died not long after they were taken," she said, running her finger over Miranda's face.

"Can I borrow them, Mom? I'll make copies for Maggie and her sisters."

"Of course. But please bring them back and put them in the photo album when you're finished. I wouldn't want to lose these pictures. They're important to me."

"I'll make sure to put them back."

Luke removed the photos and set the two side by side. Why was Miranda wearing the earrings in only the picture with Maggie? And if his mother knew the reason, why wouldn't she tell him?

Another mystery in Miranda Lindquist's mysterious life.

LUKE MET WITH ETHAN and Harper the next afternoon to go over details of the new reservation system. The company installing the system was also providing the point of sale software for the bar and the restaurant.

"The hotel I work for in Napa uses the same system and we've been very happy with it. It's easy for staff to use and whenever we've had problems, the company's been great about helping us work them out."

"That's a good enough endorsement for me. How soon do you think we'll have all our servers in place?" Ethan asked.

Luke checked the calendar on his phone. "Harper and I are doing second interviews for the front desk staff on Monday, and I should have all our servers hired by the middle of next week. Then, I'll hold training sessions on using the new systems to get people up to speed."

"Sounds good. It feels like things are really coming together."

"Yeah." Luke cleared his throat. "There's another matter I need to discuss with both of you."

"That sounds ominous. What is it?" Harper asked.

"It's nothing bad." How did he say this without revealing Maggie's financial predicament? "I think it's time for the family to be on the payroll."

"Why?" Ethan asked, obviously confused. "I certainly don't need to take money from the lodge, not that we're making money right now anyway."

"It could be a financial hardship to wait for the lodge to make money. I think it would be good practice for the family to begin to draw a salary now. No one should be left in a tough cash flow position."

Harper regarded him solemnly. "You're talking about Maggie, aren't you?"

So much for his promise. "I didn't say that."

"I should have realized she was having financial troubles. I shouldn't have expected her to go without a paycheck for so long. I was stupid and inconsiderate." Harper moved past him to get to the door. "I'll go talk to her."

Luke grasped her arm. "Don't do that, Harper. She didn't want you to know."

Anguish filled her eyes. "She's so stubborn, and so damn proud."

"Yeah. She is." He squeezed her arm before letting go. "Which is why I'm going to add all three of you to the payroll system, and you're not going to say anything about this conversation to Maggie."

Reluctantly, Harper nodded. "All right."

"Can I ask one more favor?"

"You mean there's more?"

"Nothing bad. I was wondering if I could borrow your parents' wedding picture, the one you found with your grandmother's things. I'd like to make a copy for Maggie."

"That's a lovely idea, Luke. I'm sure she'll treasure it."

Harper left to get the picture. Luke decided he'd make a copy for Scarlet, as well, and have all three put in nice frames under glass that would keep the colors from fading.

Even if he couldn't find the earrings, he owed Maggie at least that much.

MAGGIE HAD TO RESTRAIN herself from doing a little happy dance as Luke handed her a pay stub on December fifteenth.

"The money's been directly deposited into your account as of this morning."

"Thanks, Luke." The thought of having a few dollars in her bank account made her giddy with relief. "Are you still interested in going Christmas shopping?"

"Absolutely. Let me finish a couple of things and we can go right after lunch."

True to his word, Luke was waiting for her at the front door of the lodge at one o'clock. They drove to downtown Brainerd and parked near an area with some small, quirky shops. Maggie unbuckled her seat belt. "I'd like to get something for Ethan, but what do you buy for the man who literally has everything?"

"Give him something from your heart. I'm sure he'll love it because it came from you."

With that thought in mind, they entered an antique store. In a matter of moments, Maggie found some pretty glass paperweights for Harper's office, a lovely cut glass perfume bottle for Celeste, and a silver hand mirror and a couple of silver combs for Scarlet. She paused over an antique desk set with a letter opener, an inkwell and small clock, which was ticking and had the correct time. The set was made of polished brass and had lovely engraving that was decorative while maintaining a masculine vibe. She picked up the ink well and examined it from every angle. The piece was solid and substantial, like Ethan.

She checked for a price sticker on the bottom and smiled in relief. The piece was within her budget.

"That's a nice piece," Luke said over her shoulder. "Are you thinking of getting this for Ethan?"

"Yeah. Someday, once he has his own office, he can use it there. I want him to know how much he's changed my life, and how grateful I am."

"He knows."

She paid for her purchases and then went next door to a yarn and fabric arts store while Luke went shopping on his own. Maggie bought Raggedy Ann and Andy dolls for Hope and a family of teddy bears for Tessa. She found gorgeous hand knit sweaters for both Reese and Luke, a tea cozy and potholders for Phyllis, and a lovely afghan for Abby. She stroked the soft wool of the afghan and wondered how long Abby would be able to use it. She didn't have much longer...

She couldn't dwell on it or she'd cry in front of all the Christmas shoppers. Blowing out a breath, she shook off her sadness. For now, Abby was with them, and Maggie would do everything in her power to make this the best damn Christmas any of them had ever had.

No matter how hard it might be to hide her sorrow.

At a frame shop down the street, she found a couple of interesting wooden frames that she hoped Cam could use for his artwork.

As she was paying for Cam's gift, a wonderful art deco frame on a shelf behind the counter caught her eye. She pointed to it. "Could I see that one, please?"

"Of course."

The salesclerk pulled the frame off the shelf and handed it to her. Maggie loved the silver and black geometric design that somehow reminded her of Luke. Strong, steady, forthright, honest. She knew exactly the picture she wanted to put in the frame. "I'll take this one, too," she said.

The salesclerk carefully wrapped it in tissue and placed it in the bag with the other two frames. After getting Cam a couple of blank canvasses to go along with the frames at an art supply store, she was done. Fortunate, because according to her calculations she'd spent most of her paycheck.

Before leaving the art supply shop, she pulled her cell phone from her purse and called Luke.

"Hey. All shopped out already?" She heard the amusement in his voice.

"Completely. I've got gifts for everyone. How about you?"

"I'm paying for the last ones now. Would you like a coffee before we head home?"

"I'd love one. But do you think we can stow all my stuff in your truck first? I can barely carry it all."

He chuckled. "Sure. I'll meet you at my truck in a couple of minutes."

They put all their shopping bags in the back seat of the truck and locked it up before heading to a coffee shop. Before finding a table, they put in their order at the front counter.

"What will you have?" he asked her.

She smiled, happiness filling her heart. It had been a wonderful day. She'd been able to find nice gifts for her family and friends, and she'd paid for them with money she earned. It felt good.

"I want to celebrate. I'll have a hot chocolate and one of those," she said, pointing to a chocolate covered donut in the glass display case.

Luke's lips turned up in a grin. "You celebrate with donuts?"

She smiled back. "You celebrate your way, and I'll celebrate mine."

He ordered coffee and then led the way to a table near the front window. After sitting down, Maggie touched her mug to his. "Here's to a good day of shopping. I hope everyone likes the gifts I got them."

"They will, because they came from you. Everyone loves you."

She found herself drowning in his beautiful gray-green eyes. When he said everyone loved her, was he including himself? Despite her fears, she hoped he was.

But if he was, why wouldn't he tell her?

Chapter Twenty

MAGGIE SAT IN THE CHAIR next to Abby's bed. Abby didn't feel well enough to get up, but she'd insisted on the visit. Maggie still didn't understand why talking to her about her mother was so important to Abby. Nor why she couldn't tell her sisters.

Patience, she told herself.

Abby's soft snores indicated she was sleeping peacefully. Maggie closed her eyes and exhaled slowly. She had to trust Abby to reveal her purpose in her own way.

Paula entered the bedroom and straightened Abby's blanket. She smiled at Maggie. "Abby had a tough night. The night nurse said the coughing was particularly bad. It kept her awake. She's exhausted, poor thing."

"I should go and come back tomorrow. I want her to rest."

"I think that would be best."

Abby's eyes fluttered open. "Maggie?"

Maggie reached for Abby's hand and squeezed. "I'm right here."

"Your father loves you. Always." Abby's eyes blinked, and finally closed, as if she was too tired to keep them open. "Don't be angry with him."

Maggie thought it odd that Abby used the word love in the present tense. But she was exhausted, and not entirely lucid.

Her grip on Maggie's hand, however, was surprisingly strong. "Forgive."

"I will. I promise."

That seemed to satisfy her and her grip loosened. "Good, good."

In a few moments, she was asleep once more. Maggie carefully pulled her hand away and left the room. Paula gave her a smile and brief wave as she closed the door.

Forgive. What did Abby want her to forgive her father for? The murder of her mother? His blatant disregard for his daughters' futures when he ended both their lives?

Forgive.

Anger bubbled in her chest. Maggie wasn't sure she could keep that promise.

DECEMBER TWENTY-THIRD, open house day, dawned sunny and cold. Frigid, actually. As Maggie walked from the cottage to the lodge, her lungs threatened to freeze inside her chest. She pulled her thick scarf higher to protect her face from the bitter cold.

Once inside, she glanced out the French doors of the dining room to the frozen lake. The snow twinkled in the sun, and she was reminded of her grandfather's stories about diamonds in the snow.

She smiled at the memory of her grandfather. Despite the sadness and loss, she had some good memories of her childhood. She locked that thought away in her heart as she prepared for a busy day.

At least, she hoped it would be busy. If it wasn't, it wouldn't bode well for the future of the lodge.

She needn't have worried. From the moment they opened the doors to the public at one in the afternoon, they were inundated with people wanting to see what they'd done to the lodge. Most were curious locals from Minnewasta and area, but many came from farther away. Scarlet had contacted newspapers and radio stations from around the state and several reporters showed up to take pictures and do interviews, a couple from as far away as Chicago. Maggie and Celeste were too busy refilling coffee urns and setting out plates of cookies to pay much attention to the reporters, but Scarlet was thrilled with the response.

So were Ethan and Harper. Despite the cold, the sleigh rides, skating and dog sled rides Ethan organized were big hits. Harper led groups of people on tours of the renovated parts of the lodge, the newly completed guest wing and partially constructed event center. Everyone was impressed and encouraging.

As Maggie came out of the kitchen with another tray of cookies, a blonde woman approached her. "Hi. You're Maggie Lindquist, aren't you?"

The woman looked vaguely familiar, but she couldn't quite place her. "Yes, I'm Maggie."

"I'm Cheryl Johnson." She extended her hand. "Used to be Cheryl Bradley. I married Tim Johnson. He went to school in Minnewasta, too."

Maggie set down her tray and tried to mask her shock as she shook Cheryl's hand. "Hello, Cheryl. Welcome to Solace Lake Lodge."

"I think what you've done here is remarkable. I've been following the progress on your social media, and I'm really happy the lodge will be a going concern again. It's wonderful for your family and for the whole community."

"We're excited to bring it back to life." Maggie searched Cheryl's face, looking for evidence that she was laughing at her, but she saw nothing but sincerity.

"I'm a chef myself." Cheryl smiled nervously and flipped her blonde hair over her shoulder. "Tim and I were living in Minneapolis and I was working as a sous-chef." She named a well-known, and well-respected Minneapolis restaurant. "But Tim really wanted to come home to the country, so when he was offered a teaching position here, we moved back. But it's been hard for me to find work."

Maggie nodded. "I know how that is."

"I was wondering if all your sous-chef positions have been filled."

"You're asking me for a job?"

"Yes." Cheryl straightened her shoulders. "I know I'm the last person you want to hire. I was mean to you back in high school. But I'm not that girl anymore, thankfully. I managed to grow up a little."

"You married Tim Johnson?" Maggie remembered Tim as shy and smart and something of a nerd. He and Cheryl hadn't run in the same circles back then.

"Yes." Cheryl's smile was completely genuine and happy. "Tim is kind and funny and crazy smart. He's the best husband a girl could want. He wasn't what I was looking for, but he's everything I need."

"That's wonderful."

"I thought I wanted someone like Luke, the handsome, bad boy type."

Funny, Maggie had never thought of Luke as a bad boy. To her, he was simply...Luke.

"I chased him all through our last year of high school. He'd never shown me any interest until, out of the blue, he asked me to meet him at the bleachers. He kissed me, and then you were there, and it got very weird."

"Yeah, it did." Maggie fidgeted, uncomfortable with the conversation. She glanced at the door to the kitchen, trying to come up with an excuse to politely extract herself.

"That was my first and last kiss from Luke. I never heard from him again."

Cheryl's admission brought Maggie's focus back. She looked at her carefully. For some reason, she believed her. But if there hadn't been anything going on between Luke and Cheryl that summer, why stage that scene with her? To get rid of her? The thought of it continued to hurt.

"I would really like to work in your kitchen. I hope we can put the past behind us, but if you can't, I understand."

Maggie decided to go with her gut. "Send us your resume along with some references, and we'll see what happens. We're looking for at least one more sous-chef."

Cheryl let out a breath and smiled in relief. "I will, thank you. Tim's going to be so pleased. I was afraid to talk to you, but he said high school was a long time ago and you'd be reasonable."

Maggie smiled at that. High school *was* a long time ago, but sometimes it seemed like yesterday.

THE LAST VISITORS WERE preparing to leave when Maggie saw Willy Eklund stumble through the front doors, his gait unsteady. Her heart sank. It appeared his sobriety was short-lived.

"Harper! Harper, where are you? I need to talk to you." Willy's slurred voice echoed through the lodge. "I need to tell you the truth!"

Harper hurried toward him, and Maggie and Scarlet followed closely behind. While Scarlet ushered the remaining guests out the door, Maggie and Harper each grabbed one of Willy's arms and guided him to a far corner of the dining room, some distance away from the front entrance. He reeked of stale booze, his hair as wild as his eyes.

Harper's face was full of disappointment. "Oh, Willy. You were doing so well."

He hung on her arm as she made him sit on a chair. "I can't live with the shame anymore, Harper. I just can't."

"You had a setback, Willy. There's no shame in that. You need to try again."

"No, no, you don't understand."

He began to rock back and forth on the chair, his keening wails making the hair on the back of Maggie's neck stand up. There was something pitiful in the sound. No, more than that. Willy cried as if his heart was broken, as if his world had come to an end. Something must have happened since they'd last seen him. Something terrible.

Ethan, Cam, and Luke entered the dining room. Ethan pulled off his winter hat. "What's going on?"

"Willy fell off the wagon," Maggie said. "He's devastated."

"You don't understand," Willy cried. "No one understands. I can't live like this anymore. I killed her! Do you hear me? I killed her!"

Maggie's stomach roiled. Harper laid her hand on his arm. "What are you talking about, Willy?

He began rocking back and forth again. "I killed Miranda. I killed my beautiful Miranda."

Stunned silence greeted his announcement. Willy dissolved in tears, his body bent over in grief. All six of them stared at him, too shocked to utter a word.

Hope and Tessa skipped into the room, followed by Celeste. The girls heard Willy's grief-stricken cries and slowed their pace, their eyes wide and frightened. Tessa grabbed Cam's hand. "Daddy, why is that man crying?"

"Because he's sad, baby." He turned to Celeste. "Could you take the girls to your room for a while?"

She nodded wordlessly and taking the girls by the hand, led them away. Once they were out of earshot, Harper reached out to Willy. But instead of touching him, she let her hand drop to her side. "Willy, you're drunk and confused. You don't mean it. You don't mean you killed our mother."

He looked up at her and wiped his nose on the sleeve of his jacket. "I can't lie anymore, Harper. I killed her. She was my best friend and I loved her, but I killed her. I didn't mean to. I swear to God I didn't mean to."

Ethan put his arm around Harper. "Tell us what happened. All of it."

Willy wiped his nose once more and inhaled deep, unsteady breaths. "Robert showed up at the lodge unannounced, and I was worried he'd try to hurt Miranda, so I followed them out to the Point where she and I kept our canoes. I heard them arguing. I had to protect Miranda."

"I remember seeing Willy run toward them," Scarlet whispered. Cam pulled her into his arms and kissed her hair.

"Miranda told him they were over. Their marriage was over. She loved someone else, had always loved him. She walked onto the dock, intending to get into her canoe. Robert yelled at her, told her she couldn't walk away from him like that. He pushed her and she stumbled. I jumped out of my hiding place and grabbed an oar from Miranda's canoe, and I told Robert to get away from her. He came after me, screaming that I'd broken up their marriage. I swung at him with the oar, but then Miranda stood—"

Willy closed his eyes, rocking back and forth once more. Maggie looked at her sisters. Scarlet was crying quietly against Cam's shoulder and Harper appeared numb, as if his words were turning her to ice.

"What happened then, Willy?" Maggie asked. Luke's warm hand on her shoulder steadied her.

Willy turned his attention to her. "Miranda stood, and I...I hit her. I didn't mean to. It was an accident. She fell into the water. It's deep there, off the end of the dock."

"What about our father? What did he do?"

"He jumped in after her, but he couldn't find her. And then he disappeared, too."

"He couldn't swim," Harper said. "Scarlet and I used to tease him about it. We could swim the length of the pool in our backyard, but Daddy sank like a stone. He never ventured into the deep end."

"He tried to save her," Scarlet whispered.

Red dots of anger formed in Maggie's vision. "While our parents were in the water, struggling for their lives, what did you do, Willy?"

"I jumped in Miranda's canoe and paddled around and around, but I couldn't find her. I knew I needed help, so I ran to Bill's shed. I guess I forgot to tie up the canoe. They found it floating on the water and assumed Miranda and her husband had been in it." He rocked back and forth again. "I never told them I was in the canoe."

"I remember that day very clearly." Harper's words were slow and deliberate. "You came into Grampa's shed and you said, 'He hit her'. Those were your exact words, Willy. You told my grandfather that our father hit our mother with the oar."

"I don't know why I said that." Willy's voice shook. "I couldn't believe what had happened, what I'd done. I didn't want it to be true, so I lied. For many years, I even believed it. I'm so sorry."

"Sorry?" The red dots of anger fused together to form a hot, furious haze that obscured Maggie's vision. "You caused the death of both of our parents and you're sorry? You branded our father a murderer! All these years we believed he killed her. How could you let us believe that?"

Willy held out a beseeching hand to her. "I'm sorry, Maggie. I'm so sorry."

"Your apology means nothing to me. Nothing." Her body began to shake and she looked away, unable to stand the sight of him.

"I'll take him home," Luke said. He put his arm around her and kissed the top of her head. "Stay here with your sisters. I won't be long."

"I'll come with you, Luke," Ethan murmured. He reached for Harper's hand. "Will you be okay, sweetheart?"

Harper nodded, her face stony. "I'll be fine."

"I'm going to take Scarlet and Tessa home," Cam said.

"Will we see you tomorrow?" Ethan asked.

Scarlet lifted her chin. "Of course. I won't let anything ruin Christmas for Tessa."

Maggie kissed Scarlet goodnight and reached for Harper's hand. Luke and Ethan grabbed Willy's arms and dragged him away.

He twisted in their grip. "I'm sorry. Please forgive me. I need you to forgive me!"

Harper clutched Maggie's hand in a crushing grip. Neither of them acknowledged Willy as they walked away.

As soon as they reached the kitchen, Harper dissolved in tears. Sobs wracked her body and she sank to the floor. Maggie knelt beside her and held her, doing what she could to console her. But what could she say?

There was nothing anyone could say.

THE NEXT MORNING, MAGGIE was in the kitchen making breakfast with Celeste and Hope when Tessa burst through the doors.

"Auntie Maggie! It's Christmas Eve. Santa comes tonight!"

Maggie made herself smile for her little niece. Like Scarlet, she wouldn't let anything, or anyone, ruin her Christmas. She wished to God she could feel the joy and excitement the children were experiencing today. But for them, she'd fake it.

"I know, sweetheart. I've got cookies for you to leave for Santa at your house."

"Do you have carrots for the reindeer? I'll bet they'll be hungry by the time they get to my house."

"We have lots of carrots." She smiled at Hope. "And we've got cookies and carrots here for you to put out for Santa and his reindeer, too."

"Thank you, Miss Maggie. Would it be okay if I hung my stocking on the big fireplace in the dining room tonight? Then Santa can find it when he comes down the chimney."

"You sure can, Hope."

"Auntie Maggie, how is Santa going to bring me presents? We don't have a fireplace at our house."

Yikes. "What does your Daddy say?"

"He says Santa will find a way because he's magic."

Good thinking, Cam. "I think he's right. Don't you, Celeste?"

Celeste looked up from the pancakes she was flipping. "Absolutely. Santa is definitely magic."

Tessa seemed satisfied by their answers. She grabbed Hope's hand. "Let's go play Barbies in your room."

"You've got ten minutes, girls," Celeste warned. "Breakfast is almost ready. Watch the clock on the bedside table, Hope."

"Okay, Mama."

The girls left the kitchen, their excited giggles echoing through the dining room. Celeste put bacon on the grill. "How are you doing this morning, Maggie? Really."

Last night, after Ethan had taken Harper home, Maggie and Luke gave Celeste a brief account of Willy's confession. Celeste had hugged her tight and told her if she needed to talk, she was there for her. Maggie knew she could count on her friendship and she was deeply grateful for it.

"I'm..."

She was going to say she was fine, but that wasn't completely true, and Celeste deserved a real answer.

"I'm not sure how I feel this morning. I'm sad, I'm angry, I'm numb. At this point, I don't know which emotion is the strongest."

"Quite a shock, what he told you. It's no wonder you're all shook up."

"Yes." Everything she'd believed about her family history had changed. But at least now the truth could come out, and their father's memory redeemed.

By the time they brought the food into the dining room, Luke had already arrived, and Ethan and Harper were walking in the front door. Everyone was quiet and subdued. From the dark circles under Harper's eyes, Maggie could tell she hadn't slept any better than she had. Harper had always been closest to Willy. She'd been the one who'd looked out for him, especially after their grandfather no longer could.

Fortunately, Tessa and Hope talked excitedly about Christmas and Santa and kept the mood at the table from becoming too bleak. Maggie had to remind herself that Christmas was her favorite time of year, and she was with her family. She had to remember to find the joy.

When breakfast was over, everyone helped clear the table and wash dishes. With the counters wiped and leftovers put away, Celeste took Tessa and Hope by the hand. "Come on girls. We're going to dress up warm and play outside."

"Can we make a snowman?" Hope asked.

"Sure, Sugar."

She gave Maggie a brief smile as she led the little girls out of the kitchen. Luke hung his dishtowel on the rack beneath the sink. "I've got some work to do in the office. I'm sure the five of you have things you want to discuss in private."

"Don't go, Luke."

He turned to her, surprise in his eyes. She was surprised, too. All she knew was that she needed Luke's support.

And his love. But that wasn't going to happen.

She swallowed. "If we're discussing what's to be done about Willy, I would appreciate if you would stay. You already know the story. Someone who isn't quite so close to the situation will have a clearer view."

Luke's gaze was warm, giving her much needed encouragement. "As long as it's okay with everyone else."

Her sisters and their husbands nodded silently.

"You're a long-time friend of the family, Luke." Harper twisted her dishtowel in her hands. "We value your input."

"Let's sit down in the dining room next to the fireplace," Ethan said.

Several comfortable armchairs were positioned around the fireplace. Maggie perched on the end of her chair and fidgeted with the hem of her sweater, her emotions in turmoil. Cam added wood to the fire that dispelled the chill in the air, but she couldn't relax. Luke sat on the arm of her chair and placed his warm hand on her shoulder. Some of the tension left her body, and she exhaled the breath she'd been holding.

"I thought about what Willy told us all last night," Harper began, her eyes downcast. "And I can't do it. I can't go to the police and tell them what Willy told us. I can't go to court, or talk to lawyers. I can't relive their deaths."

"I feel the same way," Scarlet said. "It's too much for me right now."

Maggie couldn't believe what she was hearing. "So, you're going to let Willy get away with murder?"

"He hasn't gotten away with anything," Harper said with a sigh. "His life is in shambles because of what he's done. And he's just lost his last friend."

"Our father was accused of murder because of him." Maggie jumped to her feet, too agitated to sit any longer. "If for no other reason, we should come forward with this new information so we can clear his name."

"I want that, too, Maggie," Scarlet said. "He deserves that. But it's been more than twenty-two years. Who's going to remember?"

"We'll remember! And so will a lot of people in Minnewasta. They won't be able to whisper behind our backs anymore about how those poor Lindquist girls were the progeny of a murderer."

"What about the business?" Scarlet argued. "A scandal like this could scuttle everything we've been building here."

"I can't believe you won't fight for the truth. This is too important."

"You don't remember how it was back then, Maggie." Harper stared down at her clenched hands. "Police asking intimate questions about our parents' relationship. Journalists trying to dig up dirt. For months, reporters showed up at the lodge, sometimes pretending to be fishers. They wouldn't leave Grandma and Grampa alone."

"Or us," Scarlet added. She wiped her eyes with a tissue. "They followed us to school, questioned our teachers. How were we coping with the fact that our father murdered our mother? I don't want any of that for Tessa."

"But don't you see? If we come forward, the truth will be out there. We won't be the poor little Lindquist girls anymore. That legacy of shame won't exist for Tessa."

Harper shook her head. "I can't do it, Maggie. I just can't."

"Do you feel some kind of twisted loyalty to Willy? Is that why you won't go to the police? He doesn't deserve it! Your loyalty should be to our father!"

"Maggie," Ethan warned in a low voice. "That's enough."

Her body vibrated with rage. "To hell with you! To hell with all of you!"

She ran out of the lodge, not stopping to put on a coat or boots, too angry to feel the cold. She wasn't even sure where she was going. She ran until the frigid wind finally stopped her in her tracks, doubling her over in pain. The tears came then, with wracking sobs that threatened to rend her in two.

She hurt everywhere, body and soul. The pain was unbearable.

"Maggie!"

Suddenly Luke was there, wrapping something warm around her and pulling her into his arms. He kissed the cold tears on her face with warm lips. "It's going to be okay, baby."

She shook her head, her body trembling with cold. "No, it's never going to be okay."

"We're going back to the lodge so you can get warm. Then, you need to talk to your sisters again. You can't leave things like this."

"No, please." She didn't have the energy to fight anymore.

Luke ignored her protests. He lifted her into his arms and carried her back to the lodge. Her sisters were at the door waiting for them. As soon as they were inside, Luke set her on her feet, and Harper pulled her into a bone-crushing hug.

"I'm so sorry." Then she pushed her away and gave her a shake, tears streaming down her face. She crushed Maggie against her once more. "Don't ever do anything like that again. You could freeze!"

"I'm sorry for what I said." Maggie held her sister as if her life depended on it. Maybe it did.

Scarlet put her arms around both of them and kissed Maggie's hair. "We know, sweetheart. We know."

Harper released her enough to look into her face. "I think we need to consider our next move carefully, give ourselves some time. We're all too raw right now. We have to think clearly and a little more rationally." She swallowed and swiped at a tear that streaked down her cheek. "When Willy dropped his bombshell last night, I suddenly became a frightened ten-year-old again."

Maggie used the cuff of her sweater to wipe Harper's tears. "Don't be afraid. You have all of us now."

Both Harper and Scarlet cried as the three of them clung to each other.

Chapter Twenty-One

LATER THAT CHRISTMAS Eve, the family gathered around the Christmas tree in front of the fireplace to open presents. After the drama of the morning, Maggie was grateful for some normalcy. They'd spent the day together, skating on the lake and racing the snowmobiles along the trails. Everyone was very conscious of making this Christmas happy, one without anymore tears. Tomorrow, her sisters would spend the day with their husbands' family in Minneapolis, and she would accompany Luke to Abby and Reese's house for Christmas dinner. But she was pleased that tonight her family would be together.

And relieved. After the awful things she'd said that morning, she wouldn't have blamed them if they hadn't wanted to be with her today. She was grateful for her family's forgiveness. She believed Willy should be made to face the consequences of what he'd done, but she could understand her sisters' reluctance to bring back that painful chapter in their lives.

Pushing away the negative thoughts, Maggie watched Tessa and Hope open the gifts she got them. They seemed excited to receive them, but the sugar high from all the cookies they'd consumed might have contributed to the euphoria.

Scarlet began handing out presents from under the tree. "Time for the adults to have some fun."

Maggie gingerly pried apart the tape sealing the wrapping on the Christmas present Scarlet and Cam had given her, not wanting to destroy the pretty paper.

Scarlet grabbed the present from her hands. "Stop it! You're making me crazy!"

With a couple of tugs, she ripped the paper from the box and handed it back to Maggie. "Open it already! The suspense is killing me!"

With a laugh, she lifted the lid. A beautiful red sweater in the softest cashmere was inside the box. Maggie lifted it to her cheek and revelled in the downy texture. "Oh, this is beautiful. Thank you, guys."

Cam grinned. "You can thank your sister. Buying women's clothing is definitely Scarlet's area of expertise."

"In that case, thank you, Scarlet."

"You're welcome. But you need to open the present in the silver wrapping paper. That one is all Cameron."

Curious, Maggie reached for the box.

Scarlet wagged a finger at her. "Don't make me come over there and tear off the wrapping paper again."

"Okay, okay!"

She pulled off the bow and ribbons and tugged at the paper, rending it to pieces. Her frugal, eco-conscious side wailed at the waste, but Scarlet was pleased.

"Hurry and open the box!"

Maggie shook her head and laughed. "I'm going as fast as I can."

She opened the box and drew back the tissue paper protecting the contents. A set of wooden candlesticks, intricately turned and polished to accent the grain of the wood, was nestled in the box. She lifted one out to examine it more closely. "Oh, Cam. You made these?"

"I did. I made a set for Harper, too, but with a different turning and species of wood. Yours is in oak."

"They're gorgeous. Thank you so much." It touched her to know he'd made something especially for her.

"You made a set for me, too?" Harper sat next to Maggie "Where is it?"

Scarlet pointed to a box wrapped in the same silver paper as Maggie's. "That one."

Harper pounced on the box and opened it, revealing a set of candlesticks totally different from hers.

"Thank you so much. I love them." Harper's words wavered. "I can't tell you how happy I am to be with you all tonight. Last year on Christmas Eve, I volunteered to work a double shift at Miller's so I didn't have to be alone."

"I thought you had to work because they were short-staffed," Maggie said.

Harper shrugged. "I only took those shifts after I found out you and Scarlet weren't coming home for Christmas."

Maggie reached over and squeezed her hand. How like Harper to go out of her way to make sure she and Scarlet didn't feel guilty. She'd had to work last Christmas to make enough money for rent, but of course she hadn't told Harper that. "It's so much better to be with family at Christmas."

Harper nodded and squeezed back. "It definitely is."

The moment of connection eased Maggie's heart. She was still raw from the morning, but whatever they decided to do about Willy would be the right decision, as long as they made it together.

Luke sat beside her on the floor near the Christmas tree. "You haven't opened my present yet."

She grinned at him. "Oh, yeah? What did you get me?"

He handed her an eight by ten-inch package. "You'll have to open it to see."

"Is this a picture frame? What's the picture?"

"All I'll say is that I got the same gift for Scarlet and Harper." He leaned toward her and whispered in her ear. "I have something else I'm going to give you tomorrow at Mom and Reese's house."

"So do I," she whispered back.

Tomorrow, she'd give him the hand knit sweater she'd found at the yarn shop in Brainerd, but tonight she'd give him the silver art deco frame. She'd put a picture of Abby she'd found in her mother's photo album into the frame. Abby was young, probably about twenty-five, and she was laughing, her hair blowing in the breeze.

She opened Luke's present and found two eight by ten-inch pictures in silver frames. One was of her mother, with her sisters as little girls and herself as a baby. The second was of her and her mother alone. She blinked at Luke. "Where did you get these?"

"Mom had them. She didn't think you'd seen them before. Is that true?"

"No, I've never seen them."

Maggie ran her finger over her mother's face. She was so beautiful. And so young and happy. Perhaps it was good not to know what life had in store. "Thank you."

"You're welcome."

She held up the pictures for Harper. "Have you seen these before?"

Harper knelt on the floor beside her and closely examined the picture of the four of them. "No. But I think I remember going to the photo studio. I wore my favorite dress." She touched her mother's image. "Isn't this odd?"

"What?"

"Mom is wearing earrings in the picture with you, but not in the one with all of us. And I wonder why she took a separate picture only with you?"

Definitely odd, now that she mentioned it. One more secret, one more mystery.

Harper looked intently at the picture of baby Maggie with Miranda. "Aren't these the earrings you inherited from Mom? I remember Grandma giving them to you. I think she said they'd been a present to Mom when you were born. Daddy must have given them to her."

Maggie swallowed, hoping Harper wouldn't ask any more questions about the earrings. "Yeah, those are the ones I inherited."

"I haven't seen you wear them in ages."

"I've put them away. They hurt my ears." The lie tasted bitter on her tongue.

Her gaze met Luke's and she tried to send him a silent message to change the subject. She hated lying, but Harper would be upset if she told her the earrings were gone, and even more upset if she explained the reason why.

Fortunately, Luke got her message. He rummaged under the tree and produced two more wrapped gifts identical to hers. "I have copies of the same pictures for you and Scarlet. I thought you'd want them, too."

Harper accepted the presents from him and leaned over to kiss his cheek. "Thank you, Luke. This is very thoughtful."

"You're welcome."

Harper went back to her place on the sofa next to Ethan, and Maggie pulled the art deco frame from under the tree and handed it to Luke. "This is for you. I guess we're on the same wavelength tonight. In case you haven't guessed, it's a photo, too."

Luke tore off the wrapping paper and opened the box. When he pulled the picture frame from inside, he said nothing. Maggie was afraid something was wrong, that she'd upset him.

But then he lifted his gaze to hers, his eyes bright with emotion. "This is how I want to remember her."

She nodded. This was how she wanted to remember Abby, too. Laughing, happy, and full of life and love.

He pulled her into his arms and kissed her hair. "Thank you, Maggie. You couldn't have given me anything better."

"I'm glad you like it."

She kissed him, intending to brush a chaste kiss across his lips. But the instant she touched him, inhaled his unique scent, all she could think was that she wanted more. She touched her lips to his again and cupped his face as he deepened the kiss. She forgot that her family was in the same room watching, forgot that Abby was dying, forgot Luke would soon be leaving. In that moment, kissing him was all that mattered. She wound her arms around his neck and poured everything she had into her kiss.

She couldn't deny it any longer. She loved him, and she couldn't bear to lose him again.

A loud throat clearing penetrated her tangled thoughts. Reluctantly, she pulled away from Luke. He wore a shell-shocked expression, as if he'd been affected by their kiss as much as she had.

But she didn't know if it was enough to make him stay.

Cam got to his feet and pulled Scarlet up with him. Tessa ran to them and he lifted her into his arms. "Now that we have your attention," he said winking at Maggie, "we have something we want to share with you." He put his arm around Scarlet's shoulders.

"We're pregnant!" Scarlet blurted.

With a whoop, Harper scrambled to her feet and ran to Scarlet, throwing her arms around her. Maggie hugged both of them, tears of joy blurring her vision. "I'm so happy for you. For both of you."

She'd never thought of her career-driven sister as the maternal type. A couple of years ago, if someone had told her Scarlet would become the best stepmother a little girl could want, she wouldn't have believed it. Maggie knew friction had developed with one of Scarlet's former fiancés over having children. Scarlet didn't think she knew how to be a mother.

But that was before she met Tessa and Cam.

"When are you due?" Harper asked.

"In August," Scarlet said. "Probably not the best timing, considering how busy we'll likely be next summer."

"It's perfect," Harper said. "Absolutely perfect."

There were handshakes and hugs all around, and Celeste went in search of champagne. Maggie's eyes filled with happy tears. She was so happy for Scarlet and Cam. They were wonderful parents to Tessa, and they'd welcome this new little one with love. They deserved this happiness.

She glanced at Ethan and Harper, who toasted each other with the champagne Celeste handed around. They'd soon be parents too, she'd guess. Harper would be a wonderful mother. No one was more loving than her sister.

Maggie's gaze drifted toward Luke, and he smiled back at her. Would she ever know the kind of happiness Scarlet was experiencing? What did the future hold in store for her?

Perhaps, like her mother, she was better off not knowing.

Chapter Twenty-two

LUKE PICKED MAGGIE up at her cottage early on Christmas morning. Together, they loaded her presents and ingredients for the dishes she planned to make into the back seat of his truck. She wanted to get to Abby and Reese's house early so she could put the turkey in the oven for Christmas dinner. But despite arriving before nine a.m., they hadn't been able to beat Phyllis. As they entered the kitchen, they found her stuffing the turkey with a bread dressing.

Maggie threw her coat over a kitchen chair. "I thought I was supposed to be cooking. You're supposed to be having a relaxing Christmas day."

Phyllis waved her hand, a look of dismissal on her face. "Relaxing? That's no fun."

"Is Mom asleep?" Luke asked quietly.

"Yeah, and Reese, too, poor man. He looked exhausted last night," Phyllis said as she slid the turkey roaster into the hot oven. "We'll stay in the kitchen and try to be quiet so they can sleep a little longer."

For over an hour, they worked together in almost complete silence. Phyllis peeled sweet potatoes, while Luke washed lettuce for a salad, and Maggie worked on dessert. She'd brought all the ingredients she needed to make a pumpkin pie, not sure what was available at Abby's house. As she rolled out the pastry, Luke leaned over her shoulder.

"I haven't had pumpkin pie in ages," he said. "I'm looking forward to it."

"I hope Abby is able to have some. I made some brownies if she doesn't feel like pie."

"These days she doesn't eat much of anything," Phyllis said. Profound sadness etched the lines in her face, making her look far older than her seventy-five years. "I'm making all her favorite dishes, but I doubt she'll be able to enjoy much of them."

Neither she nor Luke replied. They all knew the days of Abby's life were winding down. If this was to be Abby's last Christmas, Maggie reasoned, then she'd do her best to make the memories of it happy. A celebration of life rather than a countdown to death. Luke and Reese and Phyllis deserved that.

"I think we need Christmas music," she said.

She wiped her hands on her apron, then turned on the small TV in a corner of the kitchen. Maggie flipped through the channels until she found one showing a fire roaring in a brick fireplace and Christmas carols playing softly in the background. When "Rocking Around the Christmas Tree' came on, she grabbed Luke's hand and twirled him around the kitchen table. Luke pulled his grandmother into their dance and together the three of them pranced around the kitchen in silly abandon, doing their best to stifle their laughter.

"And Merry Christmas to you, too."

Reese stood at the entrance to the kitchen. Even though he smiled, the lines of fatigue around his eyes told Maggie he hadn't slept well.

"I hope we didn't wake you," she said.

"No, not at all. It's nice to see some laughing faces this morning."

"Is Abby still sleeping?" Phyllis asked.

Reese dragged his hand through his hair, making it stand up on end. "Yeah, finally. She made me promise to wake her early so she could spend the day with all of you."

"We want to be with her, too, but let's let her sleep a little longer." Maggie laid her hand on his arm. "Merry Christmas, Reese."

"Merry Christmas, Maggie."

To her surprise, he pulled her into his arms for a hug. When he let her go, his eyes were bright with tears. She wished she could do something for him, say something to ease his pain. But there was nothing. The best she could do was to provide a diversion. "Now that you're here, you can help us. How are you at setting the table?"

He smiled at her, but she could see the effort in it. "Not great, but with some direction from Phyllis I think can do a passable job."

Phyllis patted his arm wordlessly and then retrieved a pretty tablecloth in Christmas red along with some crystal candlestick holders. As they set the table with Abby's best china, Maggie poured her pumpkin filling into the unbaked shell.

Reese rubbed his hands together. "I love pumpkin pie. It's my favorite."

"Mine, too." She trimmed the crust with a sharp knife. "I'll take pumpkin pie over any other kind of dessert, no contest."

He gave her a strange look that she couldn't decipher, but she put it down to the stress of Abby's illness.

"I'm going to check on Abby, see if she's ready to get up. I gave Paula the day off so she could be with her family."

"If she needs help getting dressed, give me a shout," Phyllis said. Reese nodded and left the room.

Maggie slipped her pie into the oven, shoving the turkey to one side to make room. While the oven door was open, she basted the turkey, glad to see the skin turning a golden brown.

"We're coming along," she said as she checked her watch. "We should be ready to eat in about an hour, at one o'clock."

"Why don't we sit down in the living room for a while? I'll put on some coffee," Luke said.

"You two go ahead." Phyllis banged around a couple of the pots that Maggie had washed and left to dry on the drain board. "I need to put this stuff away."

Luke looped his arm through hers. "It can wait, Grandma. I need to talk to you about something."

Sighing, she let him lead her to the living room where he made her sit on the sofa. Maggie sat beside her as Luke went back to the kitchen to make coffee. Phyllis rolled her eyes. "He's so bossy."

"I can't imagine where he gets that bossiness from," Maggie said with a grin.

"Oh, don't you start on me, too." Phyllis' light-hearted banter faded. "If I keep busy, I don't have time to remember."

Maggie clasped her hand. She couldn't imagine what it must be like for Phyllis to lose her only child. "I know."

Luke returned in a few minutes with cups of coffee for each of them. He handed Phyllis a cup and then sat in the upholstered chair opposite her. "Grandma, remember I was telling you that the cottage Maggie's staying in will soon be needed for guests of the lodge, and— "

"She could stay with me." Phyllis turned to face Maggie. "I've been thinking about it ever since Luke mentioned it. I want you to stay with me. I've got all this extra room."

"I don't want to make any work for you." Maggie's fear was that Phyllis would fuss over her too much. She didn't need to be cooking and cleaning for her.

"Nonsense. Like I said, I like to be busy. It helps. As would having a lively, young person in the house. Once Luke leaves, the house is going feel very empty."

Maggie nodded, understanding perfectly. The lodge would feel empty without him, too.

As will my heart.

"It's only temporary, until I find a place of my own."

"I know, but there's no rush."

"And I insist on paying rent."

Phyllis' mouth formed a straight, stubborn line. "Absolutely not. I won't take your money, so you might as well keep it in your pocket."

"At least let me pay for groceries."

"I'll think about it."

Phyllis' stubborn expression told her the answer would be no. Maggie crossed her arms over her chest. Two could play that game. "I'll pay for groceries, or I'll find a hotel room to rent somewhere."

"That's ridiculous! It would be too expensive."

"Those are my terms." Maggie lifted her chin a notch. "Take it or leave it."

Phyllis puffed out a breath. "Oh, all right. You can pay for groceries."

"And I'll help you with housework."

"Don't be silly. You're working all day. I'm at home with nothing to do and all day to do it."

Maggie raised an eyebrow, but said nothing. Finally, Phyllis shook her head and rolled her eyes once more. "Okay, fine. You can help with housework."

Maggie stuck out her hand. "In that case, I believe we have a deal."

Phyllis shook her hand. "You drive a hard bargain, young lady."

"What's this about a bargain?"

Reese wheeled Abby into the living room. She wore a bright blue wrap over a black turtleneck sweater and the familiar red and black plaid blanket across her knees. Despite the thinness of her face, and the dark circles under her eyes that spoke of fatigue and illness, her smile was warm.

Luke kissed his mother on the cheek. "Maggie's going to move in with Grandma for a while."

"That's wonderful!"

Reese nodded. "Sounds like a good solution. Maggie will have a safe, affordable place to live, and Phyllis will have someone to fuss over."

"I told her she couldn't fuss."

Reese laughed. “Good luck with that.”

“I think this calls for a toast. Luke, there’s some sherry in the cupboard above the stove and some sparkling grape juice in the fridge,” Abby said.

“I’ll give you a hand,” Maggie said.

While Luke retrieved the bottles, she found some brandy snifters for the sherry and wine glasses for the sparking grape juice. When she turned to look at Luke, his head was bowed as he leaned over the sink, his arms braced on the surface of the counter. Her heart constricted painfully. Without a word, she wrapped her arms around his waist and rested her cheek against his back. As with Reese, there was nothing she could do or say to make things better. All she could do was hold him and hope her presence gave him some measure of comfort.

Luke turned in her arms and pulled her against him. He buried his face in her neck and clung to her, while she held him and gently smoothed her hand over his back. Seconds later he pulled away, holding her shoulders in his big hands for a moment as he composed himself, his eyes downcast. Then, he sighed and let go. He put the glasses on a tray and carried it into the living room. Maggie followed him, willing herself to smile as if nothing was wrong.

Luke poured the sherry and the sparkling grape juice and handed the glasses around before lifting his in a toast. “To Grandma and Maggie. May you be happy roommates.”

“Hear, hear.”

Maggie watched Luke from under her lashes as she sipped her drink. He did a good job of hiding his feelings in front of his family, but losing his mother was taking a toll. If she could help him by providing a safe place where he didn't have to pretend his heart wasn't breaking, then that's what she'd do.

Once the toasts were done, Maggie and Phyllis excused themselves to put the final touches on dinner. Phyllis bustled around, checking pots on the stove that didn't need checking and rearranging table settings that were perfectly fine. Maggie knew keeping busy was her way of coping. She'd give her something to do.

"Phyllis, do you think we should have whipped cream with the pie?"

"Yes, I think that would be lovely. Abby loves whipped cream..."

Her voice trailed off. They both knew Abby was unlikely to eat much of anything. Maggie spoke quickly, not wanting her to dwell on her sadness. "I brought some whipping cream. It's in the fridge."

Phyllis' face brightened. "I'll whip it up. It'll only take a few minutes."

She set to work immediately, pulling Abby's electric mixer from the cupboard. By the time she'd finished, the potatoes were tender and ready to mash. Maggie drained the heavy pot and handed the masher to Phyllis. She pounded away at them as if they were the cancer in her daughter's body and she could obliterate it by sheer force of will.

If only it were that easy.

Maggie removed the turkey from the oven and set it on a large platter to rest while she made gravy. Once Reese carved the turkey, they'd be ready to eat.

Luke wheeled his mother's chair to her spot at the end of the table and then poured the wine he'd brought for himself, Maggie and his grandmother. He gave Abby and Reese more sparkling grape. After everyone sat, Abby lifted her glass, her hand trembling slightly.

"I'd like to propose a toast. To us, and the merriest Christmas ever. For this one day, let's forget about illness and remember how much we love each other and how much we enjoy being together. Reality will come back soon enough, but for today, let's forget. Merry Christmas."

The silence was deafening. Maggie should have known Abby would feel the tension all around her and know her family was hurting. Her cancer was the elephant in the room they couldn't ignore. They needed to address it head on. Maggie touched her wine glass to Abby's. "I second your toast. Here's to the merriest Christmas ever, with good food and good friends. Today, let's only think happy thoughts. On this happiest of days, I say cancer can go fuck itself."

Reese let out a guffaw and Abby laughed out loud. She covered her mouth with her free hand as it turned into a cough. But she was able to quickly bring the cough under control, for which Maggie was profoundly grateful.

"I'll drink to that," Abby said.

Reese lifted his own glass. Maggie hadn't seen a genuine smile on his face in some time. "I think that's a toast I can get behind."

Phyllis shook her head as she touched her glass to Reese's. "That's my roommate, potty mouth girl."

A fresh round of laughter erupted around the table. Sadness dissipated as if a window had been thrown open and a fresh breeze had blown through the house.

From across the table, Luke smiled into her eyes and lifted his glass to her in a silent salute. Maggie raised her glass and saluted back. As Abby said, reality would hit soon enough. For today, she wanted to play a game of pretend where everything was possible, like believing Abby could return to full health.

And Luke would want to stay in Minnewasta with her.

AFTER DINNER, THEY cleared the table and washed the dishes. Luke was pleased his mother felt well enough to dry a few dishes and to tell him where to store them, though she had to remain in her wheelchair to do it. Maggie turned on the TV once more and led them in singing out-of-tune renditions of the Christmas carols being played.

Thank God Maggie was there. If not for her, the day would have been gloomy and unbearable for all of them. Instead, she'd made it a fun celebration.

Once the dishes were done and the food put away, they gathered around the Christmas tree in the living room to open gifts. Luke distributed the packages, and his grandmother and mother were the first to dive in. Maggie hung back, as if she were content to watch the others open their gifts.

There were a lot of oohs and ahs and much laughter as the presents were unwrapped. Maggie seemed pleased and relieved that everyone liked the things she gave them. He knew how important buying the gifts had been to her. For his part, he loved the beautiful hand-knit sweater she gave him. It would provide much needed warmth on a cold winter day—

Once he returned to California, he wouldn't need such a warm sweater.

But if he stayed... Luke swallowed and closed his eyes. When Maggie discovered the truth about what he'd done, she wouldn't want him to stay.

With an effort, he pushed the thoughts from his mind. Today was for celebration, not to worry about the future. There'd be plenty of time for that tomorrow.

"You haven't opened any of your gifts, Maggie," his mother said.

"Open the one from me first," his grandmother said, pointing to a flat, rectangular box wrapped in bright red paper.

"Okay." Maggie slipped her fingers under the tape to open the paper, then opened the lid of the box.

"Oh, Phyllis, this is beautiful." She pulled a red knitted hat and matching scarf from the box and held it against her cheek. "It's so soft." She threw the scarf around her neck and modeled it for his grandmother. "I love it. Thank you."

His grandmother looked pleased. "You're welcome. I thought the red would look good with your coloring."

She was right. The red was the perfect contrast to Maggie's dark hair and eyes. She would look beautiful in it.

"Why don't you open the one from Reese and me next?" his mother said. Reese handed her another box.

"I could get used to this," she said with a laugh. Maggie carefully opened the wrapping paper to reveal a boxed set of knives. She stared at the box but didn't open it.

"The guy at the restaurant supply store in Minneapolis told me they were the kind of thing a professional chef would use. I hope he wasn't giving me a line," Reese said, sounding uncomfortable with Maggie's continued silence. "I can always take them back and get you something else if they're not what you want."

She lifted her head and looked at his stepfather, as a tear trailed down her cheek. "No, they're perfect, top of the line. I... I can't believe... I've looked at these knives for years, but I haven't been able to afford anything like them. I can't let you spend so much money."

"Nonsense. A good chef should have good tools," Abby said. "Use them and enjoy them."

"I don't know what to say."

Phyllis laughed. "You could start with 'thank you.'"

Maggie laughed through her tears. "Thank you. So much. You have no idea what this means to me."

She rose to her feet to hug his mother and Reese. His stepfather framed her face with his big hands and kissed her forehead in an uncharacteristic show of emotion. Maggie had that effect on all of them.

She stooped to give Phyllis a kiss on her cheek before taking her seat again. Phyllis handed her a tissue, and she blew her nose.

"I didn't expect the waterworks," she said, dabbing at her eyes.

"And you haven't opened Luke's gift yet," Phyllis said.

She turned to look at him, a half smile on her face. "Am I going to cry again?"

"I don't know," he said honestly. That hadn't been his intention. He only wanted to make her happy and give her some relief. He didn't want her to blame herself any longer.

He reached into his pocket and pulled out a small box, then handed it to her. She hesitated before unwrapping it, giving him a questioning look. His heart hammered as he waited.

"Hurry up! Open it already!" his grandmother said.

"Okay, okay!"

She ripped off the paper and then lifted the lid from the box. He heard her sharp intake of breath before she covered her mouth with her hand. Then, her shocked gaze lifted to his and tears filled her eyes once more.

"Oh-oh. The waterworks again. It must be something good," Phyllis said.

Everyone, including Maggie, laughed.

"Yes," she said through her tears, her eyes focused on his. "Very good."

Chapter Twenty-Three

MAGGIE COULDN'T BELIEVE he'd done this. "How did you find them?"

Luke shrugged. "I did some phoning around."

Not for a minute did she believe it had only taken a few phone calls to find her mother's antique earrings, the ones she'd had to pawn.

"What is it, Maggie? What did Luke get you?" Phyllis asked.

"Earrings." A tremor shook her voice. "They belonged to my mother."

"Then, how did Luke get them?"

A very good question. "I had to sell them to a pawn shop a few months ago. I...I needed the money." Emotion clogged her throat. He hadn't given any indication he'd been looking for the earrings. How much did he have to pay? She knew what she'd received from the pawnshop, and he'd have had to pay a lot more than that to get them back. More tears filled her eyes. Luke was the kindest, most generous man she knew.

"Can we see the earrings, Maggie?" Reese asked.

She wordlessly handed the box to him. Abby lifted one of the earrings and held it up to the light. "I remember Miranda wearing these. They meant a lot to her."

She and Reese exchanged a sad smile before he handed the box back to her. Maggie passed the box to Phyllis so she could take a look as well. Then, she lifted her gaze to Luke's. "Thank you. You don't know what this means to me."

"I think I have an idea."

Of course, he did. No one knew her better than Luke did, even though they'd been apart for ten years.

She went to him, kneeling in front of him and placing her hand on his cheek. She wished she had the words to express her gratitude. "Thank you."

His throat worked as he nodded. "You're welcome."

She leaned forward to kiss him. His lips were warm and sweet and welcoming, and she desperately wanted to deepen the kiss. But she was acutely aware that his family was watching. She contented herself by resting her forehead against his for a moment and breathing him in, revelling in the spicy, clean scent that was all Luke.

I love you.

With regret, she pulled away. He squeezed her hand as she got to her feet.

Maggie faced Luke and his family, her hands tightly clasped in front of her. "Thank you, all of you, for the beautiful gifts and the generosity you've shown me. It's been a wonderful Christmas day." Her smile wobbled. "I think I'm going to make hot chocolate before I start crying again."

She hurried into the kitchen, taking a moment to compose herself. She wiped her eyes once more. It had been a very good day, but bittersweet. No matter how she tried, she couldn't forget this was Abby's last Christmas.

Life was so short. After losing her parents and grandparents, she knew that better than most. But Abby's illness had really brought that message home. There was no time to waste with anger from the past. Life was for living, and she had to grab happiness with both hands and hold it for all she was worth.

"Can I help you with the hot chocolate, Maggie?"

The deep male voice surprised her. She turned to find Reese standing at the entrance to the kitchen, an uncertain expression on his face. Maggie gave her eyes one last wipe and stuck the tissue in her pocket. "Sure. Can you get the milk from the fridge?"

Together, they assembled the other ingredients – cocoa powder, sugar, salt, cinnamon, milk, half and half, and marshmallows. While Reese put the kettle on to boil, Maggie whisked cocoa powder with sugar in a pot, then added a pinch of salt and dash of cinnamon. Once the water came to a boil, she poured about a third of a cup of it into her cocoa and sugar mixture, stirred it and set it on a burner to heat.

"What else can I do?" Reese asked.

Maggie handed him a wooden spoon. "Here. You can stir till it comes to a boil."

She measured out the milk and the half and half and once the chocolate mixture began to bubble, she slowly added the milk while Reese stirred.

Reese lifted the carton of half and half. "What's this stuff? How come you use it instead of milk?"

"Half and half is half milk and half cream. The milk fat makes the hot chocolate richer and creamer. I think it tastes yummy."

"I didn't know you put cinnamon into hot chocolate," he said.

"I like a subtle hint of cinnamon under the chocolate. You might not like it as much, though."

"If you like it, I'm sure I'll love it," he said confidently. "You know food."

She chuckled. "We'll soon find out if you like it. Thanks for your help. This really is much easier to do with two people."

His smile was warm. "You're very welcome."

Maggie added the half and half. Then, she found five mugs in one of the cupboards and set them on the counter beside the stove.

"As soon as that's nice and hot, we can serve."

Before the milk mixture could reach the boiling point, she removed the pot from the heat. She added some vanilla extract, then began to pour.

"Can you top each cup with marshmallows, Reese?"

"Sure."

He stuck a couple of marshmallows into each mug. "Promise me that if you get into financial trouble again, you'll come to me for help instead of selling your mother's earrings."

Maggie spilled some of the cocoa on the counter, rattled by his words and the intense emotion in his voice. Her gaze flew up to his. "That's very generous of you, but—"

"Promise me, Maggie."

She blinked at the fervency in his dark eyes, not understanding why her promise meant so much. But she sensed its importance to him. "Now that I'm working with my family, I'm sure I'll never get into that kind of trouble again. But okay, if I find myself in a bind, I'll come to you."

Relief flashed across his handsome, weathered features. "Good."

"I appreciate your offer, I really do, but I don't understand. Why would you want to help me? We haven't known each other for very long."

"I know, but you've known Abby forever. You mean a lot to her, and Abby means everything to me."

Maggie averted her gaze, busying herself with pouring the rest of the cocoa. A wave of regret swamped her. Abby had tried to keep in contact with her over the years with cards and letters and phone calls, but she'd brushed her off. She'd let childish hurt and petty anger stop her from deepening her relationship with her mother's best friend.

And now it was too late.

"I think it's what your mother would have wanted as well."

Maggie looked up sharply. "My mother? What makes you say that?"

He cleared his throat. "It's what any parent would want, Maggie. Someone to care for their child after they're gone."

Phyllis called from the living room. "That hot chocolate is taking forever in there. You almost done?"

"Coming right up." Reese grabbed two of the mugs and left the kitchen.

Maggie hesitated a moment before following him. She didn't know what to make of Reese's out of the out-of-the blue offer. Until a few months ago, he didn't even know her.

Still, knowing she had friends who cared comforted her.

LATER, THEY BROUGHT out board games and played a couple of spirited rounds of scrabble. Around four in the afternoon, it became evident from the dark circles under her eyes that Abby's reserves of energy were waning. Luke kissed her goodbye and Reese and Phyllis helped her to bed. His heart ached as he watched them wheel her away. How much longer would she be able to hang on? His mother had been the one constant in his life, his rock. How was he supposed to live without her? He couldn't imagine not being able to pick up the phone and hear her cheery voice ever again.

Maggie slipped her hand into his and leaned her head against his shoulder in wordless support. He pulled her against him and kissed the top of her head. It was getting harder and harder to remember he was leaving soon and shouldn't start anything with her. With a sigh, he let her go.

"Let's put away the board game and clean up. Then, I guess we should go."

She nodded and helped him pick up the game pieces and put their cups into the dishwasher. As they finished, Reese and Phyllis emerged from the bedroom.

"She's already asleep," Phyllis said quietly. She turned to Reese and took both his hands in hers. "It's been a lovely day, but I'm ready to head home. This old lady has had it."

Reese kissed her cheek. “I don’t see any old lady here. I’ll get my coat and give you a lift.”

“No need, Reese. I’ll take Grandma and Maggie home.”

Reese nodded. Luke could see he was exhausted as well. He’d probably been sleeping almost as badly as his mother.

Luke pulled on his parka and went out to warm up the truck. When he returned, everyone was in the kitchen, and his grandmother was packaging up leftovers.

Maggie shook her head. “The lodge has a fridge full of leftovers, Phyllis. There's no need.”

His grandmother added dressing to the package. “You have plenty of people to feed over there.” She turned to Reese. “I’ll take home some leftovers and make turkey soup tomorrow. Abby might enjoy that. It used to be her favorite.”

Reese gave her a tired smile. “I’m sure she will.”

His grandmother and Maggie dressed in their parkas and winter hats for the drive home. Reese hugged Phyllis. “Goodnight. I’ll see you tomorrow.”

“You will. Make sure you get some rest.”

“You, too.” He turned to Maggie. “Thank you for all your work today. We had a lovely dinner and a beautiful Christmas day. I’m so happy you were here.”

She hugged him, and Reese wrapped his arms around her and closed his eyes as if he never wanted to let her go.

Luke knew the feeling well. He cleared his throat. "I'll see you tomorrow, too."

Reese let go of Maggie and nodded his head. "Your mother will be pleased.'

They left the house and drove the short distance to his grandmother’s house in silence. Maggie reached into the back seat to grasp Phyllis' hand as they arrived. "I had a wonderful day. Thank you for everything."

"It was fun working in the kitchen with you, dear," she said. "Let me know when you're ready to move in."

"I will. Goodnight."

"Goodnight."

Luke carried the turkey leftovers to the front door for his grandmother and made sure she got in safely. "Make sure you lock the door. I'll be home after I drop Maggie off."

She waved her gloved hand. "There's no hurry. Take all the time you need. In fact, stay the night if you want to."

Before closing the door in his face, she gave him an impish grin. Luke shook his head in amusement. His grandmother was definitely one of a kind.

Maggie said little on the drive back to the lodge, but her tension communicated itself to him. He glanced at her profile as she stared out the windshield. She'd seemed happy today, and she'd comforted him when he needed it. If not for her humor and positive energy, it would have been a very somber Christmas. They'd all been too aware this Christmas would be his mother's last.

He drove past the lodge and up the small incline to the cottages, driving by Ethan and Harper's cottage and coming to a stop in front of Maggie's place. He left the motor running.

"Would you like to come in?" she asked.

He looked away. "Thanks, but I think it's best if I don't."

"Oh." Disappointment made her voice flat and colorless. She reached for the door handle, her gaze averted. "Good night."

He touched her arm, stopping her. She deserved the truth. “If I go inside with you, if I’m alone with you, I won’t be able to stop myself from touching you. I’m not that strong. That’s why I have to go.”

She lifted her gaze to his, her eyes bright in the dashboard lights. “What if I want you to touch me? What if I want you to make love to me?”

His heart pounded. “I can’t promise you anything. I can’t promise I’ll stay more than a few weeks.”

“I know. I want you anyway.”

Desire exploded inside him. He turned off the ignition. “I want you, too.”

They rounded the truck and as they reached the front porch steps, he held out his hand to her. She clasped it and, smiling, they ascended the stairs together.

Chapter Twenty-Four

MAGGIE'S HANDS SHOOK as she unlocked the front door of her cottage. Luke stood silently behind her, his hand on her shoulder. The simple touch made her blood sing.

As soon as they were inside, he turned her and pulled her into his arms, his mouth descending on hers. She rejoiced in the way his tongue swept her mouth and tangled with hers, the way his arms pulled her tight against him, his hands kneading, caressing. *He wants me.* Maggie wound her arms around his neck, her body shaking with need. How she wanted him. She'd waited so long for him to want her again.

He'll be leaving again. Don't forget.

Maggie pushed the voice of caution from her mind. She didn't care what happened tomorrow. All she wanted was this moment with Luke.

Luke stripped off his winter coat and then hers and tossed them to the floor. They kicked off their boots and Luke lifted her into his arms, surprising her and making her laugh. Joy filled her heart.

"I'm liking the caveman routine."

He laughed and the sound warmed her heart. He was once again the boy she'd loved. *My Luke.*

He carried her to the bedroom and set her on feet. They undressed each other, their hands fumbling in their haste to touch warm skin. When they were both naked, Luke lifted her once more and set her on the bed. He laid beside her and skimmed his hand over her stomach.

"You're beautiful. Even more than I remember."

His kiss was full of need and promise. She whimpered as his lips left her mouth, but then he trailed kisses down her neck and chest, making her breathless. When he ran his tongue around her taut nipple, then pulled it into her mouth to suckle, a shaft of desire shot straight to her core. She pressed against him and revelled in the exquisite sensation.

With one last kiss to the underside of her breast, he moved his exploration lower. Excitement built, making her tremble. Wetness pooled between her legs as he kissed her stomach, then the inside of her thighs. Ten years ago, they'd explored each other with trembling hands. They'd been too innocent, too green, to experiment with oral sex. But now, with Luke, it was exactly what she desired. His tongue delicately licked the sensitive folds at the entrance to her body, and heat raced through her. She wouldn't be able to hang on long, even though she wanted to prolong the ecstasy.

He gently sucked, finding the spot she needed him to. Her orgasm was instant and overwhelming. She screamed his name, her body writhing on the knife-edge between pleasure and pain.

Pleasure won.

When the spasms slowed, Luke gave her one last lick that made her shiver and then rolled off the bed. Maggie pushed herself onto her elbows to watch him as he rifled through his discarded clothes.

"Please tell me you've got a condom somewhere in there."

He flashed her a wolfish smile. "I was a Boy Scout. We're always prepared."

"Yay for the Boy Scouts."

He pulled a condom package from inside his wallet. "Yay, indeed."

As he ripped open the package, her memory flew back ten years. She and Luke were in their hiding place in the forest, naked and shaking with need. They'd touched each other before, explored each other's bodies, but they planned to go all the way, the first time either of them had gone that far. Both were nervous, and a little scared. Especially Maggie. But she trusted Luke implicitly. He'd take care of her.

Luke had gone to Brainerd to purchase a box of condoms; if he'd bought condoms at the drug store in Minnewasta, the news would have spread all over town. He'd struggled with putting on the condom. In his inexperienced, shaking hands, the condom had refused to smoothly roll over his throbbing penis. Maggie had been transfixed at the size of him and when he entered her, there had been pain at first. But Luke had been so gentle, so kind, that the pain had gradually lessened.

Now, as Luke rolled the condom over his engorged penis with quick efficiency, she wondered how many women he'd slept with in the intervening years.

Maggie cursed herself for her doubts. Of course he'd been with other women in the last ten years, just as she'd been with another man. But he was here with her now, and the past didn't matter.

Maybe if she kept telling herself that, she'd actually believe it.

She pushed her doubts away and reached out her hand. He kissed the palm, then in one quick move straddled her. He hovered over her, his cock nudging the entrance to her body. Maggie arched her back, trying to get closer, but Luke remained out of reach, teasing her until she was wild with excitement and need. Suddenly, he plunged into her and the pleasure nearly forced her over the edge. For a moment, he held himself immobile, and they stared into each other's eyes. Beads of sweat dotted his forehead.

"I've wanted this for so long." He began to move, setting up a rhythm she followed eagerly. "I've dreamt of this."

"Yes." She'd dreamt of this, too. The dreams had lessened in frequency over the years, but they continued to have the power to wake her in the middle of the night, still had the ability to make her sweat and writhe and ache.

Luke's gaze became unfocused as his pace increased. Her hands roamed restlessly over his back and buttocks. Her climax hovered, teasing her with its closeness. And then, he reached between them and inserted his finger inside her. She came immediately with shattering force. A moment later, Luke shouted his release. His body shook from the spasms, and she held him close, never wanting to let him go.

But soon, she'd have to. Until then, she wanted him here, in her bed. Until then, she'd pretend they had forever.

LUKE WOKE WITH A START, disoriented and unsure of where he was. The only illumination in the pitch darkness came from the glowing red numbers on a clock beside the bed that registered five minutes after two in the morning. Then, the warmth of Maggie's body tucked up against his side reached him. Memories of the night flooded back. Tenderness filled his heart, his soul. Maggie had responded to him with such passion and total abandon that he was reminded of the way it had been for them the first time they'd made love, when they were kids.

Except, they weren't kids anymore. Maggie was an incredibly beautiful, desirable woman, and he wanted her with a passion that frightened him. He'd hurt her then, and he couldn't bear to do it again. But if he gave in to the desire pulsing through his blood right now and made love to her again the way his body was demanding, how could he not? He was leaving in a few short weeks.

Unless I stay.

Guilt and hope battled in his head. The only way he could stay was if he told her the truth about why he'd left ten years ago. Once she knew, he wasn't sure she could forgive him.

Luke closed his eyes. He had to leave Maggie's bed while he still could.

Carefully, he swung his legs over the side of the bed and got to his feet. He fumbled in the dark, searching for his clothes, remembering how they'd undressed each other in a flurry of excitement. He stifled a curse when he stubbed his toe against the frame of the bed as he pulled on his pants.

"Luke?" Maggie's voice was husky with sleep.

"It's all right, baby. Go back to sleep."

The sheets rustled and the bedside lamp snapped on, creating a small pool of light that illuminated her tense face. "You're leaving?"

He heard the disappointment in her voice, saw it in her eyes, even in the dim light.

"If I don't leave now, my grandmother will know I've been with you all night. Harper and Ethan will see my truck here in the morning, and they'll know we slept together."

"Harper and Ethan are staying in Minneapolis tonight, but even if they were home, it wouldn't matter. I don't give a damn what anyone thinks, not even my family. We're grownups now. We don't have to sneak around to be together like we did when we were kids." She lowered her gaze, her hands clutching the sheet to her breasts. "Unless you don't want anyone to know. Unless you'd rather not be here."

"Maggie—"

"It's okay, really." She looked away and shrugged a small shoulder. "It's no big deal."

He couldn't leave her like this. He sat on the bed beside her and stroked her hair. "It's a big deal to me. There's nothing I want more than to stay, but it wouldn't be fair to you."

Her eyes flashed in disbelief. "Wouldn't be fair to me? What are you talking about?"

"In a few weeks, after my mother is...gone, I'll go back to my job in California. And you'll be here."

"And never the twain shall meet?"

"It's not what I want, but it's reality."

"What about what I want, right here, right now? Maybe we don't have forever. Nobody does. If I've learned anything from your mother's illness, it's that we can't take anything for granted. We can't let uncertainty and fear stop us. If we only have a short time together, so be it. At least, we'll have had that time. I won't regret it."

She was amazing. She was still the strong, forthright, vibrant girl he'd fallen in love with that summer.

And he had loved her. Deeply. They'd been far too young to sustain a lasting relationship. But that didn't mean he hadn't loved her.

I still love her. I never stopped.

The sudden insight rocked him. When he'd left Minnewasta, he'd not only buried his guilt, he'd tried to bury his feelings for Maggie. But she'd taken up residence in a tiny corner of his heart and refused to leave. She'd been with him every day, even when he'd refused to acknowledge she was there.

Now he realized that whenever he'd tried to start a new relationship with a woman, he'd look inside that corner of his heart and remember, and he knew he was never going to love any woman the way he'd loved Maggie. No one could compare.

"Stay with me," she whispered. "Please."

He kissed her softly, a tremor of need racing through him. "I'll stay. If you want me to."

"I do," she said simply.

He let his hands glide over her satin-smooth skin. He wanted to explore her, to discover her body once more. He wanted to learn what made the grown-up Maggie sigh with pleasure and writhe in passion.

But Maggie had her own agenda and was as eager to explore his body as he was to explore hers. She slid down his body, kissing her way down his chest, his stomach, and then the inside of his thighs. When she took his cock into her mouth, his control nearly snapped. The exquisite pleasure of her warm, wet mouth surrounded him. Her tongue swirled and licked and worked his cock until he was on the edge of climax. He needed to be inside her. Now. With a growl, he lifted her head.

"Baby, stop, or this is going to be over real quick."

"We can't have that." She gave him a seductive smile as she reached for the condom he'd left on the bedside table, the last one in his wallet. "We can't have that at all."

She kissed her way down his body once more and rolled the condom on him. She then straddled his hips and impaled herself on his cock. Luke nearly exploded inside her. But the look of rapture on her face, the closed eyes, the partly open mouth, made him hang on to make their joining special for her. With a moan, she threw back her head and rode him. He was deep inside her, her inner muscles clenched around him. He reached up to palm her small, perfect breasts, rolling the nipples between his thumb and forefinger. She sucked in a breath.

"Oh, yes. Luke, it feels so good. It's been so long..."

Her body stiffened as her release came. He followed her immediately, his climax more powerful than any he'd ever remembered. When they both stopped shaking, Maggie folded herself over his chest, and he wrapped his arms around her, too spent to do much else. He loved this moment of connection with her, the feeling of skin on skin, his body inside hers. He held her a little tighter, not ready to lose this tie. Not yet.

Their breathing slowed and heartrates returned to normal, but they remained joined together. Luke couldn't have said how long. At last, Maggie began to stir.

She lifted her head and smiled down at him. "Wow."

Wow indeed. He tenderly brushed the hair from her forehead. "You're amazing."

"You're not so bad yourself." Though her voice sounded amused, he read an undercurrent of sadness in her eyes. She dropped a kiss onto the corner of his mouth before sliding off him. A chill immediately followed her departure, and Luke shivered as he covered himself with the sheet.

A moment later, Maggie returned from the bathroom and Luke pushed himself up to sit on the edge of the bed, preparing to go to the bathroom to dispose the condom. Maggie sat beside him and linked her fingers with his.

"This was different, wasn't it?" she said.

"You mean making love?"

"Yeah. I thought making love with you was wonderful when we were kids. But this was so much more."

Luke brought their joined hands to his mouth and kissed her fingers, his heart so full it threatened to burst from his chest. "Like you said, we're grown-ups now. We don't have to hide or feel like we're doing something wrong. And we have a little more experience."

Her mouth curved at that. "A little more. But I wouldn't trade my first experience with you for anything, no matter how awkward we might have been." She averted her gaze. "It was honest. At least for me."

He grasped her chin and made her look at him. "It was honest for me, too. Don't ever doubt that."

She stared at him, her dark eyes unblinkingly. Finally, she nodded. "Will you be coming back to bed, or are you going home?"

Luke's heart gave a painful kick. Even though they'd made love again, she still expected him to leave. But then, he hadn't given her much reason to expect anything else. "I'll be right back."

When he returned from the bathroom, she was under the covers, her eyes closed. Luke turned off the bedside light and slid into the bed beside her. He pulled her to him, her back to his chest, and she snuggled against him, her bottom pressing against his cock. It flared to life, but he willed it to behave. From the cadence of her breathing, she was nearly asleep. He kissed her hair and rested his chin on her silky head.

He loved her. That much he knew for sure. What he didn't know was what he was supposed to do now. Did he give up his life in California and move back here? Did he ask Maggie to move to Napa with him? Or did he stick with his original plan and leave after his mother was gone? His mind whirled in confusion.

Maggie had spoken of wanting him in the here and now, but gave no indication of what their future held. Or if they had a future. He had no idea what her feelings were for him. She'd always guarded her heart, even as a teenager. She'd never told him she loved him, and he'd hung back as well, afraid to be the first to say the words.

He'd hurt her so badly in the past. Maybe that hurt could never be repaired. And she didn't know the worst of it...

Luke held her a little closer as despair washed over him.

Chapter Twenty-Five

MAGGIE'S SENSES WENT on full alert as Harper stepped into the kitchen and asked, "Hey, need help with anything?"

Harper knew full well she didn't need help with a simple family dinner. "No thanks. I've got it under control."

"Good, good."

She prowled around the kitchen, examining jars of dried pasta, lentils and beans. Moving to the range, she opened the lid of one of the pots and peeked inside. "Something smells good. What are we having for dinner?"

"Exactly what I told you yesterday. Roast beef, mashed potatoes, green beans and a tossed salad."

"Oh. Okay, right. I forgot."

She wasn't fooling her for a minute. "Spit it out, Harper. What's on your mind?"

Harper turned to her with troubled eyes. "I'm worried about you. I've seen Luke's truck parked in front of your cottage the last several mornings. Has he changed his mind? Has he told you he plans to stay?"

Maggie moved to the sink, busying herself by washing lettuce for the salad. She couldn't look her sister in the eye. "His plans haven't changed. He's going back to his job in California."

"Honey, you know I love Luke like a brother, but it's not wise to get so involved with him. I don't want you to get hurt."

Scarlet entered the kitchen. "What's going on? Who's going to hurt Maggie?"

"She's sleeping with Luke."

"Harper!" Maggie spun around to face her sisters.

"Are you being careful? Using birth control?" Scarlet rubbed a hand over her small but growing baby bump. "If not, you too could develop an unsightly bulge like this."

"It's not funny, Scarlet. Luke isn't planning to stay." Harper turned to Maggie in alarm. "You *are* using birth control, aren't you?"

Maggie rolled her eyes. "Of course, we are. You gave me the birds and bees lecture when I was twelve. It stuck."

"I'm all for sex, Maggie, but I don't want to see you get hurt either." Scarlet laid her hand on her arm. "You're my favorite little sister."

"I'm your only little sister, you dork." Maggie put her hand over Scarlet's. "I'm perfectly fine. We're two consenting adults having an adult relationship. I went into it with my eyes wide open knowing that Luke's stay comes with an expiration date. Why shouldn't we enjoy each other while he's here?"

Harper folded her arms across her chest. "Because, I think there's more to your relationship than you've ever told us. Because, I think you're in love with him."

Maggie blinked and looked away. "I'm a big girl now, Harper. You don't have to protect me anymore."

Harper sighed, and when Maggie looked at her again, she gave her the same anxious expression she had when Maggie was sixteen and had done something stupid. "You know I love you, and what I want most in the world is for the three of us to work together, but if you want to go to California with Luke, you should go. I don't want you to feel obligated. You have to do what's right for you."

Maggie swallowed, her bravado slipping. She couldn't go to California because Luke hadn't asked her to. "This is where I want to be. I want to see the kitchen and the lodge succeed, and I want to be part of that success. I'm not going anywhere."

Harper nodded, not looking convinced. "That's what I want for you, too. But if you ever change your mind—"

"I won't."

Even if she wanted to change her mind, that option hadn't been presented to her.

JERRY FIELDS HIT A few keys on his keyboard, then gave Luke a satisfied nod. "That should do it. Your internal computer network and guest Wi-Fi are set to go. I've also added more security levels to keep anyone from hacking into your network."

"Thanks for your help, Jerry. I really appreciate it." He cleared his throat. "Will you be able to keep an eye on things here, help out with computer problems after I leave? I want to make sure things go smoothly in the future."

Jerry's smile slipped. "I was hoping you'd changed your mind about leaving."

"No. That's still my plan. I'll stay until..."

He couldn't make himself say "until my mother dies". The inevitability of that event stared him in the face every day.

"I know." Jerry nodded, understanding what he meant. "Please tell Abby she's in my thoughts and prayers."

"She'd appreciate that."

"The way I treated her is one of the regrets of my life. I should have been there for her, done more than give her money."

I should have been there for her. His father's words echoed his own feelings. For the last ten years, he hadn't been around for his mother or his grandmother.

Or Maggie.

"She doesn't hold you responsible. In fact, she accepts some of the blame for keeping us apart. She says she discouraged you from seeing me."

Jerry shrugged and shook his head. "She did, but I didn't protest too hard. If I'd pushed, she might have come around. It's on me."

Looking into his father's eyes, it suddenly occurred to Luke that Jerry wasn't the villain he'd made him out to be most of his life. He was simply an ordinary guy. An ordinary guy who'd made mistakes he regretted.

Just like him.

"Jerry, is that offer to have dinner with you and Denise still open?"

His father sat up straighter. "Of course. How about tomorrow night?"

He had to put old hurts aside. He and Jerry were probably never going to be close like some fathers and sons, but, with some work, they could forge a new relationship.

"I'd like that. I'd like that very much."

"I'VE BEEN THINKING," Harper said, lifting her teacup. "You were right, Maggie. We can't ignore what Willy told us. He caused our parents' deaths. It might have been an accident, but he lied about it."

"I've been thinking the same thing." Scarlet sipped her camomile tea. She'd sworn off caffeine for the duration of her pregnancy, so Maggie made sure to keep a selection of herbal teas on hand for her. "We have to defend our father's name. The media coverage might affect the business, but if we're forthright and come out with all the facts before the media jumps all over it, we'll be fine. Eventually, they'll move on to something else."

"You're sure?" Maggie asked.

Harper nodded.

Scarlet set down her teacup. "Yes, I'm sure, too. We have to do this."

"So, what happens now?"

"I asked Ethan to find a lawyer who can guide us. They'll know what we should do next."

Maggie nodded, relieved they were no longer on opposing sides. As long as they stuck together they'd be okay, no matter how tough things got. She'd let herself forget that truth but never would again.

LATER THAT DAY, LUKE quietly entered his mother's room and closed the door behind him. The sight of the hospital bed jarred him, even though Reese had told him he'd rented one. The bed was more comfortable for his mother because it could be raised or lowered, and the nurses found it easier to care for her in it. But it served as a reminder she was losing her battle with cancer.

Abby's eyes were closed and, at first, he thought she was asleep, but then she opened her eyes and gave him a tired smile.

"Hello, sweetheart."

"Hi, Mom." He kissed her forehead, inhaling her perfume. Even in her sick bed she insisted on wearing her favorite scent. He sat on the edge of her bed. "How are you feeling today?"

She waved her hand. "Oh, fine."

She never complained, not once. "I saw Jerry earlier today. He asked me to tell you he's thinking about you."

"That's kind of him."

"He says the biggest regret of his life is not doing right by you."

"Tell him he has nothing to regret. He gave me you and I'm very grateful."

"I'm going to dinner at his house tomorrow."

Abby grasped his hand. "Luke, that's wonderful! I'd so hoped you'd give him a chance to be your dad."

"Don't get too excited. It's only dinner." He set some magazines on the bed. "I thought I could read some magazine articles to you."

She grinned knowingly. He was changing the subject and she knew it. "That sounds nice."

Luke read some short articles, mostly about Hollywood stars. They laughed over some of the pictures and his mother shook her head over others.

"I hope they learn that family and friends are much more important than money or fame. You figure out what's really important in life you're dying."

Her words made his heart lurch in pain. His head knew she didn't have long to live, but his heart was having difficulty accepting it. He set down the gossip magazine. "I brought a National Geographic. I know how much you love the pictures. There's an article here about the Arctic I could read to you."

"Perhaps later. Can we talk for a minute?"

"Sure, as long as it's not about Jerry."

"No, not Jerry. I want to talk about you and Maggie. Now that the two of you are together, are you going to stay in Minnewasta?"

He was taken aback by her direct question. "What makes you think we're together?"

"Please. Have you ever known my mother to keep a secret? She says you haven't spent a night in her house in more than two weeks."

It wasn't exactly a secret they'd been sleeping together, but some privacy would have been nice. "We're not really together, Mom." He hopped off the edge of her bed and began to pace the small bedroom. "We haven't talked about the future past the grand opening of the lodge. Honestly, I don't know if we have a future beyond that."

"Do you want a future with her?"

He looked into his mother's red-rimmed eyes. Though now sunken from illness, they were the same vivid blue, still full of life. They compelled him to tell the truth. "I want that more than anything."

"Have you told her that?"

"No."

"Why not?"

She waited silently for him to explain. He'd never told her the complete story of his move to California so long ago, and he was ashamed to tell her now. "I did some things I'm not proud of, Mom. I don't know if Maggie will understand."

"Did you rob a bank or something?"

He laughed in spite of the ache in his chest. "You don't have to worry. I didn't do anything illegal."

"But you did something you consider immoral, like lying to her."

Luke looked away. "Yes." There was no point hiding anything from her any longer.

He sat on the edge of her bed once and made his confession, pouring out every detail and regret. Unburdening himself should have made him feel lighter, but instead he only felt empty.

"She loves you. If you tell her the truth, she'll understand. It might not happen right away, but eventually."

Luke wasn't so sure. And he wasn't sure Maggie loved him. But he wouldn't upset his mother with his worries. He reached for her hand. "You're right."

She grinned and for a moment she was her old self. "I know when I'm being patronized." She gripped his hand, her grin disappearing. "Don't lose her, Luke. I know she loves you. She has since you were kids. Trust me, first love is a powerful thing. It never leaves you."

"What do you mean?"

"Reese was my first love. I fell for him when I was a fourteen-year-old with braces. But he was nearly nineteen and crazy in love with someone else. It took him years to realize I was the one for him. But no matter what was happening in our lives, or who we were with, he was always in my heart."

He'd never heard this story before. "You fell in love with Reese at fourteen?"

"Yeah, like Maggie fell in love with you. But unlike you and Maggie, Reese barely knew I existed back then."

She closed her eyes, her head sinking into her pillow. His visit had depleted her energy. Luke kissed her forehead once more. "I'll let you sleep for awhile. I'll be back tonight for a few minutes."

She opened her eyes once more and clutched his hand, her strength surprising him. "Don't be afraid to tell her you love her. Love is worth the risk."

He nodded, mostly for her benefit. He didn't know if he had the courage to take such a monumental risk.

Chapter Twenty-Six

LUKE ENTERED THE LODGE'S kitchen and as his gaze connected with hers, Maggie couldn't help the warm glow of happiness that started in her heart and radiated throughout her body. Seeing him made her feel alive, and somehow *better*. She was a better person for loving him, as crazy as that sounded.

"It's official, ladies. Ten days to the open house and we're completely booked, including all the completed cottages and the hotel room where you're currently staying, Celeste."

Celeste grinned. "So you're throwing us out, is that what you're saying?"

Luke grinned back. "I'm afraid so. But don't worry. The suite in the event center is ready for you and Hope to move into. We've brought in the beds and other furniture."

Last week, Maggie helped Harper and Ethan move out of their cottage and into a three-bedroom bungalow in Baxter that they'd rented. She was excited that they'd also bought a piece of land near the lodge where they planned to build their forever home. As soon as Cam completed the rest of the cottages, he was going to design and build their house.

"We'd like to paint Hope's room before they move in," Maggie said. "We picked up paint in her favorite shade of pink the other day but haven't had a chance to do the job yet."

"Why don't you leave the paint with me? I'll get one of Reese's guys to paint the room. If we get the painting done today, you and Hope and can move in tomorrow, Celeste."

"It won't take us long. All we have to do is pack a couple of suitcases."

Luke nodded, then turned his attention to Maggie. "What about you? Can you be packed up by the end of the day? Grandma can't wait for you to move in."

"I think so. I'll start packing after lunch. Do you mind taking over in the kitchen for the afternoon, Celeste?"

"No, of course not."

"Thanks." She shook her head. "I'm going to miss that little cottage."

The soft smile in Luke's eyes told her he'd miss it to. They'd spent every night together there since Christmas, often making love, but sometimes simply talking and holding each other. The cottage was their little haven, a cocoon of warmth and privacy. They'd be together at Phyllis's house, but it wouldn't be the same.

Phyllis didn't strike her as the prudish type, but she hoped she wouldn't be offended by her and Luke sleeping together. Maggie's face burned with embarrassment at the thought. She told herself the same thing Luke had told her. They weren't kids anymore, and they weren't doing anything to be ashamed of.

Even so, Phyllis was Luke's grandmother and her opinion very much mattered to Maggie.

Luke checked his watch. "I'd better get going. I'll let you know as soon as that room is painted, Celeste."

"Sounds good."

He gave Maggie a kiss on the cheek, then smiled and kissed her on the lips. His kiss was warm and chaste, but held an edge of desire that made all her nerve endings sing. She wanted to lean into him, wrap herself around him. But it was the middle of the morning and they had work to do. She contented herself with brushing another kiss across his lips before letting him go.

After he left, Celeste quietly asked, "Has he changed his mind about staying?"

Maggie crashed back to Earth with a jarring thump. "No. Nothing's changed."

"Have you asked him to? Have you told him how you feel about him?"

She shook her head, unable to speak. She had tried, but she couldn't say the words. The idea of telling him she loved him filled her with fear, dread. Even in the solitude of her own mind, she couldn't explain why.

Maggie prayed he could feel her love.

THE NEXT MORNING MAGGIE sipped coffee at Phyllis's kitchen table. She stared out the window as fat flakes of snow drifted to the ground. Luke sat across from her reading the newspaper while Phyllis bustled around the kitchen, washing dishes, wiping counters, and sweeping the floor, somehow all at once. The little domestic scene made her smile. She was home.

Yesterday, Maggie had moved into the bedroom on the second floor next door to Luke's room. He'd come to her during the night, and they'd made love. They'd tried to be quiet, but after the solitude they'd enjoyed in the cottage, quiet wasn't in their repertoire. Fortunately, Phyllis's bedroom was on the main floor, which afforded them some privacy. Maggie had been relieved he'd stayed with her the rest of the night. She'd been afraid he'd find sleeping with her too awkward in his grandmother's house.

Neither of them spoke of a future beyond the grand opening on Valentine's Day. Maggie poured her emotions into their lovemaking each night, trying to tell him with her body the things she couldn't bring herself to say.

Last night, she'd bordered on desperate. She'd been wild in his arms, giving herself over completely. He'd been equally as wild, his hands and mouth and tongue bringing her to climax over and over. He'd turned her so she was on her hands and knees and entered her from behind, his fingers strumming the delicate folds of her sex till she exploded in orgasm. She'd had to cover her face with a pillow to keep from screaming down the house. The thought of Luke touching her so intimately made her tremble and burn.

"Would you like more coffee, Maggie?"

She blinked and looked up at Phyllis in confusion, her face as hot as her thoughts. "Um, no thanks, Phyllis. We should probably leave for work."

Luke folded the newspaper. "I'll start the truck."

Phyllis put her hand on his arm, preventing him from rising from his chair. "Reese phoned me early this morning. He said Abby wants to speak privately with Maggie today."

He exchanged a startled glance with Maggie. "Privately? Did he say why?"

Phyllis turned to Maggie. "Only that Abby wants to continue the story about her mother."

Luke turned to her. "The story about your mother?"

"Yes. Abby's been telling me things she knows about my mother and her first love, someone she knew before my father. We haven't had a chance to talk since before Christmas, but it seems important to her, so I want to hear what she has to say."

"Of course," Luke said with a decisive nod. "You can use my truck to drive into town."

"Thanks." She turned to Phyllis. "Did Reese say when I should come?"

"The usual, about one in the afternoon. That seems to be a good time for Abby."

Later, they said goodbye to Phyllis and got in the truck. As he turned the ignition, Luke asked, "What's this about your mother's old boyfriend?"

Maggie brought him up to speed on everything Abby had told her so far. "I don't know why Abby wants to tell me these stories."

"Mom usually has a reason for the things she does. Maybe today she'll let you know what it is."

A shiver of unease coursed through Maggie's bones. "Yeah. Maybe today."

The morning flew by in preparations for the Grand Opening. Around twelve-thirty, Maggie removed her white jacket and prepared to leave, frowning as she looked at the dirty lunch dishes lining the counters. "I'm sorry to leave you with this mess."

Celeste waved her hand. "Don't worry about it. Go see Abby. That's more important."

Maggie nodded and gave her a brief hug. Celeste was fast becoming her best friend. "I'll make it up to you tonight. I'll do all the clean up."

"It's a deal. I can hardly wait until the rest of the kitchen staff starts working, especially the dishwashers."

"In a couple of days," Maggie said as she headed to the door. "Just before the grand opening."

"It's gonna get crazy in here," Celeste said with a grin. "Drive safely."

"I will."

The roads were covered with a fresh layer of snow, but Luke's truck navigated them without a problem. She stopped in front of Abby and Reese's house and turned off the ignition. She gripped the door handle and for a moment, concentrated on calmly breathing in and out. Watching Abby's continued deterioration was more and more difficult, and today would be especially hard being on her own. In the past month, she'd visited Abby often, but always with Luke.

With one final deep breath, she left the truck and walked up the sidewalk to the door. Reese greeted her with a smile.

"Thank you for coming," he said, as he closed the door behind her.

"Phyllis said Abby wanted to see me alone today."

He nodded and hung her coat in the front hall closet. "She's in her room, waiting for you. Paula and I will be out here if you need us."

In the privacy of the hallway, Maggie closed her eyes and let out a breath, one hand on the knob. Then she forced herself to smile and opened the bedroom door. The head of Abby's hospital bed had been raised so that she was in almost a sitting position. She opened her eyes as Maggie approached.

"Hello, sweetheart."

"Hello." Maggie intertwined her fingers with Abby's and kissed her cheek. Her face was gaunt, the cheeks sunken, but her eyes were bright. "How are you feeling today?"

Abby lifted her free hand in a feeble wave. "I'm training to run in the next Boston marathon. How 'bout you?"

Maggie laughed, struggling to keep from dissolving into tears.

"What? You're not doing the Ironman Triathlon in Hawaii?"

"Not this year." She let go of Maggie's hand and patted the empty spot next to her on the bed. "Sit beside me, sweetheart."

Maggie did as she asked. "Reese said you wanted to talk about my mother again."

"Yes."

"Why didn't you want Luke to come?"

"You should hear the story first."

"I hope you don't mind, but I've told him the story so far."

"No, I don't mind at all." The corner of her mouth lifted. "You love him, don't you?"

There was no point lying to Abby, especially now. "Yes."

"Good. You two need each other. I don't want my boy to be alone. Or you."

Maggie nodded, for a moment unable to speak around the lump in her throat. Letting Abby believe they'd be together might be a lie, but if it made her happy, what did it matter?

She cleared her throat. "You were going to continue the story."

"Right. We should get started before I'm too tired."

Abby's waking and lucid hours were steadily decreasing. Maggie squeezed her hand in encouragement and waited.

"Did I tell you how Miranda met her old boyfriend again one summer, and he fell in love all over?"

"Yeah. That's where you ended. What happened next?"

"At the end of the summer, her old boyfriend begged her to leave her husband. He wanted her and the girls to live with him. Once she was divorced, they would marry.

"Miranda wanted to, but she was scared. After all, he'd left her once before. Would he do it again? Would she break up her family, tear her daughters away from their father and everything familiar to them, only to find herself alone again? She had a good life with Robert. Though she didn't have the passion she had with her old boyfriend, she couldn't ruin her daughters' lives for passion's sake. So, at the end of the summer, she went back to Robert."

"Okay," Maggie said. "So, she went back to my father and they had me nine months later."

Abby inhaled a shaking breath, expelled it, and then lifted her gaze to Maggie's. "Not exactly, sweetheart. Soon after she went back to Robert, she realized she was pregnant. They both knew the baby couldn't be his."

Maggie stared at her, her powers of speech temporarily deserting her. She shook her head. "No, that can't be right. Robert is my father."

"I'm sorry, sweetheart, but he's not. Miranda's boyfriend is. He was the love of her life."

Maggie shook her head. "No."

Abby gripped her hand. "Your mother and Robert tried to reconcile, but the evidence of her infidelity was in front of him every time he looked at you, and he couldn't get past it. They knew they couldn't make their marriage work any longer. And Miranda was still desperately in love with your father. She contacted her boyfriend to tell him you were his and then she brought you three girls to the lodge. The plan was for the four of you to stay there while her boyfriend found a place to live. And then Robert showed up at the lodge. Even though he agreed to a divorce, I think he must have changed his mind and wanted Miranda back."

"No!"

She let go of Abby's hand and slid off the bed. Everything she believed about herself was a lie. "No, this can't be right."

"It's the truth, Maggie. I swear."

"No!" She covered her ears with her hands as if that would stop Abby's confession. "No! I have to go!"

She fumbled for the door and wrenched it open. Blindly, she ran down the hall, needing to escape. Reese met her at the front door.

"Maggie? What's wrong?"

"I have to go." She grabbed her jacket from the closet and shoved her arms through the sleeves. "I can't...I can't stay."

"Don't go. Not like this. Let's talk about it."

She shook her head and reached for the doorknob. She couldn't talk, couldn't think. She had to get away.

He touched her arm. "Maggie—"

She didn't wait to hear what he had to say. She threw open the door and ran to Luke's truck. Turning the ignition, she stepped on the gas and raced out of town. She swiped angrily at her tears. *No more tears.* She was done crying.

They'd lied to her. The people who should have loved her best had lied to her – Abby, her grandparents. Was anything about her life true? Had her sisters known?

Her sisters. Dear God, were they really her sisters?

Maggie stepped on the gas and fishtailed on the icy road.

Chapter Twenty-Seven

WHEN LUKE'S PHONE RANG and he saw that Reese was calling, his heart fell into his stomach. *God.* Reese calling could only mean... He hesitated, unwilling to hear the words that his mother was gone. The phone rang again and he reluctantly hit the talk button. "Hello?"

"Luke, is Maggie there?"

"Maggie?" Relief poured through him. Then Reese's words registered in his brain. "I thought she was with you and Mom this afternoon."

"She left. There was some...upset, and she ran off. Can you check whether she made it back to the lodge all right? I've phoned Phyllis and she's not at her house."

Luke pushed his chair away from the desk and got to his feet, frightened by the alarm he heard in his stepfather's voice. "What happened? What kind of upset?"

Reese hesitated. "I think it's best if you talk to Maggie. Please, Luke. Check if she's there and phone me back right away. If I don't hear from you in ten minutes, I'm going out to look for her."

"I'll get back to you as soon as I can."

He ended the call and stuck his phone in his pocket. He ran to the front entry to see if his truck was in the parking lot, but there was no sign of it.

He ran to the kitchen, where he found Celeste icing a cake. "Celeste, have you heard from Maggie?"

"No, not since she left to go to your mother's house. What's wrong?"

"I'm not sure. My stepfather says she left after some sort of argument. I've got to find her. If you see her or hear from her, call my cell right away."

"I will."

He hurried back to the office for his jacket. *Please, please, please don't let anything bad happen to Maggie.*

He needed a vehicle, fast. Harper was working in the dining room, but he didn't want to alarm her, at least not until he knew what was going on. He found Ethan shovelling snow off the front step.

"I need to borrow your truck. It's an emergency." He gave him a brief account of his conversation with Reese.

Ethan stuck his hand into the pocket of his parka, pulled out a set of keys and tossed them to him. "Find out what's going on. Call me as soon as you can."

Luke nodded and sprinted to Ethan's truck.

Once he reached the main road, he didn't know which way to turn. Would she be somewhere between the lodge and Minnewasta? Or had she passed the lodge and continued up the road?

Something told him she'd need time to think through whatever his mother had said. He turned left, taking the road going away from Minnewasta, deeper into the forest and lake country. As he sped away, he hoped to hell his intuition was right.

His heart slowed its frantic pace when he found his truck parked in a lookout spot at the top of a hill overlooking a lake. The view of the lake was obscured since snowplows used the small parking lot as a snow dump. He pulled up beside her. Maggie was behind the wheel staring at the snowbank in front of her, the ignition turned off.

He called both Reese and Ethan to tell them he'd found her, then left Ethan's truck and slipped into the passenger seat of his truck. Maggie acknowledged his presence with a brief turn of her head. Then, she stared straight ahead once more.

"They lied to me, Luke. Everyone lied to me. Why would they do that?"

"Who lied, Maggie? What happened?"

She turned back to him, her eyes bleak. "Your mother, my grandparents, everyone who knew the truth. I don't know who I am anymore. Who am I, Luke?"

"Sweetheart, you're not making sense. Tell me what happened."

"Apparently, my father is not who I thought he was my whole life. Abby told me I was born of an affair my mother had with an old flame of hers. She says he was the love of Miranda's life." She gave a bitter laugh, the sound angry. "You want to know the funny part? Miranda and her boyfriend began their affair when she was fourteen and he was eighteen. Sound familiar?"

Luke's head whirled with this news. No wonder she was upset. "Yeah."

"My grandparents did their best to keep them apart. I'll bet they couldn't believe their bad luck when the same exact scenario happened with us. How fascinating that my story so echoed my mother's. I might have appreciated the irony if I'd known."

"I'm sorry, Maggie." He didn't know what else to say.

Her mouth twisted. "You know what else is similar? This so-called love of her life left her at one point. Isn't that amazing? Talk about history repeating itself."

Luke couldn't move and barely breathed. He was afraid to speak. Afraid that whatever came out of his mouth would be wrong. Afraid she would demand to know the truth, a truth she had every right to know.

"For ten years, I've wondered what I did to make you go away." She took a shuddering breath, her hands gripping the steering wheel. "You were everything to me. When I found you with that girl, and you told me you didn't want me, my heart was ripped from my chest. A part of me died that day."

Her anguish hit him like a physical blow. "I'm sorry, Maggie. I never wanted to hurt you."

"But you did. Why? And what are we doing now? Am I a convenient bed warmer until something better comes along?"

"No! You're everything to me, too." He caressed her cheek. "I love you, Maggie. I always have."

She pushed his hand away. "You love me? You've *always* loved me? How am I supposed to believe that? You tell me you don't want anything to do with me and then I don't hear from you for ten years. Not a word. No explanation, no 'How are you doing?' Nothing."

"I wanted to talk to you, to hear your voice. You don't know how many times I picked up the phone those first couple of years."

"Then why didn't you?"

Luke closed his eyes in surrender. He couldn't evade the truth any longer. She deserved to know. "You were right when you said history repeated itself with us. Your grandparents did their best to keep us apart, too."

"What do you mean?"

"After your grandfather found us together, he told me if I didn't leave you alone, he was going to have me charged with rape. You were underage and it didn't matter that the love we made was consensual."

She averted her eyes. "So you left for California."

"No. I told him if I left, you would follow me. You'd never believe I would abandon you."

Maggie lifted her gaze to his, her brow furrowing in confusion. "But you left. I don't understand."

"Your grandfather knew as well as I did that you wouldn't leave me, even if he sent me to jail. I was scared, but I stood my ground. I told him if he sent me to jail, you'd never forgive him."

"You're right. I wouldn't have," she whispered.

"Bill understood that, too. So, he dangled a carrot."

Her eyes turned wary. "What did he do?"

Luke swallowed, his throat closing. This was the hardest part. "He made me a deal. He said if I made you believe I wasn't interested in you anymore, he'd pay for me to go to school in California." Luke swallowed again. Aside from leaving Maggie, confessing the reason he'd left was the hardest thing he'd ever had to do. "I took the deal."

"You what?"

"I took the deal. I accepted money from your grandfather so I could get away from Minnewasta. So I could have a life."

She stared at him, first in disbelief, and gradually in revulsion as the truth sank in. "You sold me out."

"You know how it was for me here. If I'd stayed, I would have been Jerry Field's bastard son for the rest of my life. The bastard son of a bastard son. I needed to make a life for myself."

"So you sacrificed me to get it."

"I couldn't see any other way out!" Even as he said the words, he knew she was right. No matter how often he'd told himself they were both too young and he'd done the only thing he could, he knew he'd sacrificed her to get the life he wanted.

Except, the life he'd created had been empty without her.

She turned away from him, her hands dropping from the steering wheel into her lap where she clutched them tightly together. "I think you should go. I'll bring your truck back to the lodge as soon as I get my things from Phyllis' house. I'll stay with Harper and Ethan until I can find a place of my own."

"Don't do this. Don't hurt my grandmother because of me."

She closed her eyes and inhaled sharply as if holding back a torrent of emotion. "I'll talk to Phyllis. Once you're gone, perhaps we can be roommates again. All I know is I can't stay at her house while you're there."

He grabbed her arm, desperate for her to listen, to forgive. "Please, can't we talk about this?"

She jerked her arm away as if she couldn't stand his touch. "There's nothing to talk about. Please go, Luke."

The sting of her rejection cut deep. He watched her profile as she stared out the windshield, her expression as cold as the snowbank in front of his truck. She wasn't going to get over this. He squeezed his eyes shut, as if that could stop his world from crumbling at his feet.

"I'm sorry, Maggie."

There wasn't anything more to say. He opened the door and pushed himself out of the cab. Numbly, he opened the driver's side door of Ethan's truck and slid behind the wheel. He watched as Maggie put his truck into reverse and sped out of the parking lot.

Luke rested his head against the steering wheel. It was over.

ETHAN GENTLY TOUCHED Maggie's shoulder and she jerked in alarm, too deep in agony to notice he'd entered the living room. Harper held her tighter and stroked her hair in a soothing caress.

"Sorry, Maggie," Ethan said quietly. "I didn't mean to startle you. Scarlet's here." He turned to Harper. "I'm going out for a while, sweetheart. I'll be back later."

Maggie sat up and shook her head. "You don't have to do that, Ethan. This is your house."

He leaned forward and kissed the top of her head. The gesture was so tender, and so brother-like, it made her eyes sting.

"I think I do. Whatever's going on, you need to talk to your sisters about it."

He left the room, patting Scarlet's arm as he passed her on his way out. Scarlet walked toward her, her brows knitting together in concern. "Honey, whatever's wrong, we'll figure it out it. Okay?"

Maggie jumped off the couch and went to her, letting her sister wrap her arms around her and give her comfort. Until that moment, she'd kept the tears at bay, even as she'd said goodbye to Phyllis. She'd come to Harper's house with all her belongings, only telling her she couldn't stay in the same house as Luke. Harper comforted her and didn't pry.

But now there was no stopping the tears. She cried for her mother and for the man she'd believed all her life to be her father. And she cried for herself and Luke, for the life they could never have together.

"Oh, baby girl. I'm sorry." Scarlet led her back to the couch and made her sit. Harper held her close and murmured soothing words in her ear. Maggie cried until she was empty inside.

Scarlet stroked her hair. "I'm so sorry you had a falling out with Luke. You looked so happy together, I'd hoped he'd decided to stay. Is that why you argued? Because he's determined to go back to California?"

Maggie shook her head. Time for the truth. The whole truth.

She told them about the intense relationship she and Luke had had ten years ago, about his desire to go away to school, and how she'd learned he'd taken money from their grandfather to leave Minnewasta. To leave her.

"Oh, Maggie. I'm sorry you were hurt like this," Harper said.

"So am I." Tears shone in Scarlet's eyes. "I wanted you to be happy the way Harper and I are."

Maggie nodded and squeezed her eyes shut to stop the tears. She'd wanted that, too.

Harper linked her fingers with hers. "I know you don't want to hear this, but I think I understand why Grampa did what he did. You weren't even fifteen, and you were having a sexual relationship with Luke. Grandma and Grampa were trying to protect you. Their methods were heavy-handed, but I know they acted out of love."

Scarlet squeezed her arm. "And I can see why Luke took the money. Right or wrong, he saw it as his only chance to make something of his life. Luke was a little younger than me, but I remember kids teasing him in school about who his father was and how he'd deserted him."

Maggie knew all the reasons why Luke wanted to get away. But had lying to her, humiliating her in front of Cheryl Bradley, been his only choice?

Maybe later, when she was thinking more clearly, she could better understand his decisions. Right now, she had to tell her sisters the rest of the story.

"The day Grandma died was the day Luke told me he didn't want me. But I was determined to find him and make him see we belonged together. Grandma and I argued, and I said some horrible things to her. And then she had the heart attack. If I hadn't fought with her, if I hadn't threatened to run away—"

"Stop right there." Harper put up her hand. "You are in no way responsible for Grandma's heart attack. She was sick, Maggie. She'd had heart trouble for years, and she'd had a heart attack a couple of years previously. Another attack was going to happen whether you argued with her or not."

Maggie was shocked to learn about the previous heart attack, but it didn't excuse her behavior. "If I hadn't put her under so much stress—"

"Harper is right," Scarlet said. "You were a teenager trying to cope with a terrible situation. No one blames you, so stop blaming yourself."

Maggie wasn't sure she could ever stop blaming herself, but she was relieved to know they didn't hold her responsible. But even this confession wasn't the total truth. "There's more. Much more."

Scarlet put her hand over her belly as if to protect her unborn child. "All right. Let's hear it."

Maggie told them everything Abby had told her about their mother's affair, starting with the teenage love and the difference in ages that so mirrored events in Maggie's life. She swallowed hard as she came to the crucial part. "At the end of the summer, Miranda went back to Robert, but she discovered she was pregnant. With me. And both she and Robert knew he couldn't be my father."

Harper and Scarlet stared at her as the implications sunk in. Harper's lips moved but she couldn't seem to find words. Maggie swallowed and looked at her hands folded neatly in her lap. How odd they appeared so calm when she was churning with anxiety.

"So this means we're not real sisters," she said. Tears welled up in her eyes again.

Scarlet sat up straighter. "Not real sisters? What are you talking about?"

Harper gripped her hands. "This information changes nothing. We're sisters, period."

"But now we know we have different fathers. We're only half sisters—"

"I don't give a damn about fractions." Harper got on her knees in front of Maggie, squeezing her hands hard. "We're sisters. We've always been sisters and that's the way it's always going to be."

"That's right." Scarlet slipped her arm around her shoulders. "Nothing can change the sisterhood of the Lindquist girls."

"I don't even know what my last name is supposed to be. I ran away before Abby could tell me Miranda's boyfriend's name."

"You mean the name of your father," Harper said gently.

"Yes." She had difficulty thinking of this unknown man as her father.

"I have to admit I'm a little envious," Scarlet said on a sigh. "You have a chance to get to know your father. That's something not open to Harper and I."

"I don't even know if he's still alive. And if he is, why has he never come forward?"

Harper cupped her cheek. "You need to find out from Abby. She may be the only person who knows the truth."

She didn't need to add that time was quickly running out to discover the secrets that Abby had kept hidden for so long. Heaviness hung unspoken in the air, weighing down their thoughts.

Chapter Twenty-Eight

LUKE HANDED THE GUEST an envelope. "Here's your key card. Your room is down the hall and to your left, number one twenty-seven. Enjoy your stay."

"I'm sure we will. We can't wait to get out on the cross-country ski trails."

"We've had a lot of snow. The trails are in great shape."

The guest held his young daughter's hand. "Sounds wonderful. Thanks."

The little girl gave Luke an impish grin that made him smile. She had dark eyes and dark braids that hung beneath her knitted hat. She reminded him of Maggie...

Everything reminded him of Maggie.

He pushed down a lump of guilt and greeted the next group of guests in line. He, Harper and their new desk clerk had been working steadily at the front desk to check people in. Despite a few minor glitches, the grand opening celebrations were going well. The packed house meant every staff member was working flat out. The jury was still out, but it looked like the Lindquist sisters would make a success of the new Solace Lake Lodge.

He was happy for them, and proud of their accomplishments. It would have been fun to see this venture through, to be part of their ongoing success. But it wasn't to be. Maggie didn't want him at the lodge, and he couldn't blame her.

Thinking about Maggie made his chest ache. In the last few days, they'd only spoken about matters concerning the business. But despite their lack of communication, she'd made it perfectly clear they were over.

After he finished checking in another family, Harper quietly turned to him. "Reese is on line one, and he's asking for you. I think you should take this call in the office."

The bottom fell out of his stomach. He nodded briefly to Harper and left for the privacy of the office. He sat behind the desk, his hand shaking as he picked up the phone. "Reese?"

"Luke. Your mother is asking for you and Maggie. The nurse says...she says it won't be long now."

Luke bent his head, barely suppressing a groan. He wasn't ready. He'd never be ready. "I'll come right away."

"Please ask Maggie to come, too. I know how busy you all are, but seeing her once more is important to Abby. She can't rest until she does."

"I don't know if Maggie will come with me."

"Please, Luke. It's important that Maggie comes." His mother likely wanted to tell her the name of her biological father.

He squeezed his eyes shut. Maggie needed to know as much as his mother needed to tell her. "I'll make sure she does."

He hurried out of the office and past the front desk, giving Harper a nod. She nodded back, understanding and sorrow in her eyes. Luke wove his way past the guests filling the restaurant and bar and entered the kitchen. The room was thrumming with organized chaos. Maggie plated food with a quick, efficient hand while calling orders to Celeste and the two new line cooks they'd hired. Luke touched her arm.

"Maggie. Reese called. Mom wants to see us. He says it won't be long now."

As she stared at him, a rainbow of emotions crossed her face, each one speaking to him in silent words. He saw surprise, indecision, resignation, and finally sorrow and a touch of fear. Was she afraid of what his mother had left to say?

She turned to her sous-chef, her face bleak. "Celeste? I have to go."

Celeste understood immediately. She wrapped Maggie in a hug, then gave her a little push toward the door. "Go. Don't worry about us, honey. We'll be fine."

Maggie expelled a long, slow breath as she hung her apron on a peg near the door, then turned to Celeste once more. She looked so lost Luke had to clench his fists to keep from touching her. "I don't know when I'll be back."

"It doesn't matter. We'll take care of everything here."

She nodded before turning to face him. He could almost see the armour she was building around her heart, to protect herself from what she was about to face, or possibly from him. He squeezed his eyes shut against the pain.

"I'm ready."

They made it to his mother's house in less than fifteen minutes. Reese met them at the door and captured Maggie's hands in his. “Thank you for coming. I know this is not easy for you.”

Maggie only nodded, her gaze slipping to Luke’s. She was scared. Without thinking, he reached for her hand and was relieved she didn’t try to pull away. Instead, she held on tight.

Reese led them to the bedroom where Paula was taking his mother’s pulse. His mom looked frail and small in the hospital bed, like a tiny, wounded bird. She opened her eyes as they entered and, despite her weakness, managed a smile.

“My darlings.”

His throat threatened to close. “Hi, Mom.”

“Luke, my sweet boy. Maggie, dear, come sit beside me. Please.”

She did as his mother asked. “I’m sorry about running away before. I didn’t know what to do or what to think. Your news caught me completely off-guard.”

“I know. I’m sorry I had to tell you like that, but you needed to know. You deserve to know.”

“Yes.”

“Are you ready to hear the end of the story?”

Maggie’s gaze locked briefly with his. Then, she lifted her chin and smiled for his mother. “I’m ready.”

Luke had never been prouder of her, of her strength, her grace, her kindness. And he’d never loved her more.

Reese stood on the other side of the bed. “Paula, would you mind leaving us for a few minutes?”

“Of course, Reese. I’ll be in the living room if you need me.”

Paula left the room and quietly closed the door. Maggie reached for his mother's hand. "I'd like to hear the rest of the story, Abby."

"All right." She rested her head against her pillows. "Miranda and Robert tried to work things out when they found out you were on the way. I know they went to marriage counseling, but things got even worse after you were born. I believe Robert loved her very much, but the strain of knowing you were another man's baby was too much. You were a living, breathing reminder of Miranda's infidelity, and worse, a reminder that her heart belonged to someone else. Cracks began to form in the marriage and they argued constantly.

"It soon became obvious to both of them that they couldn't go on because the tension was beginning to affect Harper and Scarlet. So Robert moved out, and Miranda contacted your father and told him about you. He was overjoyed. He told her he didn't care that she'd gone back to Robert. The five of them could now be together as a family. There was nothing standing in their way any longer.

"Miranda was thrilled to finally be able to start a life with the man she'd loved for so long. She planned to leave Robert the house, so as soon as school was out, she packed up you girls and headed to the lodge. She had to tell her parents about her upcoming divorce and about Robert not being your father."

Maggie grasped her hand. "She never told Harper and Scarlet why they'd come to the lodge, did she?"

Abby's sigh was long and tired. "I tried to tell her keeping the girls in the dark was a mistake. But she wanted to wait until your father got to the lodge so they could tell them together.

"Your father was working in Ohio on a construction crew, and he moved back to Minnesota right away and started looking for a house near Minneapolis where they could all live. Miranda wanted Harper and Scarlet to be close enough to their father to be able to see him often.

"Unfortunately, finding a house took longer than he planned. Before he could take you away to your new home, Robert showed up at the lodge. I guess he had a change of heart and went there to try one last time to win Miranda back. And now we know the truth about what happened. He didn't kill Miranda. He loved her to the end and died trying to save her."

"And my father? What happened to him?"

"He was grief-stricken. He'd lost the woman he loved, and you, with one fatal blow."

"Is he...is he still alive?"

"Yes."

Maggie's throat worked. "Abby, can you tell me who my father is? Like you said, I have the right to know."

"Yes, you have the right to know." Her gaze flickered toward her husband. "Doesn't she, Reese?"

"Yeah."

In that one, barely audible word, Luke heard the pent-up emotion in his stepfather's voice. Maggie must have heard it, too. She lifted her gaze to Reese, and he reached out to touch her shoulder.

"I hope you're not disappointed, Maggie. It's me. I'm your father."

MAGGIE STARED AT HIM. All these years, it had been Reese. He'd known he was her father since she was less than two years old and he'd done nothing. Why hadn't he told her?

Abby's voice was barely a whisper. "I know you don't understand. You have to let him explain. Let him be your father. I've always known he'd be a wonderful father."

Her confessions had taken a toll. Her hand fell limply to her side and lines of fatigue etched grooves between her brows. Reese kissed her forehead and gently tucked the blanket around her. "Rest now, sweetheart."

Her eyes flickered open. "I love you, Reese. I've always loved you. My first love and my last."

"I love you, too, Abby." He caressed her cheek with a gentle hand. "You're the best wife, the best partner a man could ever have."

When Reese raised his head, tears streaked his face. Answering tears filled Maggie's eyes, but she wouldn't let them fall. She needed answers.

"Let's go into the other room and let Mom sleep," Luke said quietly.

Maggie and Reese followed him to the living room. Reese wiped his eyes with a tissue and addressed the nurse. "Paula, would you mind sitting with Abby for a while?"

"Of course."

As soon as she heard the door to Abby's room close behind the nurse, Maggie turned on Reese. "Why didn't you tell me? Where were you when I was growing up?"

"I don't blame you for being angry." Reese lowered himself into an armchair, his movements slow. "Please, Maggie, sit down and I'll try to explain. You too, Luke. You need to hear this."

She perched on the edge of the sofa cushion, too full of questions to relax. She wanted to shout at Reese, to demand answers. Instead, she folded her hands in her lap and forced herself to wait for him to speak. Luke sat next to her, his pale face telling her he was as shocked at this news as she was.

"I loved your mother very much, Maggie. Abby told you how we fell in love as teenagers?"

"Yes." She glanced at Luke. "Your story was eerily similar to mine and Luke's."

"I guess it was. Strange how history repeated itself." He closed his eyes a moment before continuing. "I never stopped loving Miranda, even after she went back to her husband. When she told me you were my child and that she was leaving Robert, I was ecstatic. We were finally going to be together, and we were going to be a family.

"And then I heard she was dead. I couldn't believe it. I went crazy. I drove to the lodge and demanded that your grandparents hand you over to me. Of course, they wouldn't. Miranda's will gave them legal custody of you and your sisters. In the eyes of the law, you were Robert Lindquist's child. And to be honest, I was in no shape to raise you. I was consumed by grief and anger and guilt."

"Why did you feel guilty?"

Reese scrubbed a hand across his face. "If only I'd come for Miranda and you girls immediately instead of trying to find someplace nice for us all to live. If I'd taken her away, she wouldn't have died."

"You couldn't have known what was going to happen. No one could," Luke said.

"I struggled for years before I realized that, before I could forgive myself. I spent nearly ten years trying to ease the pain with booze. I was no fit parent for you, Maggie."

"What made you finally get sober?" Despite her anger, she could appreciate what he'd gone through. She could understand, but she didn't know if she could forgive.

"Abby. About nine years after Miranda's death, she talked to my brother Glenn and he told her I was drinking myself to death. I happened to be working in Minneapolis, and she came looking for me. She didn't pull any punches. She told me to stop feeling sorry for myself and start living again. If I wanted a chance to be in your life, I had to get clean and sober. I had to rebuild my life.

"She got through to me. I checked myself into a rehab center. Once I got out of there, I joined Alcoholics Anonymous and worked hard on staying sober. It was tough, but I always knew Abby was only a phone call away. She was a friendly shoulder to lean on, someone to listen to my problems. She never wavered in her support, but she wouldn't let me wallow in self-pity either. Gradually, I fell in love with her."

"She told me you were her first love," Luke said. Maggie turned to look at him in surprise. "She said she'd loved you since she was a girl."

"Yeah." Reese smiled in remembrance, closing his eyes briefly. "She told me the night I asked her to marry me. I had no idea. I'd been so in love with Miranda all those years ago I hadn't noticed anyone else. While your mother was alive, Abby avoided me, even though Miranda was married to Robert. She was wracked by guilt because she was in love with the man her best friend loved. After Miranda died, she felt even worse, as if she was somehow responsible for her death because of her feelings for me. Abby was completely loyal to the people she loved.

"She probably wouldn't have sought me out if Glenn hadn't told her about my drinking. But she wanted to help. And she continued to help me, right to the end. She insisted on being the one to tell you I'm your father because she thought it would be easier for both of us if she gave you the news." A smile trembled on his lips. "I've been privileged to love, and be loved, by two incredible women. I'm a very lucky man."

Maggie swallowed back her tears. But she still had unanswered questions. "Why didn't you come to see me once you got sober?"

"I tried. When you were about thirteen, I came to see your grandparents while you were at school. I wanted the two of us to get to know each other, and I wanted you to know I was your father. I didn't ask for custody or anything like that because I didn't want to take you away from your sisters and everything you'd known. But your grandparents wouldn't hear of it. They forbade me from seeing you and threatened to tell you I'd caused your mother's death if I tried to contact you. I was afraid they'd make you and your sisters hate me, so I backed off. I'm sorry I did that now.

I should have fought them. But they were getting old, and they'd already lost so much."

"So you had Abby step in to keep tabs on me in your place." Anger and sorrow and regret for all the wasted years swirled in her head. Maggie didn't want to be angry with Abby, especially now. But she'd kept the truth from her for years.

"That was all Abby," Reese said with a fond smile. "She was your friend because she loved you. Things got very complicated for her when the two of you got together."

Maggie glanced at Luke. Abby must have been torn between her love for her son and her desire to care for her. She took a shaky breath. All those times she'd gone to Abby for comfort and solace, all the confidences she's shared with her. Abby had never judged or been disappointed in her, no matter what she'd done. She'd always tried to be her friend, no matter what. Love for Abby swamped her.

"If you wanted to see me so badly, why did you and Abby move away when you got married?"

"By then, I had a construction business established in Minneapolis. And frankly, living so close to you without being allowed to talk to you was hard. I reached out to your grandfather again after your grandmother died, but he was as adamant as ever that I should stay away from you. I thought it would be best to leave things alone until you were an adult and could make up your mind about me for yourself. I'd hoped that through your relationship with Abby, I could maintain a kind of contact with you."

Maggie glanced down at her hands. "But then I cut Abby off because I was angry she'd left me. I thought she'd abandoned me, like so many other people abandoned me."

Luke placed his hand on her shoulder and squeezed. Whether he was trying to apologize for abandoning her or lend support, she didn't know. Despite her lingering anger with him, she didn't push him away.

"Abby never gave up on me. She continued to write to me all those years, even though I didn't write back. I was angry with her, but I always looked forward to her letters."

"If I had to do it over, I would have stayed here in Minnewasta and tried to get to know you. That was one of the many mistakes I've made, Maggie." Reese sank against the cushions of his chair. "When we found out Abby's cancer was terminal, she wanted to come home and bring all the secrets out into the light. She wanted you to know the truth."

The truth. Lately the truth had been hitting her like a tsunami. First Willy's confession, then learning Robert Lindquist wasn't her father, and now discovering that Reese was. But most of all Luke's bombshell. Truth upon truth piled on her until she couldn't breathe. She wasn't sure she could handle much more.

She got to her feet. "I need to get back to the lodge. I'm sure the kitchen is swamped."

Luke also rose. "I should get back, too."

Maggie nodded at him, not quite meeting his eyes. Luke's truth had hit her hardest of all. It hurt so much to know he'd taken her grandfather's money to leave her. And he said he loved her, had always loved her. She had no idea what to do with that declaration. After so many lies, she didn't think she could start believing him now.

Reese walked them to the door. “I hope some day you can forgive me, Maggie. I hope we can forge some kind of relationship from all the pain we’ve been through.”

She nodded, not certain how to respond. She needed time to process everything she’d learned.

Reese put his hand on Luke’s shoulder. “It won’t be long now.”

Maggie swallowed and closed her eyes, knowing he was referring to Abby. Time was a luxury she didn’t have.

Chapter Twenty-Nine

HIS MOTHER DIED TWO days later. In the end, her passing was peaceful and with little pain, for which Luke was grateful. He and Reese and his grandmother had taken turns sitting with her around the clock. Maggie joined them often, spelling them off and bringing them food. Together, they watched his mother's life force slowly ebb from her body. Her lucid moments gradually became fewer and fewer but at one point, while he was alone in the room with her, she opened her eyes and looked directly at him.

"Don't ever forget. Love is worth the risk."

They turned out to be her last words to him, words he would never forget.

Abby had made all the arrangements for her own funeral during her illness. Right until the end, she'd tried to make things easier for the people she'd left behind. But then, that was his mom.

On the day of the funeral, the clouds cleared and the sun shone brightly, though the temperature was frigid. Luke moved through the day like a sleepwalker. Through the ordeal of the service itself, and the bitter cold of the internment, he watched the proceedings as if from a distance, feeling like his spirit had left his body the way his mother's had. The only thing that kept him grounded was having Maggie nearby. She stood beside him at the graveside and though she said very little, her presence comforted him.

Abby had arranged for a luncheon to take place in the church basement after the internment, and the whole town showed up. Friends, acquaintances, neighbors and former co-workers of his mom's stopped by his table to pay their respects and offer condolences. He and Reese and his grandmother murmured their thank yous and listened to their reminiscences about Abby. She'd been universally loved by everyone. He appreciated their sympathy, but all Luke wanted was for the day to end.

Jerry Fields and his wife approached their table, Denise carrying a small bundle in her arms. Jerry said a few words to Reese and his grandmother and then turned to Luke. "I'm so sorry. Abby was a wonderful person and wonderful mother. She was taken from you too soon."

"Yes, she was." His throat closed. He couldn't believe she was gone.

Luke cleared his throat. He needed to talk about something, anything, before he broke down in tears. He turned his attention to Denise. "You've had your baby. Congratulations. Boy or girl?"

"Girl. Jerry is getting outnumbered by females in our house."

Jerry put his arm around her shoulders. "I couldn't be happier about it."

Denise adjusted the bundle in her arms. "Would you like to meet your new baby sister, Luke?"

He blinked, taken aback by her words. Of course he knew Jerry's children were his half-siblings, but somehow hearing it put that way made it real. "Sure."

Denise pulled back a blanket so he could get a better look at the sleeping baby. Her features – miniature nose, tiny fingers, rosebud mouth—were perfect and beautiful. He touched her blonde hair with one finger, the texture as soft as down.

"She's beautiful," he murmured. "What's her name?"

"Grace Marie, after my mother. Emily was named after Jerry's Mom."

Luke looked up at Jerry, suddenly aware that he knew nothing about his heritage on his father's side. He hadn't even known his grandmother's name.

"I hope you'll come for dinner again soon. We so enjoyed having you over, and so did Emily. She's been asking about her big brother ever since you were at our house. You can bring a friend if you'd like."

He immediately thought of Maggie. She'd get a kick out of meeting his baby sisters...

Maggie didn't want to go anywhere with him.

"Thanks, but I don't know how long I'll be staying in Minnewasta."

Denise's face fell. "Oh. I thought you were staying to work at the lodge. Jerry was so hoping..." She glanced at her husband and then turned back to Luke with a forced smile. "All the more reason for you to come to dinner soon."

She was right. "I'll call you in a day or two, Denise. I promise."

The smile she gave him was more genuine this time. "That's good. Family needs to stick together in moments like these."

Luke nodded, unable to respond.

Jerry clapped him on the shoulder. "We need to get the baby home. Goodbye, son. We'll talk to you soon."

Luke watched them leave. *Family*. He had co-workers and a few good friends in California, but no one he could call family. Losing his mother taught him how precious family was. Did he really want to live so far from the family he had left?

The crowd began to thin out, and Harper and Maggie approached their table. Harper held out her hands to Reese. "We're going to miss her terribly."

Reese nodded, a wan smile on his lips. "We are."

"Once everyone leaves, would you all like to come out to the lodge? We're having a family dinner and we'd like you to join us. We've closed the dining room to the public for the evening, so we'll have privacy."

Reese glanced at him and his grandmother. Phyllis gave a tired nod. "That sounds lovely, Harper. I don't think I'm ready to be alone yet."

Luke reached for her hand and squeezed. He wasn't ready either.

"Ethan and Maggie and I are heading off now. Come out whenever you're ready."

"Thank you."

As Harper said goodbye, Maggie's gaze met his. Apart from the sadness he saw in her eyes, he couldn't read her. He wished he knew what her feelings for him were. Had he ruined any chance of a relationship with her? He had no idea.

After the last mourners left the church basement, he drove his grandmother and Reese to the lodge in his truck. Harper and Scarlet met them at the door with warm hugs. Scarlet looped her arm through his as they headed into the dining room.

"Where's Tessa?" he asked.

"She's having dinner with Celeste and Hope in their apartment. Celeste thought it might be easier for her than being with us tonight. We're all in a somber mood."

He sighed. "That's true."

"Maggie's busy in the kitchen preparing dinner, or she would have greeted you herself."

Luke wasn't so sure about that. He didn't know if she even wanted him here. "Really?"

"Yes, really. She insisted on cooking dinner herself. She wouldn't let me or Harper or even Celeste help. I guess it's her way of working through her grief." She tightened her hold on his arm. "Give her time, Luke. So much has happened in the last few weeks. It's shaken all of us, but Maggie got the brunt of it. Her world's been turned upside down. And then there's you."

"Yeah." The things he'd told her about the past had delivered her a heavy blow.

A fire was roaring in the dining room fireplace, lending a welcome warmth to the room. Ethan and Cam were setting the table closest to the fire. Ethan stepped forward to shake his hand. "I'm glad you came, Luke. Do you think we could have a quiet word after dinner?"

"Yeah, sure." He probably wanted advice on how to proceed once he left.

There was nothing holding him in Minnewasta any longer. He could go back to California whenever he wanted to.

But did he want to?

All the reasons he'd stayed away from Minnewasta for so long seemed meaningless. There was nothing left to hide. No secrets to maintain. He was beginning to forge a relationship with his father now, and he'd like to get to know him and his family. And he couldn't imagine leaving his grandmother or Reese. They needed him.

Maggie. He definitely needed her, but he didn't think she had anything left for him.

As if he'd summoned her, Maggie appeared in the dining room carrying a platter with a roast chicken. Their gazes met and held a moment before she looked away to set the platter on the table. She turned to his grandmother. "Phyllis, I could use a hand. Would you mind carving the chicken?"

His grandmother's expression brightened. "I'd love to."

Maggie could handle dinner preparations on her own, but she understood Phyllis needed to be useful and busy, especially today. Luke shot Maggie a grateful smile. She simply nodded and headed back to the kitchen. He watched her leave, his heart heavy. He missed the easy relationship they'd established while working together. He missed her, in his bed and in his life.

Harper touched his arm. "She'll come around."

He nodded, hoping she was right.

Dinner was somber. Conversation centered on the success of the lodge's grand opening and events planned for the upcoming months. But, even though no one mentioned it, Abby's death weighed heavily in their thoughts. Luke felt her loss like a stone pressing against his heart.

After dinner, everyone pitched in to clean up and put leftovers away. Maggie made hot chocolate and they sat in the lounge to drink it.

Ethan turned to him. "I'd like to have that word with you now. Can you join me in the office?"

"Of course."

As soon as they reached the office, Ethan quietly closed the door. "I'm not going to beat around the bush. Not today of all days. Harper and I want you to stay on permanently as our manager. I think we all work together well, and we make a hell of a team. We need you."

Ethan named a figure that exceeded his salary in California. Luke shook his head. "I don't know what to say."

"Maybe we don't have everything that California has to offer, but we have one thing it can't give you – family."

"You're not playing fair."

"Probably not, but that's because we want you to stay. Is there anything about the job that's causing you to hesitate? Because if there is, we can work it out."

"No, there's nothing. I'd like to be a part of making the lodge a success, but..." He couldn't finish.

"You're not sure about Maggie."

"I can't stay here if she doesn't want me to."

"Have you talked to her?"

"No, at least not about us. I don't even know if there is an us." Unsure if Maggie had told her brother-in-law, he came clean with Ethan about taking money from Maggie's grandfather to leave.

"You were both so young. Maggie's not unreasonable. Eventually, she'll understand you did the only thing you could."

"Understanding and forgiving are two different things."

One was done with the head and the other with the heart. Even if she came to understand, she may never feel the same way about him again. He believed she'd loved him years ago, though she'd never told him. How he wished he could look into her heart and know her feelings now.

"Do you love her?" Ethan asked.

There was no point denying it. "Yes."

"Have you told her?"

"No."

"What are you waiting for? I almost lost Harper because I waited too long to tell her the truth about my life and my feelings for her. I can't imagine living without her now."

"What if she doesn't feel the same way?"

"Then, you'll know for sure. I think Maggie is worth taking that risk."

Luke heard his mother's voice in his head, encouraging him to step to the edge of the precipice and jump. *Love is worth the risk.* He would need all of his courage to take that leap of faith.

MAGGIE WATCHED LUKE follow Ethan out of the dining room. She didn't need a crystal ball to predict her brother-in-law was trying to convince Luke to stay. He'd be an asset to the lodge, a necessary piece of the puzzle for its success.

Longing swamped her. How she wanted him to stay. If only they could go back to before she knew he'd accepted money to leave her.

But she did know. She honestly didn't think she could trust him. If she gave him her whole heart once more, he might leave her in the future. How many times could she love and lose? She couldn't bear the pain of being left behind again.

Too restless to play what-if games with herself, she refilled cups of hot chocolate with the carafe she'd brought from the kitchen. When she approached Reese, who sat off by himself near the fireplace, he declined. Instead, he patted the seat beside him.

"Do you think we can talk for a moment?"

"Sure." Maggie set the carafe on a side table, then sat beside him and folded her hands in her lap. Nerves made her heart race. Though she'd known Reese for months, it was like meeting him for the first time.

In a way, she was. For the first time, she was learning about him as her father.

"I wanted to say I'm sorry for not telling you the truth long ago."

"I had a good life, with grandparents and sisters who loved me, so I don't regret anything. But it would have been nice to know I had a father who cared about me." She sighed. "I wish my grandparents had let me get to know you."

"That's on me. I should have found a way. The truth is, I was afraid."

That surprised her. "Afraid? Why?"

He swallowed and lifted his gaze to look in her eyes. "I was afraid to be a disappointment to you. I still am. I've had my share of demons, Maggie. Depression, alcoholism, hopelessness."

She laid her hand on his. "But you've overcome those things."

He put his callused hand on top of hers. "For the most part. That was Abby's doing. She was all sunshine. She came into my life and swept away the gloom."

Maggie smiled, though her heart ached. "She did that for all of us. She was a remarkable person."

"She certainly was."

"What was my mother like, Reese? I mean, what was she *really* like? My grandparents only told me things they thought I should know, and my sisters were children when she died. They knew her as a mother, not as a woman. Tell me about her."

He smiled sadly. "Miranda was one of a kind. She was determined, headstrong, ambitious, and smart as a whip. But she was also the kindest person I'd ever known. She wasn't afraid to stand up to bullies or to speak up for what she believed. She was a lot like you."

"Like me?" His words stunned her. "I'm not sure I'm any of those things."

"Yes, you are. You're your mother's daughter." Reese looked at their joined hands. "That picture that Luke found of you with your mother? Miranda had that taken for me. She told me you were mine, and I sent her the earrings through Abby. They'd been my mother's, and Miranda knew they were special to me. I was so damn thrilled you were my baby."

Maggie couldn't speak around the lump in her throat, so she nodded and clutched his hands tighter.

"When you were fourteen, Abby told your grandmother she'd given the earrings to Miranda as a gift when you were born, and she wanted you to have them."

She gave a laugh that teetered on the edge of tears. "She must have been pretty convincing. Grandma Dorothy could sniff out a lie from a mile away."

One corner of Reese's mouth turned up. "I'm glad Luke was able to get them back for you."

"Yes, so am I. I'm sorry I lost them. I didn't want to pawn them, but—"

"It's okay, sweetheart. I understand. Remember what I told you. If you're ever in trouble again, come to me. You're not alone anymore."

Hearing those words was like a balm to her soul. "Thank you. You're not alone either, Reese."

He shook his head, his mouth trembling. "Losing Miranda was unbelievable agony. And now losing Abby...I don't know what I'm going to do without her."

"I know how difficult it's going to be. But she'd want you to have a good life. She'd want you to be happy."

"She wanted all of us to be happy. Especially you and Luke."

Maggie looked away, her eyes stinging. "I don't know if there's a me and Luke."

"If you're angry that he accepted money from your grandfather to leave town, you need to put it behind you."

"You knew about that?"

He nodded. "Abby told me. We had no secrets between us. That's what made our relationship so special."

"Luke and I have nothing *but* secrets between us." She heard the bitterness in her voice.

"Then you both have to lay out all your cards and tell each other what you really want and how you feel." He squeezed her hands again. "Try to put yourself in Luke's position. Considering your age, what else could he have done?"

Maggie looked into deep brown eyes so similar to her own. Maybe he was right. Maybe she was being selfish and childish. But she'd been hurt badly by Luke's actions, and she wasn't sure the wound had completely healed, no matter how much she loved him. "It's not easy for me to tell people how I feel."

"I understand. It's never been easy for me either. I guess it's a trait we share." He patted her hand before releasing it. "I hope...I hope eventually we can be friends, Maggie."

"I'd like that, too." Longing overwhelmed her. She wanted to know him, to know her history and her heritage, but mostly she wanted to belong. For the first time, she had a chance to know a parent. "But what I really need is a Dad."

Reese nodded as his eyes filled with tears. “Say the word. I’m all yours.”

Chapter Thirty

LUKE DREW IN A FORTIFYING breath before knocking on the door of Ethan and Harper's rented house. He was taking a big chance. Ethan had told him Maggie would be home today on her day off, but Luke wasn't sure she'd want to see him. In the five days since the funeral, he and Maggie had been scrupulously polite to each other, but had managed to say very little.

He needed honesty. And he needed to know where he stood.

Maggie answered the door, and he noted the way her eyes widened in apprehension. "Luke, hi. What are you doing here?"

Not exactly the welcome he'd been hoping for. "I came to talk to you. Can I come in?"

She stepped aside. "Of course, come in. It's cold out there."

As she closed the door behind him, she wrapped her sweater a little more securely around herself as if fending off the cold. Or protecting herself. From him.

The thought made his stomach lurch.

"Can I make you some coffee?"

Luke pulled off his knitted hat. "No, thanks. I came because I wanted to talk to you in private. I think we have some things to say to each other."

"I see." She averted her gaze. "Do you mind if I make myself tea?"

"Sure. Go ahead."

Maggie looked relieved to have something to do rather than talk. As she filled a kettle with water, Luke pulled off his coat and tossed it over one of the kitchen chairs and took a seat. She moved around the kitchen like a dancer, totally in tune with her surroundings, belonging there, even though she'd only lived in the house a short while. He smiled when he noticed her bare feet. As a girl, she'd loved to go without her shoes. Some things didn't change.

Like his love for her.

"Ethan asked me to work permanently at the lodge. He made me a very generous offer."

Her hand trembled and her shoulders bunched with tension as she spooned loose tea leaves into a pot. "Ethan told me he wanted to ask you to stay. What did you say?"

"That I'd have to talk to you before I could make a decision."

"You don't need my permission. I told Ethan that."

"I think I do."

She carried a small teapot and cup to the kitchen table and set them down carefully before taking the seat across from him. Finally, she looked at him, her dark eyes wary. "Is staying in Minnesota what you really want to do? Honestly? I love Minnewasta, but I know it's not the Napa Valley."

"I want to stay. Reese and Grandma need me."

"I know you want to be here for them, but what about you? You have to be happy, too."

"I will be. It's truly what I want. I need my family right now."

Her brows knit together and he got the feeling his answer disappointed her. "If that's what you want, then you should stay."

"I have to know how you feel about me staying."

"What do you want me to say, Luke?"

That you love me, and you don't want me to go. "I can't take the job if working with me makes you...uncomfortable. I'm sorry I hurt you. I don't want to make you unhappy, Maggie."

She waved her hand as if dismissing his apology. "Do you want to take the job? I thought you were happy in California."

"I was, but things are different now. I don't like the idea of leaving Grandma and Reese on their own." *I don't like the idea of leaving you.*

"No, of course not." She drank her tea and avoided his gaze.

She could have been discussing whether to wear white socks or blue ones. She acted as if she didn't care about him at all. That their relationship meant nothing. That everything was a lie.

"Dammit, Maggie." Luke exploded out of his chair, too agitated to sit. "We were lovers. Doesn't that mean anything to you?"

She set down her cup and lifted her chin. "Of course, it does. But don't make this about me. If you want to take the job, then take it. If you want to go, go. I don't want you to be unhappy either. I'm not going to stand in your way whatever you choose."

Luke's heart sank. He wanted her to stand in his way. He wanted her to tell him he should stay because she needed him. Because she loved him.

The closed expression on her face told him wishing for such a thing was pointless. Perhaps, he had his answer. Whatever had been between them was truly over. Acknowledging that truth stabbed him in the gut so hard he was momentarily dizzy.

He grabbed his coat and pushed his arms through the sleeves. "I should go."

He headed for the door and pulled on his winter boots, not bothering to lace them. Maggie followed him.

"Luke?"

Her arms were around herself again, making her look small and vulnerable. He fought the urge to gather her in his arms and hold her close.

"I meant what I said. I want you to be happy, more than anything in the world." She stopped talking, her lips pressed together as if she were afraid of saying too much. Of revealing too much.

He couldn't resist one touch. He traced his finger down the curve of her cheek, revelling in the softness of her skin. "I want that for you, too, Maggie."

She nodded and stepped away, breaking the tenuous connection between them.

"Goodbye, Luke."

Her words had an air of finality to them.

"Goodbye."

He closed the door and walked quickly to his truck, hunched over against the cold.

Time to go.

"MAGGIE, HAVE YOU GOT a minute?"

Maggie finished plating the grilled whitefish and looked up at Harper in disbelief. "Kind of busy here. The restaurant is full of dinner guests. Can it wait?"

"Actually, no. It's urgent."

Cheryl Johnson took the plate from her and slid it under the warming light. Maggie and Luke had hired her the previous week, one of the last things they'd done together. "The rush is nearly over. I can handle dessert and anything else that comes up."

"But—"

Harper untied her apron and pulled it over her head. "You heard the woman. Let's go."

She steered Maggie out of the kitchen. Once they reached the office, Harper closed the door and turned to her. "Luke's leaving."

The bottom fell out of Maggie's stomach. Even though she'd known all along this was coming, the intensity of the pain robbed her of breath.

"He told Ethan today he plans to leave for California by the end of the week."

For a moment, she could only stare at her sister. Of course, he was going to California. She'd always known he would.

Still, she'd hoped. When he'd asked her how she felt about him staying, she wanted to tell him she needed him to stay because she loved him, but the words stuck in her throat, frozen in fear. He had only said he wanted her to be happy, not that he loved her. She was too afraid to put her feelings out in the open, especially if her feelings weren't returned.

Would he leave without even saying goodbye?

Harper grabbed her by the shoulders. "Maggie, do you love him? Do you want him to stay?"

Her throat closed and all she could do was nod.

"Have you forgiven him? Do you understand why he accepted money from Grampa Bill?"

She nodded again.

"Have you told him how you feel?"

She swallowed hard. "No."

Harper shook her. "You have to tell him. I know how hard it is. I was so scared when I went to Ethan's condo in the city to give him the shares in the company. I was afraid he'd turn me away, or laugh at me. But the thought of living the rest of my life without him...I had to find the courage to fight for him."

"I'm a coward," Maggie whispered. "I've never told Luke how much I love him, not even when we were kids. I can't say the words." She gave a bitter laugh. "I'm more like our grandmother than I ever wanted to believe. Do you know she never once told me she loved me? I can't even say the words to you and Scarlet."

"Grandma had a lot of demons. Don't make them yours, too." Harper ran a soothing hand down her back. "If you love

Luke and you want him to stay, you have to tell him. I think he feels the same way."

"What if he doesn't?"

"Then, you'll know for sure. Do you want to spend your life wondering 'What if?'"

Harper was right. She couldn't let Luke walk away believing she didn't care. She'd lost him once because of secrets and lies. She couldn't let it happen again. "I have to go. I have to tell him."

Harper gave her a relieved smile as she pulled her keys from her pocket. "Here. Take my truck."

"Thank you. For everything." Maggie's throat threatened to close, but she forced the words out, knowing she was long overdue in saying them. "I...I love you, Harper."

Harper cupped her cheeks. "I love you, too, Maggie Cat. See? That wasn't so hard, was it?"

"No, not so hard." It had been the most difficult thing she'd ever said to another human being. Telling Luke the depth of her feelings would be even harder.

MAGGIE'S HAND SHOOK as she knocked on Phyllis' front door. A moment later, Phyllis answered, her smile welcoming.

"Maggie! Come in, come in."

She stepped over the threshold on unsteady legs. Phyllis pointed to the blue cardboard box Maggie held in her hands. "Is that a going away gift for Luke?"

"Something like that."

"You'll want to say goodbye to him, I expect." As Maggie nodded, the older woman's smile disappeared and she whispered, "I don't want him to go."

Maggie struggled to keep tears at bay. "Neither do I."

Phyllis gripped her arm. "Good. Maybe he'll listen to you."

Phyllis led her into the living room where Reese and Luke were drinking coffee. Luke immediately got to his feet. "Maggie, hi. I didn't expect to see you."

"Harper told me you were leaving. I wanted to talk to you."

He shrugged and looked away. "It's time for me to go."

"Don't say that."

Reese got up from his chair. "Phyllis, why don't I make you a cup of coffee at my place? I bought some donuts we can have with it."

Phyllis looked from Maggie to Luke and back again. "That sounds lovely. Let me get my coat."

Reese kissed Maggie's forehead. "Goodnight, sweetheart." In a soft whisper, he added, "Good luck."

Maggie could only nod. A moment later, she heard them leave through the front door. She lifted her eyes to Luke's, her body trembling. "I have something I want to show you." She held out the blue box to him.

He accepted it from her and then sat down. "What is it?"

She sat on the sofa across from him and clutched her hands in her lap, her knuckles white. "Open it and see."

He opened the lid and pulled out the second box and then rummaged through the tissue paper until he uncovered the glass unicorn. For a moment he stared at it, his brow wrinkling. "I remember this. I thought of you the minute I saw it. Beautiful and unique, and rare." He lifted his gaze to hers, incredulity in his eyes. "I can't believe you still have this. I would have thought you'd have smashed it against a wall years ago. I wouldn't have blamed you if you had."

"I couldn't do that. The unicorn was all I had of you. And no matter how many times I moved, that little guy came with me." She swallowed. "You came with me."

"Maggie."

"All the years we were apart, I never stopped caring about you, Luke."

Luke got to his feet and began to pace. "I never stopped caring about you either. I wish you could believe that."

"I do." She held out her hand to him. "Sit with me, Luke."

He sat next to her, keeping his gaze averted as if he was afraid to look in her eyes. She laid her hand on his and squeezed his fingers. "You were right. If Grampa had gone to the police and had you charged with rape, I never would have spoken to him again. Everyone in town would have found out, and there would have been a firestorm of gossip. I'm sure Grampa knew all that, and he didn't want it to happen anymore than we did. When his idle threats didn't work, he resorted to bribery."

"Being charged with rape didn't feel like an idle threat."

"No, I'm sure it didn't. You were young and scared. And you wanted out. Grampa knew that, too."

He nodded. "I didn't want to leave you, but I couldn't stay. I had no future in Minnewasta."

"I know." She sat up straighter. "You were pretty convincing. You made me believe you and Cheryl were an item and that you were seeing her even while we were together. I thought the two of you were laughing at me."

"No, never." He gripped her hand and looked into her eyes "I was never with her. The first and last time I kissed Cheryl Bradley was on the day you found us together. I staged the whole thing so you'd believe I didn't want you."

"Cheryl told me you only kissed her that once." She lowered her head and blew out a breath. "That hurt more than anything. I think I could have understood you needing to get away, but the way you did it..."

"I had to make you believe I didn't want you. I was afraid you'd try to follow me to California, and I think your grandfather was, too. You weren't even fifteen, Maggie. I could barely take care of myself back then." He looked at their joined hands. "If I'm completely honest, I didn't want you to come with me. Instead of going to school, I would have had to find a job and look after you."

Maggie lifted his hand to her lips and kissed his fingers. "You would have resented me for holding you back. Whether you'd stayed in Minnewasta for me, or if we'd somehow managed to run away to California together, eventually you would have come to see me as a burden."

"Maggie, no—"

"Yes," she said firmly. "That would have been the worst for me. Maybe Grampa did us a favor."

"Some favor."

She couldn't help but smile at that. "I'm sorry it took me so long to work things out."

"You don't have to apologize."

"I think I do." She kissed his fingers once more, then brought his hand to her cheek. "I've never told you what you mean to me, then or now. It's hard for me to talk about the things in my heart."

He gently caressed her face. "I know."

"I don't want you to go."

"Then give me a reason to stay."

He wasn't going to make this easy for her. She lifted her chin and looked deeply into his grey-green eyes. Despite her shaking hands and pitching stomach, despite the fear threatening to turn her tongue to stone, she had to find the courage to tell him the truth.

"I want you to stay because I want to make a life with you here in Minnewasta. I want you to stay because no one else in the world makes me feel the way you make me feel. I want you to stay for the best reason of all." She paused, her mouth impossibly dry. "Because I...because I love you. I've always loved you."

Her little speech exhausted her. She was as winded as if she'd run a marathon. But seeing the smile blossom on his face instantly energized her.

"I love you, too, Maggie Cat."

His lips descended on hers and, finally, she knew she was truly home.

Epilogue

MAGGIE HELD SCARLET'S left hand securely as they walked along the shore of the lake while Harper did the same on her right. Making sure their pregnant sister didn't slip on the remaining bits of snow and ice was paramount for Maggie. Now that April had arrived, the ice was beginning to break up on the lake, leaving patches of open water. But winter wasn't ready to give up the fight. Overnight, a strong north wind had pushed great chunks of ice onto the southern shore. The wind continued to roar its fury, making her pull her knitted hat a little more securely over her ears.

"Willy went to the police today," Harper said. "He went on his own and told them about what happened to Mom and Daddy, and how he was responsible for their deaths. The police called to tell me."

Maggie gripped Scarlet's arm. "What's going to happen? Will he go to jail?"

Harper shook her head. "I'm not sure. Their deaths were an accident, but he lied and pointed the finger at Daddy. He has to atone for what he did."

"I'm glad Willy confessed," Scarlet said. "At least we don't have to turn him in ourselves. But if there's a trial—"

"If there's a trial, we'll get through it together. We've got our family now," Harper said, putting her arm around

Scarlet's waist. "Whatever happens, the truth will come out and Daddy's name will be cleared. The important thing is that *we* know the truth."

"I wish Grandma and Grampa could have known the truth." Maggie wondered if knowing how and why her daughter died would have been easier on Grandma Dorothy.

She shivered at the thought. Nothing would have made her daughter's death easier to bear.

Scarlet snuggled close. "You're shivering. Are you cold, Maggie?"

"A little. The wind coming off the lake has quite a bite." Maggie checked her watch. "I should head back to town soon. Phyllis will have dinner waiting for us."

"How's your deal with Phyllis working out?" Harper asked.

Maggie grinned. "It's perfect."

She and Luke had been living with Phyllis since they got back together, and the arrangement suited all three of them. Luke and Maggie handled maintenance and cleaning around the house, and Phyllis enjoyed cooking for them. Since Reese lived down the block, he was a frequent visitor, giving her and her father the opportunity to forge a relationship. Someday, she and Luke would get a place of their own but for now, it was more important they all be together.

"We should go back to the lodge," Harper said.

"In a minute," Maggie said. "There's a reason I asked you to come for a walk with me. I wanted to show you this."

She pulled off her glove to reveal the engagement ring Luke had given her the previous evening. The gold band and solitaire diamond sparkled in the dying rays of the sun.

Scarlet sucked in a breath and grabbed Maggie's hand. "Oh, my God! Our baby sister is getting married, Harper!"

Tears shone in Harper's eyes. "I'm so happy for you, sweetheart. Luke is perfect for you."

"He is. He's the best man I know, and I love him so much." The joy Luke had brought into her life made her happier than she'd ever been. She only hoped she made him just as happy. Somehow, she knew Abby was looking down on them with approval.

"I'm glad you don't have trouble saying those three little words anymore," Harper said with a laugh.

"No, no trouble at all. I've had a lot of practice over the last few weeks. And if I haven't told the two of you lately how much I love you, I'm telling you now."

Scarlet kissed her cheek. "We love you, too, Maggie Cat. Let's head back to the lodge."

As they turned around, the sound of a woman's laughter drifted across the lake. *Abby's laughter*. Maggie abruptly stopped walking. "Did you hear that?"

"What?"

"A woman laughing."

"Are you sure? I didn't hear anything." Scarlet tucked her hand into hers once more. "We'd better get you home. The excitement of your engagement is making you hear things."

"Very funny."

Maggie continued walking, but as she looked back at the lake, two women in a yellow canoe waved at her. She jerked to a stop and sucked in a breath.

Harper steadied her, concern in her eyes. "Are you okay?"

Maggie glanced toward the lake once more, but all she saw was late afternoon sunlight glinting on a patch of open water.

"It's crazy, but I swear for a moment I saw a canoe out there."

Scarlet swallowed. "Was it a yellow canoe?"

Harper gasped. "You saw it, too?"

"I did. Once. Last winter. We were all out skating on the lake, remember? But I was the only one who saw it. It happened just before my wedding."

"I saw the yellow canoe last summer, a few days before my wedding. And now Maggie's getting married..." Harper's voice trailed off.

Holding hands, they gazed out at the lake, letting the cold wind whip around them. But the wind no longer sent a chill up Maggie's spine. Warmth enveloped her. Comforting peace wrapped around her heart, filling her with love and thankfulness.

"They're happy for us," she whispered.

Her sisters didn't ask who she meant. Instead, they nodded in understanding.

Several minutes passed. Finally, Scarlet squeezed her hand. "We need to go. Our families are waiting for us."

Together they walked back to the lodge, hand in hand.

The End

Thank you for reading "Truth and Solace". Want to read another story in the Love at Solace Lake world? How about CHRISTMAS AT SOLACE LAKE? Celeste and Drew are two of my favorite characters from the series and I wanted them to have their own story, and their own happy ending:

IT'S CHRISTMAS TIME at Solace Lake Lodge, but a series of thefts threatens everyone's holiday spirit.

Widow Celeste Bishop has made a good life for herself and her nine-year-old daughter in the three years she's worked, and lived, at Solace Lake Lodge, an inn located deep in the Minnesota woods. But this Christmas, a series of thefts puts the lodge at risk and has staff suspecting one another.

An emergency brings Drew Barnes to Solace Lake Lodge. He's sure desperation is the only reason his aunt and uncle, the owners of the lodge, allow him to fill in as their bookkeeper. No one in his family has trusted him since his mistake got him fired from his previous job.

When Drew gets to know Celeste, the pieces of his life tumble into place. He doesn't care that she's nine years older. But while he's falling in love, she's pulling away. She can't risk loving and losing again.

As Christmas approaches, the thefts increase. Can Drew stop the thief and redeem himself in his family's eyes—and his own? And can he convince

Celeste they deserve the gift of a happily-ever-after this Christmas?

Scan the QR for your copy of CHRISTMAS AT SOLACE LAKE!

A Note from Jana

REVIEWS ARE THE LIFE BLOOD for authors. I hope you enjoyed this book. If you did, I would appreciate you letting other readers know. Please leave a review at the retailer where you purchased the book, on Goodreads, or on your own blog. If you leave a review, I would love to read it! Please email me the link at Jana@JanaRichards.com.

You can stay up to date with me and my upcoming new releases, sales, giveaways and contests by joining my newsletter. You'll receive a FREE ecopy of **HOME TO SOLACE LAKE** as a thank you for signing up. This romantic novella is available only to newsletter subscribers. I'd love to have you on board! Here's the blurb for **HOME TO SOLACE LAKE**:

> After Jerry Fields buried his mother twenty-two years ago, he cut all ties to the small town in Minnesota where he grew up. He swore he'd never return. But when his biological father, a man who never acknowledged him, leaves Jerry his entire estate, curiosity has him returning to Minnewasta. Why did Earl Rogers will him everything he owned when during his lifetime he didn't give Jerry a minute of his time?

Denise Rogers wants to save the business that her deceased husband loved so much. But when her father-in-law Earl leaves all his property to his illegitimate son, saving the business gets much more complicated. Denise is determined to buy the property from Jerry Fields to keep it from being demolished and turned into condos. She wants to continue to run the business as a marine repair shop, knowing it's what her husband would have wanted. But events throw her plans into disarray and she has to give up on her dream. Until Jerry offers to work with her over the summer to help her buy the property.

Jerry can't stomach the idea of putting his half-brother's widow out of a job and a home, so he decides to stay in Minnewasta to help her. At the end of the summer, Denise will purchase the property from him and they'll go their separate ways. But as they work together, their feelings for each other deepen into love, and they uncover long-held secrets that force Jerry to question everything he thought he knew about his parents. Can Jerry overcome past hurts and fears for a chance at love?

Sign up using the QR code below for Jana's newsletter and receive your FREE copy of **HOME TO SOLACE LAKE!**

Don't miss out!

Visit the website below and you can sign up to receive emails whenever Jana Richards publishes a new book. There's no charge and no obligation.

https://books2read.com/r/B-A-YISD-ANMZC

BOOKS 2 READ

Connecting independent readers to independent writers.

Also by Jana Richards

A Left at the Altar Romance

Her Best Man

There Goes the Groom

Always a Bridesmaid

Love at Solace Lake

Lies and Solace

Secrets and Solace

Truth and Solace

Christmas at Solace Lake

The Victorian Mansion Series

Rescue Me

Take a Chance on Me

Twice in a Lifetime Series

I'll Be Seeing You
Never Can Say Goodbye
When I Was Your Man

Standalone
A Long Way From Eden
Seeing Things

Watch for more at https://www.janarichards.com/.

About the Author

When Jana Richards read her first romance novel, she immediately knew two things: she had to commit the stories running through her head to paper, and they had to end with a happily ever after. She also knew she'd found what she was meant to do. Since then she's never met a romance genre she didn't like. She writes contemporary romance, romantic suspense, and historical romance set in World War Two, in lengths ranging from short story to full length novel. Just for fun, she throws in generous helpings of humor, and the occasional dash of the paranormal.

In her life away from writing, Jana is a mother to two grown daughters, grandmother to an amazing granddaughter, and a wife to her husband Warren. She enjoys golf, yoga, movies, concerts, travel and reading, not necessarily in that order. She and her husband live in western Canada with a senior calico cat named Layla and an acquarium full of unnamed fish. She loves to hear from readers and can be reached through her website.

Read more at https://www.janarichards.com/.

www.ingramcontent.com/pod-product-compliance
Lightning Source LLC
LaVergne TN
LVHW020654110826
845149LV00012B/1989

* 9 7 8 0 9 9 5 2 7 9 1 5 5 *